PRAISE FOR

FINDING LAURA

"You always know you are in for an outstanding read when you pick up a Kay Hooper novel, but in *Finding Laura,* she has created something really special! Simply superb!"
—*Romantic Times* (gold medal review)

"Hooper keeps the intrigue pleasurably complicated, with gothic touches of suspense and a satisfying resolution." —*Publishers Weekly*

"A first-class reading experience."
—*Affaire de Coeur*

"Ms. Hooper throws in one surprise after another. . . . Spellbinding." —*Rendezvous*

AFTER CAROLINE

"Harrowing good fun. Readers will shiver and shudder." —*Publishers Weekly*

"Kay Hooper comes through with thrills, chills, and plenty of romance, this time with an energetic murder mystery with a clever twist. The suspense is sustained admirably right up to the very end."
—*Kirkus Reviews*

"Peopled with interesting characters and intricately plotted, the novel is both a compelling mystery and a satisfying romance."
—*Milwaukee Journal Sentinel*

"Kay Hooper has crafted another solid story to keep readers enthralled until the last page is turned."
—*Booklist*

ALWAYS A
THIEF

KAY HOOPER

BANTAM BOOKS

This is a work of fiction. Names, characters, places, and incidents either are the product of the author's imagination or are used fictitiously. Any resemblance to actual persons, living or dead, events, or locales is entirely coincidental.

2009 Bantam Books Mass Market Edition

Copyright © 2003 by Kay Hooper

Published in the United States by Bantam Books, an imprint of The Random House Publishing Group, a division of Random House, Inc., New York.

Bantam Books and the rooster colophon are registered trademarks of Random House, Inc.

Originally published in mass market in the United States by Bantam Books, an imprint of The Random House Publishing Group, a division of Random house, Inc., in 2003.

ISBN 978-0-553-59271-9

Cover art copyright © 2003 by Alan Ayers

Printed in the United States of America

www.bantamdell.com

9 8 7 6 5 4 3 2 1

AUTHOR'S NOTE

About ten years ago, I wrote a series of short contemporary novels for Bantam's Loveswept romance series. That's right—romances.

But a funny thing happened while I was writing those books. Although I enjoyed all the characters, one in particular was, quite literally, difficult to keep offstage when he wasn't supposed to be active in the story. My cat burglar Quinn practically walked off the pages, and even at the time my agent told me that "one day" I'd have to do more with him.

One day came.

Sometimes a writer is lucky enough to be able to look back at older work and be granted the opportunity to rewrite it as she wanted to write it at the time; I was writing series romance then, and there were simply things I couldn't do in the books because of what they were—and when they were. I am very proud of those books, but they were definitely stories written for a particular audience at a particular time.

At the time, I was unable—because of both the length of the books and the genre itself—to make the characters as complex as I wanted, to give them shades of gray, ambiguities of motive and personality. And since I was already, by then, feeling the need to stretch my wings, to write bigger, more complex books, I was very conscious that I was not providing Quinn and some other characters the wider canvas they deserved.

Which brings me to the second reason I wanted to include this note in the "Thief" books: *Once a Thief* and *Always a Thief* are not the books you remember if you read the original versions. They've been, in a sense, reimagined. I haven't just added a few thousand words here and there—I have restructured the stories in several ways.

Some scenes remain from the originals, but even those have been shifted, sometimes slightly, to provide a different perspective or provide that wider canvas for the characters. Some characters have either stepped back out of the spotlight or disappeared entirely from the narrative, and new ones are introduced. The same goes for some plotlines.

This is Quinn's story, or at least the beginning of it. And since he continued to be a lively presence in my writer's imagination long after his story was supposedly told, I gather he has more adventures in mind. We'll see.

If you've enjoyed my more recent suspense novels, I hope you'll give this one a try. It's not as dark and gritty as the Bishop books, and if there are any psychic elements—well, we'll just have to wait and find out about that—but Quinn is a lot of fun, and he's allowed me to show a lighter, more playful side of my writing.

My agent calls this sort of story a "caper, a bright, fun, witty adventure that holds on to its sense of humor even though there might well be deadly danger lurking about."

Might well be . . . and there is. Because there's a spectacular collection of gems and artworks about to go on display, and more than one person is ready and willing to do whatever it takes in order to possess it. Even kill.

Come meet Quinn, and let me know what you think of him. I like him a lot. And I hope you do too.

PROLOGUE

The fog could have made it easier for Quinn to shadow his quarry without giving away his own presence, but he had already discovered that the shifting gray mist could be as unpredictable as a living creature, thick as pea soup one moment and wispy thin the next, so he stayed as far back as he could without losing the target.

It made things more difficult.

His foot slipped a bit on a fog-wet roof tile, and he made a mental note to look for a pair of newer, better soft-soled shoes for these nighttime excursions. That went through his mind even as his gloved hands reached for—and dislodged—another of the slippery tiles.

Quinn froze.

He had excellent night vision, but through the

swirling fog it was difficult to be certain the man moving yards ahead of him on the same roof hadn't heard the faint sound. Quinn squinted, concentrated all his senses, and decided finally that the man was still moving slowly, cautiously, away from him.

Hardly breathing, testing every foothold, Quinn continued to follow his prey.

As he followed, from one rooftop to another across an expanse of several huge office buildings, something nagged at him. What? What was bothering him?

This was the third night he had managed to locate and stalk his prey, and so far nothing was different. Just a trip across rooftops, silent and cautious, in the darkness. Tonight there was a fog, but otherwise it was the same.

The same.

Exactly the same.

Quinn froze again, this time with realizations gathering in his mind. The same. The same goddamned route. The same time of night, to the hour. The same rooftops, none of them sheltering anything of interest to a thief of gems or artworks. The same difficult, physically demanding path testing both his nerve and his skills.

He was playing follow the fucking leader.

And he wasn't the leader.

He was being tested.

A rare anger swept over Quinn, but even

stronger was the instinctive urge to break off immediately. Someone else was playing a dangerous game, and until Quinn knew the rules he had no intention of playing along.

He eased back and began his retreat, automatically planning the best path to take.

And he almost made it.

Avoiding an iron fire escape, as he did whenever possible because he'd found them to be unacceptably noisy, Quinn fastened a grappling hook securely and used the gear he usually carried to rappel down the side of the building and into the dense darkness of an alleyway.

He was no more than ten feet from the pavement when all his senses screamed a sudden warning that someone was nearby, too close—and he was dangling helplessly like a worm on a hook.

He barely had time to turn his head, had only an instant to see the shadowy outline of a man on the fire escape not far away, see the gleam of faint light on dark steel, and then a sound like a soft sneeze reached his ears in the same moment that Quinn made an instinctive effort to push himself away from the building and drop to the alley below.

He felt the bullet hit him, and the shock caused his legs to buckle as he reached the pavement. Hot pain washed over him, pain he fought to ignore as he looked up, searching the fire escape for the man who had shot him.

The fire escape was empty.

Quinn pressed a gloved hand to his chest, and when he brought it away he could see even in the darkness of the alley a wet gleam.

"Son of a bitch," he muttered.

CHAPTER
ONE

Morgan West was beginning to get tense about the entire situation. The Bannister collection of priceless artworks and gems would be moved to the museum within days, which meant the bait would be in the trap. Neither Max Bannister nor anyone else had deigned to inform her that there *was* a trap, information she knew only because of an overheard conversation. And she hadn't seen—or felt—a sign of Quinn in weeks.

It was maddening.

She didn't fool herself into believing that Quinn wasn't uppermost in her mind. Once she'd gotten over her fury at having been presented with a concubine ring (though she fully intended to give him a piece of her mind about *that* little item when next they met), she had gone back to spending an hour or two of her evenings parked outside some likely museum or jewelry store, hoping to be able to sense him, feel him, whatever the hell she'd been able to do before. But he hadn't been kidding when he'd said if he didn't want to be found, not even she would be able to find him.

The most elusive thief in the world seemed to have no difficulty in eluding her.

Dammit.

She had read the newspapers front to back and had kept her ears open during her days at the museum, but if Quinn had robbed anybody they apparently didn't know it. There had been no splashy headlines about the world-famous cat burglar, and no breathless news bulletins on television.

In fact, nobody had reported a jewel or art robbery of any kind since Max Bannister, his half brother Wolfe Nickerson, and Interpol agent Jared Chavalier had captured a psychotic thief bent on murdering Storm Tremaine, the exhibit's computer expert.

With that leader of an organized gang of thieves out of business and the gang scattered and inactive, anybody with valuables to protect in the city had heaved an almost audible sigh of relief.

In Morgan's own museum, the *Mysteries Past* exhibit space was nearly ready for the priceless collection of gems and artworks now being cleaned and appraised in its vault. And barring a definite undercurrent of tension between Wolfe and Jared, things had been downright *peaceful*.

Morgan told herself she should be happy about that state of affairs. It was best for all concerned. Quinn had quite probably gone back to Europe, especially after she'd warned him about the trap.

Something she hadn't mentioned to Max.

Still, in spite of common sense and logic, she had the nagging feeling that Quinn hadn't left San Francisco. He was here somewhere, and if he hadn't committed a robbery it was probably because he was waiting for a chance to grab Max's collection—trap or no trap.

That was why she kept looking for him, she told herself. Because if the first warning hadn't worked, maybe she could come up with one he would pay attention to. It was, after all, her responsibility to guard the forthcoming exhibit from harm, and Quinn undoubtedly posed a threat she should guard against.

Yeah, right! she sneered at herself.

She was an idiot, there was no doubt about it. She should be doing everything possible to put his ass behind bars and never mind warning him.

She could have provided the police with a very accurate description of him. Did he know that? Of course he did. Did he worry about it? No, because he knew all too well she wouldn't say a word to the police about being able to describe him.

Dammit.

She refused to wear the concubine ring—no matter how beautiful it was—but she hadn't exactly dumped it in the garbage either. In fact, she had a habit of taking it from her jewelry box and staring at it for long minutes each night before she went to bed.

And wouldn't Freud have a field day with *that*.

On this particular Thursday night, Morgan had, with difficulty, talked herself out of her usual search for Quinn. She had occupied herself with paperwork and a late movie, then showered and dressed for bed in her usual comfortable sleepshirt. She paid a brief visit to her jewelry box and studied the glowing, square stone of the concubine ring, said a few heartfelt words about Quinn's probable ancestry out loud, and, her feelings vented somewhat, went to bed.

When she woke with a start, the luminous display of her alarm clock proclaimed that it was twenty minutes after three in the morning. It was very quiet, but she found herself lying rigidly beneath the covers, wide awake, her ears straining. Something had awakened her, she knew that. Something—

There. A faint sound from the front of the apartment, from the living room. A scratching sound, then a very soft creak, the way a floorboard protested weight.

Morgan held very strong views about guns. She believed that the vast majority of the people who owned guns probably shouldn't have been trusted with a slingshot, and she believed that anyone who had both a gun and a child of any age in the same house was guilty of criminal stupidity.

But she had also been on her own for too long to take dumb chances. So she had learned to handle guns, from experts, and she had bought an automatic to keep in her apartment. Twice a month, she went to a target range and practiced scrupulously to keep her aim true. She was, in fact, a crack shot.

So it was almost a reflex to slide very carefully from the bed, ease open the drawer of her nightstand, and take out the gun. It was another reflex to thumb off the safety and hold the weapon in a practiced two-handed grip.

Of course, it probably would have been smarter to creep into the bathroom with the gun and her portable phone—also on the nightstand beside her bed—lock the door, and call the police. But she didn't even think of that until much later. Instead, she crept toward the door of her bedroom, ears straining, trying to be utterly silent.

The hallway was short, and she lingered close to the wall just outside the living room, searching the dark room for any sign of movement. There—by the window. It was only a shadow, indistinct, but it didn't belong there.

Remaining close to the wall for cover, her eyes fixed on the shadow, Morgan managed not to startle herself with the clear strength of her own voice. "I have a gun," she warned in a grim tone. "And I'll use it, believe me."

"I believe you." The voice was deep, masculine, and somewhat dry. "However . . . since American authorities haven't yet . . . put a price on my head . . . I'd rather you didn't. Shooting me for profit . . . makes perfect sense . . . to me . . . but I'm not . . . quite . . . ready for a mercy killing."

She slumped. "Quinn."

"Don't sound . . . so damned relieved, Morgana," he reproved in an even dryer voice. "I may not . . . be a murderous fiend, but you should . . . at the very least . . . consider me . . . dangerous. I am . . . a known felon . . . after all."

"You're a lunatic." Automatically, she pointed the pistol at the floor as she eased the hammer back down and thumbed on the safety. She stepped into the living room and put the gun on a table by the wall, then turned on the lamp there.

It took a moment for her eyes to adjust to the sudden light, but when they did she found him near the window, his gloved hands resting on her high-backed reading chair. More disappointed than she wanted to admit to herself, she noted that his usual all-black cat-burglar costume included the ski mask that effectively hid his face. Why was he hiding his face from her when she'd already seen it?

"What are you doing here, anyway?" she demanded.

"Happened . . . to be . . . in the neighborhood," he murmured.

Morgan took a step toward him, then another, frowning. He was standing too still, she thought, too stiffly. And something about the way he was speaking wasn't right. "Oh, really? And you just *happened* to climb up my fire escape and pick the lock on the window?"

"Lousy lock," he said, his voice growing softer, almost slurring. "You . . . ought to get another."

Forever afterward, Morgan was never certain at what moment she knew what had happened. But she began moving toward him more quickly, covering the space between them with hasty steps. Maybe it was pure instinct that told her what was wrong—the primal sensing of blood and weakness—but she knew with utter certainty that he was very badly hurt. As soon as she was closer to him, the fact was obvious.

"No police, Morgana," he muttered in that soft, thickened voice. "Doctors have to report . . . report—" He swayed, and she was barely able to reach him in time to keep his head from striking the floor when he fell.

A light breeze was clearing out the fog, but the night retained that swathed-in-cotton silence the mist usually provided, so she was careful to make no noise as she glided away from Morgan West's apartment building.

Interesting. Very interesting indeed.

And surprising. So the seemingly infallible Quinn had a weak spot? An unexpected vulnerability in the armor of his heart—and his brilliant mind?

She made her way to the car parked several blocks away and slid inside, only then allowing a soft laugh to escape her. She had come to San Francisco with one goal.

Now she had two.

"Quinn? *Quinn?*" The black of his sweater showed a dull, wet gleam high on his chest and on his left shoulder. A spreading gleam. And when she pulled the ski mask off, his lean, handsome face was ghostly pale and beaded with sweat, his flesh chilled. His eyes were closed.

Morgan had never felt so cold with fear, but first-aid training took over as she felt for the carotid pulse in his neck. His heart was beating, but faintly and the rhythm was all wrong; he was going into shock.

He was far too heavy for her to move. *Keep him warm and elevate his legs,* she told herself with a calm inner voice that came from God-knew-where. She dragged a heavy blanket from her bed and covered him, then lifted his legs carefully until they rested across a low hassock.

She didn't want to look at the wound but knew she had to, and Quinn's last mumbled words kept ringing hauntingly in her ears. She couldn't call a doctor, because doctors had to report violent wounds to the police, and the police wanted Quinn in the worst way.

Even so, Morgan knew with absolute certainty that Quinn alive and in jail would forever be her choice over Quinn dead and still an enigma to the police; if she had to make that decision, it was already made.

She used her sewing scissors and carefully cut his sweater open far enough to expose the wound. She didn't know much about this kind of thing, but she was certain she was looking at a bullet wound. One glance was enough; she made a thick pad of several clean cloths and pressed it gently over the sluggishly bleeding wound, fighting a queasy feeling. But that cool inner voice remained calm inside her head.

Not so bad. The bleeding's nearly stopped. Unless there's an exit wound . . . She slipped a hand under his shoulder and didn't know whether she should be relieved that the bullet was still lodged in his body. *It isn't near the heart or lung. I think.*

"Damn you," she muttered, hardly aware of speaking aloud. "Don't you die on me, Quinn. Damn you, don't die."

Those absurdly long lashes of his lifted and, even now, a gleam of amusement lurked in the darkened green eyes. "If you're going to swear at me," he said in a voice little more than a whisper, "then . . . at least use my first name."

"I don't know it," she snapped, holding on to her ferocity because she suspected it was the only thing that kept her from falling apart.

"Alex," he murmured with the ghost of a laugh.

Morgan didn't feel any sense of triumph at all, even though she was certain he wasn't lying to her. Alex was his name, his real name, and that knowledge put her several jumps ahead of just about everybody who was chasing Quinn. But she didn't feel any elation because he'd trusted her with the information. She was very much afraid that it might well be along the lines of a deathbed confession. Her voice held steady and grim.

"You die on me, *Alex,* and I'll hunt your ghost to the ends of the earth."

His eyes closed, but a faint chuckle escaped him. "I can save you . . . the search. You're quite . . . likely to find me . . . in the neighborhood . . . of perdition's flame . . . Morgana."

She tasted blood and realized she'd bitten her bottom lip. "I have to get a doctor for you—"

"No. The police. I can't . . . let them put me away . . . not now . . . I'm too close."

She didn't know what he was talking about. "Listen to me. You're in shock. You've lost a lot of blood. You have a bullet in you, and it has to come out." When his eyes opened again, she was even more alarmed by the feverish glitter stirring there. Quickly, she said, "Max. I'll call Max. He'll be able to get a doctor here quietly, without the police having to know."

It didn't strike her until much later how wonderfully ironic her solution was: a wounded cat burglar bleeding in her living room, and the only man who might be able to help him was the man who owned a priceless collection that would soon bait a trap designed to catch that cat burglar.

Ironic? It was insane.

Quinn looked at her for a long minute, and then a sigh escaped him. Relief, acceptance, regret, or something else—she wasn't sure what it was. But the smile that briefly curved his lips was a strange one, twisted with something other than pain.

"All right. Call him."

Despite the fact that it was the middle of the night, Max answered his private phone line in a clear, calm voice and listened to Morgan's hasty explanation without interruption. When she was through, he simply said, "I'm on my way," and she found herself listening to a dial tone.

Quinn seemed to be unconscious, but he was still breathing. She tucked the blanket more securely around him and went back to her bedroom to quickly strip off her sleepshirt and scramble into jeans and a sweater. Then she returned to kneel beside him. Her fingers trembled as she stroked his thick golden hair and then his cool, damp cheek.

"If you die I'll never forgive you," she whispered. He might have heard her, or he might have been too deeply unconscious to hear anything, but his head moved just a bit as if he wanted to press himself more firmly to her touch.

It was ten interminable minutes before she heard a quick, soft knock at her door and went to let Max in. She had turned on more lamps, so he was able to see Quinn clearly the moment he stepped into her apartment.

"The doctor should be here any minute," Max told her, shrugging off his jacket and tossing it over the couch before moving quickly toward Quinn. "How is he?"

"The same." She followed and knelt on one side of the unconscious man while Max knelt on the other. His long, powerful fingers checked the pulse, and then he eased the blanket back and looked under the cloths with which she had covered the wound. His hard face rarely showed emotion of any kind no matter what he may have been feeling, and his voice remained dispassionate.

"Nasty. But not fatal, I think."

If a doctor had said the same thing, Morgan probably would have doubted him, but she had known Max long enough to have implicit faith in his judgments. The cold tightness of fear eased inside her, and she felt herself slump a little. "He—he looks so pale."

"Loss of blood." Max replaced the cloths and drew the blanket back up to Quinn's throat with a curiously gentle touch. "And shock. The human body tends to resent a bullet."

"It's still in him."

"I know. Lucky for him that it is. If it had gone straight through him, he probably would have bled to death by now." Max looked at her for a moment, then said, "I think he'd be more comfortable off the floor."

"If we can get him to my bed—"

"You go get the bed ready. I'll bring him."

Quinn was by no means a small man, and unconscious he was a deadweight, but Max was unusually large and unusually powerful, and he seemed to feel little strain as he carried the thief into Morgan's bedroom and eased him down on the bed. Morgan helped pull his soft-soled boots off, then eyed the remainder of his lean, black-clad form hesitantly.

"Maybe I'd better do the rest," Max said.

She nodded and backed toward the door. "Maybe you'd better. I'll—go make some coffee."

She had just filled her coffeemaker and turned it on when the doctor arrived. He was a middle-aged man, with steady eyes and a soft voice, and seemed quite matter-of-fact about having been pulled from his bed to secretly treat a gunshot wound. If Max said it was the right thing to do, he told her comfortably, then that was all he needed to know.

Someone else with implicit faith in Max's judgment, it seemed.

Morgan pointed the way to the bedroom but retreated to the kitchen herself. She didn't know how much more she could take but was fairly sure her fortitude would crumble if she had to watch a bullet being extracted from Quinn.

She could hear the low voices of the doctor and Max, and once a faint groan caused her to bite down hard on a knuckle. She turned the television on to CNN but remained in the kitchen and was working on her second cup of coffee by the time Max came out of the bedroom a few minutes later.

"The bullet's out," he reported quietly. "It went in at an angle, apparently, so it was more difficult to get at than it would have been otherwise. But if it hadn't entered the way it did, it probably would have killed him."

Morgan poured him a cup of coffee and gestured toward the cream and sugar on the counter, then said rather jerkily, "I heard him— Did he—"

"He came to in the middle of it," Max explained. "It wasn't very pleasant for him, I'm afraid. But he doesn't want anything for pain, and he's still conscious."

"He'll be all right?"

"Looks like it." Max sipped his coffee, then added with a hint of dryness, "So you'll have a wounded cat burglar in your bed for a few days."

It occurred to Morgan that Max had been amazingly incurious about all this, and she felt heat rise in her face. Clearing her throat, she murmured, "I . . . uh . . . sort of ran into him a few times, and he . . . more or less . . . saved my life. Twice, probably."

"Did he?"

She nodded. "So I owe him. Giving up my bed for a few days isn't much of a price to pay."

Max was watching her steadily. "No, if he saved your life I'd say it was a bargain."

"You won't—" She cleared her throat again, and said with difficulty, "I overheard something I probably shouldn't have at the museum, Max. The night you got back to town after your honeymoon."

"I thought you might have." He smiled slightly. "I saw your name in the museum's security log when I signed out, Morgan. I had a hunch you'd overheard Jared and me talking and had figured out what we were planning."

"Yeah, well . . . after Quinn saved my life, I . . . warned him. About *Mysteries Past* being bait for a trap."

"I see."

"I'm sorry, Max, but—"

"It's all right," he soothed, but before he could say more, the doctor emerged from the bedroom with positive news.

"Constitution of an ox," he said, gratefully accepting the coffee Morgan offered. "And an unusually high tolerance for pain. He's also a quick healer, unless I miss my guess. Probably be on his feet in a day or two." He looked at Max and added, "He wants to see you, and I doubt he'll rest until he does."

Max set his cup on the counter, gave Morgan a slight, reassuring smile, and left the kitchen as the doctor was beginning to give her brisk instructions on how to care for the patient during the coming days.

When he entered the lamplit bedroom, Max stood for a silent moment studying Quinn. His upper body was slightly raised on two pillows, the covers drawn just above his waist so that much of his broad chest and the heavily bandaged shoulder was clearly visible. His eyes were closed, but they opened as Max looked at him, clear and alert despite the pain he was undoubtedly in.

Curiously, he didn't look incongruous in Morgan's bed. She hadn't gone overboard with frills in decorating her bedroom, since she wasn't a frilly woman, but it was quite definitely a feminine room; despite that, Quinn seemed to fit among the floral sheets and ruffled pillow shams without sacrificing any of his maleness. It was an interesting trait.

After a minute or so, Max reached behind him to push the door shut. Quinn watched silently as the big, dark man moved gracefully over to the window and stood looking out on the dimly lighted street below.

"I gather Morgan doesn't know," he said quietly.

"No, she doesn't," Quinn responded, his voice subtly different from the careless one Morgan was accustomed to hearing.

"What kind of game are you playing with her?" Max asked, still without turning.

There had been no particular inflection in that deep voice, but Quinn shifted restlessly on the bed nonetheless, grimacing slightly as his wound throbbed a protest. "You must know it isn't a game." There was an inflection in his voice: defensive, maybe even defiant. "I don't have the time or the emotional energy for games."

"Then keep her out of it." This time, the tone was Max Bannister's boardroom voice, the sound of an authority rarely challenged and even more rarely defeated. But a quiet challenge came from the bed.

"I can't," Quinn said.

Max stiffened just a little. "In some ways, Morgan's fragile. And she always roots for the underdog. You could break her heart." His voice was flat.

Quinn said even more quietly, "I think she might break mine."

"Stop it. Now, before . . . either of you has to pay too high a price."

"You think I haven't tried?" Quinn laughed, a low, harsh sound. "I have." He cleared his throat, and went on with a stony control that did nothing to diminish the meaning of what he was saying. "I've tried to stay away from her. You'll never know how hard I've tried. I don't even remember deciding to come here tonight. I just . . . came. To her. If I was going to die, I needed—I had to be with her."

Max turned then, leaning against the window frame, and the defeat was in his voice. "It's a hell of a mess, Alex."

Quinn's long fingers tightened their grip on the covers drawn up to his waist, and his mouth twisted as he met that steady, curiously compassionate gaze. "I know," he said.

Morgan had begun to worry when Max still hadn't left the bedroom after more than half an hour. The doctor had gone, leaving her with instructions, antibiotics and pills for pain, and a list of supplies she'd need to care for the patient, and all she could do was pace the living room and eye that closed bedroom door nervously every time she passed the hallway. She couldn't hear a thing; what was going *on* in there?

It was nearly dawn, well after five o'clock, when Max finally came out. As usual, he didn't show whatever he was feeling, but she thought he was a bit tired.

"How is he?" she asked somewhat warily.

"Ready to sleep, I think."

Morgan was nearly dying of curiosity, but before she could ask why Quinn had wanted to see him, a sharp knock at her door distracted her. "Who could that be? The doctor coming back for something?"

"No, I don't think so." Max went to open the door, and Jared Chavalier strode in.

Morgan moved almost instinctively to put herself between Jared and the door of her bedroom, but her eyes went to Max, and it was to him her thin question was directed.

"How could you—"

"It's all right, Morgan," he said quietly with a reassuring smile. "Trust me."

Before she could respond, Jared's low, angry voice drew her attention. He looked a bit pale—probably, she thought, from fury, since his eyes blazed with it.

"Has anything changed from what you told me on the phone?" he asked Max.

"No," Max replied. "Serious, but not fatal. He'll be all right in a few days."

Jared laughed shortly. "I might have known—he has more lives than ten cats."

Still calm, Max said, "You'll want to talk to him. He got close this time. Too close. He believes that's why he was shot."

Morgan stepped away from the hall and into the living room as she realized there was no threat to Quinn from the Interpol agent, her bewilderment growing. "I don't understand," she said to Max. "What's going on?"

Max replied, "The exhibit *is* bait for a cat burglar, Morgan, but it isn't Quinn. He's working with Interpol to help catch another thief."

CHAPTER
TWO

Slowly, she began to smile. "How about that."

Jared looked at her and, harshly, said, "Don't get any fool romantic notions about nobility into your head. Quinn's helping us to keep his own ass out of jail—and that's it. If we hadn't caught up with him, he'd still be looting Europe."

Morgan met that angry glare for a long moment, her smile fading. Then, speaking pointedly to Max, she said, "I'll go and make some fresh coffee."

"Thank you," Max said. When she was out of the room, he looked at the other man. "Was that necessary?"

Jared shrugged, scowling. He kept his voice low, but the anger remained. "Don't tell me you *want* her to fall for a thief. Aside from the fact that he's about as stable as nitro and damned likely to end up in prison or executed—not to mention shot by someone with a better aim—he's just perfect for her. Hell, Max, you know he'll drift right out of her life the minute this is finished—if not sooner."

"Maybe not," Max said quietly. "He was hurt bad last night. Bleeding, in shock. He didn't come to me for help, and he didn't come to you. He came here. To Morgan. He doesn't remember consciously making that decision."

"Then," Jared said crudely, "all his brains are below his belt."

"I hope you know better than that."

After a moment, Jared's eyes fell. "All right, maybe I do," he said. "But I thought I knew him ten years ago, and I was sure as hell wrong about that."

Max sat down on the arm of a chair near Jared and looked at him steadily. "What makes you more angry—that he became a thief, or that he didn't confide in you about it?"

"Does it matter?"

"Of course it does. If you're angry at what he chose to do with his life, that's concern for him. If you're angry because he didn't tell you, that's your bruised ego."

"Ego, hell. I'm a cop, Max, an officer in an international police organization. So how do you think I felt to find out that my brother was the crafty thief who had topped our most-wanted list for the better part of ten years?"

Morgan came back into the room just in time to hear that astonishing information and was so startled she spoke without thinking. "Brother? You mean, you and Quinn are—"

He looked at her with those pale, angry eyes, and for the first time she saw an elusive resemblance between his handsome features and Quinn's. "Yes, we're brothers," he confirmed flatly. "Do us all a favor and forget you know that."

She didn't get angry at him in return, because she was both perceptive enough to see the anxiety underneath his simmering fury and shrewd enough to have a fair idea of what a difficult position Jared must have found himself in when the infamous Quinn turned out to be his own flesh and blood. There was, clearly, reason enough for him to be a trifle put out.

"Consider it forgotten," she murmured.

Jared didn't look as if he believed her but directed his question to Max. "Is he awake?"

"He was a few minutes ago."

"Then I'd better talk to him."

"Max, you said he was ready to sleep. Can't it wait until later?" Morgan protested.

"No," Jared told her briefly, and headed for the bedroom with a determined stride.

Morgan stared after him for a moment, then looked at Max. "Don't you think you'd better go in there too? Jared has blood in his eye, and Quinn's lost too much of his own to be able to defend himself."

"You're probably right." Max was frowning slightly, but he didn't waste any time in following Jared.

*   *   *

It was after eight o'clock that morning before Max and Jared emerged from the bedroom.

"Wolfe'll have a fit when he finds out what happened," Jared muttered gloomily, his anger apparently gone but his mood not much improved.

"I'll handle Wolfe," Max told him.

"Good. He's still pissed at me."

"Why should he have a fit?" Morgan asked curiously. "Good lord, does *he* know Quinn too? I mean really know him, the way you two do?"

"Ask Quinn," Jared growled, and stalked from her apartment.

Morgan was feeling her virtually sleepless and very eventful night by then, a state not helped by numerous cups of coffee, and nearly wailed at Max, "And all this time I felt guilty because *I* knew him!"

One of his rare smiles swept across Max's hard face. "Morgan, since Alex is asleep and will probably sleep for hours, why don't you stretch out on your couch and take a nap. I think you need one."

That suggestion held too much appeal for her to argue, and it wasn't until she'd closed the door behind Max, briefly checked on her sleeping patient, and curled up on the couch with a pillow and blanket that something occurred to her.

Max had directly referred to Quinn by name only once, and then it had been his real name—Alex. She tried to think about that, but she was just too tired, falling asleep almost instantly.

* * *

Storm Tremaine, tiny and blond, with fierce eyes and a lazy Southern drawl, didn't look anything at all like a cop—or even a technical specialist. But she happened to be both—an agent with Interpol, specializing in computers and security.

In any case, Jared Chavalier, senior Interpol agent and her boss on this assignment, had known her too long not to know that she was small only in physical stature, not ability or self-confidence.

"So Max is talking to Wolfe, huh?" She glanced at the computer screen on her desk from time to time as the security system she had designed and installed was currently running its diagnostic program. But otherwise she kept her gaze on Jared, who was moving rather restlessly around the very small room.

"Yeah."

"And since you know Wolfe is still furious at you, you're hiding back here with me."

"I am not hiding."

"Right. You just love pacing about six square feet of floor space. Where I come from, that's what we call going nowhere in a hurry."

Jared turned to stare at her, but after meeting her amused gaze, he finally sat down in her visitor's chair with a sigh. "I've been expecting him to pull the plug ever since you were attacked and he found out about the trap. After what happened last night . . . God knows what he'll do."

"Whatever Max wants him to do."

Jared knew that Wolfe was completely in love with Storm and she with him, and he also knew there were—now—no secrets between them, so he said bluntly, "He knew about Quinn before this, didn't he?"

"Yeah, but not because I told him."

Jared lifted an eyebrow, but Storm shook her head with a smile. "I gather he got in touch right after he found out about the trap, but he didn't say how. Just that he and Quinn had a little . . . meeting."

"And Quinn told him the truth?"

"Wolfe thinks he did."

"What do you think?"

"I think . . . Quinn is the sort of man who always has an ace or two up his sleeve. Maybe even a rabbit. And never tells anybody the whole truth."

Jared grimaced. "That's what I'm afraid of."

"But you do believe he's working with you rather than against you this time?"

"Christ, I don't know. Before all this started, I would have said Max was the last man on earth who'd have to worry about Quinn stealing anything from him. Now . . . I just don't know."

"This trap . . ." Storm pursed her lips, then went on slowly. "Interpol doesn't know about the bait, do they?"

"Interpol isn't in the habit of using priceless private collections of gems and artworks to bait traps."

"Umm. That's what I thought. But they do know that Quinn is working with you to catch this thief they're calling Nightshade, an arrangement they approve because Nightshade is by all accounts way more vicious and deadly than Quinn is. Yes?"

"Yes."

"And because when he finally did get caught, Quinn was quietly given a choice between rotting in prison for the rest of his life or putting his skills to good use playing on Interpol's team. So you're supposed to be holding the leash."

"Supposed to be," Jared said grimly, "is a good description. He claimed to need more freedom in order to do his *job*, so I let the leash play out and gave him what he wanted. God knows if I could even reel him in now."

"Mixing your metaphors," Storm murmured, then went on before Jared could do more than glare at her. "His working with Interpol is recent, right?"

"Right. Other than some . . . intelligence he's provided, this is the first active case he's been on. First time out on a leash, so to speak."

"So you can't really know if this is going to work on any level. But you said he gave you his word he wouldn't try to escape you—or Interpol."

"He did."

"You also said his word was worth something, that he never breaks a promise."

"That's what I keep telling myself."

"You think he'd run if he got the chance?"

"Not before we catch Nightshade. It's personal for him."

"How—"

"Don't ask; I don't know the details. I only know that Quinn wants Nightshade. Badly."

"Umm. Well, in the meantime, I can see how Interpol might be a bit upset with you if they find out exactly what's going on over on this side of the pond. And I imagine Lloyd's of London wouldn't be very pleased if they knew about the trap either, since they insure the collection. And Wolfe is definitely risking his job with them. I guess I'm most surprised at Max being willing to take the risk. It took his family five centuries to build the collection, and every piece is irreplaceable."

"Don't remind me. I think it's a lunatic idea and I have from the beginning."

"Then it wasn't your idea. Why did you agree to it?"

"Max agreed. Once he did, there was nothing I could do about it except go along."

Storm couldn't help but smile. "Sounds like you've got a pit bull at the other end of that leash. It was Quinn's idea, wasn't it? His plan?"

Jared nodded, and hesitated for an instant before saying, "If it had been anybody but Nightshade, I never would have even allowed Quinn to approach Max. But to stop a thief and murderer like Nightshade, almost any risk can be justified."

"Even your brother's life?"

Jared's face tightened slightly, but he replied in a steady voice. "He's been risking his life for ten years or more. The only thing that's changed is the reason why."

"Has he ever been shot before?"

"No. He says not. Injured a few times and beaten up more than once, but never shot."

"So that's changed. And one more thing has changed, Jared."

He waited, silent.

"This time, Quinn's on a leash. Something a man accustomed to total freedom might well find to be a problem. A deadly problem."

"Yes," Jared said. "I know."

"The doctor said you have to take the pills. They'll help prevent infection."

"Not with milk," Quinn said firmly, frowning up at her. "I hate milk, Morgana."

She sighed, faced with the first real mutiny from her patient after slightly more than twenty-four hours of tranquillity. He had slept most of that time, waking only briefly every few hours and accepting without protest the broth she had spooned into him. He had watched her steadily, his green eyes quiet, thanked her gravely for any service she performed for him, and was otherwise a model patient. Until now, anyway.

Given his personality as she knew it, she hadn't expected the placidity to last, of course, but she had hoped for at least a couple of days before he began to get restless.

"All right, no milk," she said agreeably. "But you have to take the pills. How about juice?"

"How about coffee?"

"The last thing you need is caffeine."

"Coffee," he repeated, softly but stubbornly.

Morgan debated silently, then decided it wasn't worth a fight. It was more important that he take the pills—no matter what he washed them down with. Besides, she was almost sure she had a can of decaffeinated. "All right, coffee. It'll be a few minutes, though; I have to make some."

He nodded, those absurdly long lashes veiling his eyes so she couldn't tell if he was gloating over her capitulation. She retreated from the bedroom with the unwanted milk, vaguely suspicious although she didn't know why.

Fifteen minutes later, she returned to the bedroom to find the covers thrown back and the bed empty and realized she must have read his intentions subconsciously if not consciously. His minor rebellion was escalating. The bathroom door was closed, and there was water running in the sink.

She set the cup of coffee on the nightstand, went to the door, and knocked courteously. "Alex, what are you doing in there?"

"It's not polite to ask that, Morgana," he reproved in a muffled but amused voice.

She leaned her forehead against the door and

sighed. "You're not supposed to be out of bed. The doctor said—"

"I know what the doctor said, but I'll be damned if I ever let myself get *that* helpless. There are some things a man prefers to do for himself. Do you have a razor?"

"You aren't going to shave."

"Oh, yes, I am."

Morgan took a step back and glared at the door. "All right. I'll just wait out here until you get dizzy and fall on your ass. When I hear the thud, I'll call Max and ask him to come over here and drag your carcass back to bed."

There was a moment of silence, and then the water stopped running in the sink and the door opened. He stood there a bit unsteadily, a towel wrapped around his lean waist, his green eyes very bright, and that crooked, beguiling smile curving his lips. He had slid his left arm from the sling meant to ease the weight on that shoulder and braced his good shoulder against the doorjamb.

Judging by the dampness of his tousled hair, he had washed up a bit, doing the best he could when he could hardly stand and couldn't get his bandaged shoulder wet. As for the towel—he probably hadn't felt steady enough to get into any of the clothing Max had sent over, even though the stuff was neatly folded in plain view on the storage chest at the foot of Morgan's bed.

When Max had stripped him, he had removed

everything; Morgan knew that because she had washed the pants and shorts and thrown the ruined sweater in the trash.

"You're a hard woman, Morgana," he murmured.

She wished she was. She had been trying rather fiercely to see him only as a wounded body needing her help, and as long as he'd remained in the bed she had more or less succeeded. But he was on his feet now—however unsteadily—and it was impossible for her to look at him wearing only a towel and a bandage and not see him as utterly male and heart-catchingly sexy.

He's a thief.

She remembered too well how that hard body felt against hers and how his beguiling mouth had seduced hers until she hadn't cared who or what he was. She remembered his murmured words, when he'd told her that he thought she was going to break his heart.

He's just a damned thief.

She also remembered the mocking gift of a concubine ring.

It was that last memory that steadied her. Calmly, she said, "Look, if you really have to shave, there's an electric razor around here somewhere. I'll get it for you. But you have to go back to bed."

After an instant, he nodded slightly and took a step toward her. He would have fallen if she hadn't quickly slid an arm around his waist and put her shoulder under his good one.

"Dammit, you tried to do too much," she muttered as he leaned on her heavily.

"I think you're right." He sounded definitely weakened. "If you could help me to the bed . . ."

Halfway across the room, Morgan got the distinct feeling that he wasn't quite as frail as he seemed, but she didn't try to call his bluff. What else could she expect, after all? she asked herself somewhat wryly as she helped him those last few steps. His humorous, mischievous, and careless nature had been obvious from the first time she'd met him, and she doubted very much if he had a sincere bone in his body; he was perfectly capable of pretending weakness simply because he enjoyed leaning on her.

She batted his amazingly limp but wonderfully accurate hand away from her right breast and more or less dumped him on the bed.

Quinn grimaced as his shoulder was jolted, but he was also laughing softly. "All right, but you can't blame me for trying," he said guilelessly.

Hands on her hips, Morgan glared down at him. Damn the man, it was so *hard* to stay mad at him. "Next time you get out of that bed, you'd better make sure you can get back under your own steam. I meant what I said about calling Max."

Quinn eased himself farther up on the bed, then glanced down at the towel still wrapped around him. "I suppose you wouldn't want to help me—"

"No. Like you said, there are some things a man should do for himself. I'll go find the razor." He was laughing at her again when she left the room, but Morgan didn't yell at him. She didn't even turn around to look at him, because he would have seen her smiling completely against her will.

Even if he *was* on the side of the angels this time, she told herself, he was still a thief and a scoundrel. Charming, but still a scoundrel. She needed to remember that.

She really, really needed to remember that.

When she returned to the bedroom a few minutes later, he was propped up on the pillows, the covers drawn up to his waist, sipping the coffee she'd brought him. The towel was crumpled up on the floor by the bed.

She retrieved it and returned it to the bathroom. Silently. She unwound the cord from the electric razor, plugged it into an outlet by the nightstand, and set the razor within easy reach for him. Silently. Then she gave him his pills and waited until he swallowed them.

He eyed her somewhat warily, then said, "You aren't mad at me, are you, Morgana?"

It cost her, but she managed to remain at least outwardly unmoved by his wistfulness. "No, but you're walking a fine edge," she warned him mildly.

He was silent for a moment, then set his coffee cup on the nightstand and nodded gravely. For once, his green eyes were perfectly serious. "I know—I can't help pushing. And . . . I hate having to depend on anyone else. For anything."

Morgan could feel her resolve weakening. As dangerous to her composure as he was in his playful, amusing mode, this—apparent—painful honesty was devastating. She had the sudden conviction that unless she was very, very careful, Quinn would steal far more from her than she could afford to lose.

From somewhere, she summoned an award-winning portrayal of calm reason. "Why don't we make an agreement. I'll do my best not to threaten your independence in any way, and you shelve Don Juan for the duration. Okay?"

Smiling, he nodded. "Okay."

"Good. Now, I'm going to do something about lunch while you shave. And afterward, if you don't feel like resting, there are a host of alternatives, beginning with reading or television and ending with a card game."

"You play cards?" His eyes gleamed at her. "Poker?"

"Any kind except strip," she said gently.

"Oh, shoot," he murmured, not Don Juan now but the mischievous boy who was nearly as seductive.

She shook her head at him and turned toward the door, but halted there when he spoke softly.

"Morgana? Thank you."

Again she found her resolve threatened, and again she managed to shore it up. "Oh, you can pay me back easily, Alex. Just return the necklace you stole from me."

He laughed at her as she left the room, completely unrepentant and utterly shameless.

Inspector Keane Tyler of the San Francisco Police Department scowled down at the virtually nude body of Jane Doe (#3 for this month) and said to no one in particular, "This is not my favorite way to spend a Saturday afternoon."

"Don't imagine it's hers either." Inspector Gillian Newman, new to San Francisco but clearly not to the job, spoke with the slightly wry detachment common to cops who saw too much of the darker side of life's streets. "Preliminary estimate says she's been dead awhile, but when's difficult to pin down."

"Why?"

"Doc says she's spent some time in a freezer."

Keane's scowl disappeared and his eyebrows lifted. "That's an unusual wrinkle. So somebody wants to mess with our heads."

"Looks like. Could be somebody she knew, trying to make the time of death as vague as possible because he—or she—can't establish an alibi."

"Any evidence the killer knew her?"

"Not so far."

"Was she raped?"

"Doc says no."

"Stripped to her panties but not raped. Maybe because her clothes could have given us an I.D.—or at least a place to start looking for an I.D."

"Or maybe the killer is a boob man. Gets his rocks off looking or copping a feel, and took the clothes as a trophy."

"Equally as likely," Keane admitted. "At least until we have some solid evidence either way."

"It's clear he didn't want her identified. The doc says her fingers were burned with a blowtorch."

"That'll do it," Keane said grimly. "Maybe forensics can get something resembling a print, but it'll take time if it's even possible at all."

"In the meantime, back at the office they're checking her description against the missing-persons file," Gillian reported briskly. "Nothing so far. We're doing the usual door-to-door, but so far nobody saw a thing. Not surprising, considering how remote this place is. Area's being searched, but I think we both know this is just where the body was dumped. Nothing else happened here."

"Great," Keane muttered. "So unless she turns up in our files as missing or we get wildly lucky and somebody recognizes a photo, we don't have a hope in hell of getting an I.D."

"Well, there is one thing that might point us in a specific direction. Or at least point us where the killer wants us to go."

"What do you mean?"

"During the preliminary exam, the doc found something. In her panties. It's a strip of paper torn from one of those guides you pick up when you visit a national landmark—or a museum. You know, information, a map. I sort of doubt it got in her underwear accidentally."

Keane began to feel queasy for the first time. "Ah, don't tell me. Please don't tell me."

"Sorry. It's the Museum of Historical Art."

CHAPTER
THREE

W hat I don't understand," Storm Tremaine drawled somewhat absently as she typed commands into the computer, "is why you're still snapping at Jared. He's just doing his job."

"What I don't understand is why you have to work on a Saturday. Max told you to take weekends off." Resting a hip on the corner of her desk and wearing her little blond cat on his shoulder, Wolfe Nickerson, security expert and representative of Lloyd's of London, was waiting for his lady to finish the work she insisted had to be completed today.

"I just wanted to fix this glitch before Monday. Now tell me why you're still pissed at Jared."

Jared had left the room only moments before, and though a security problem had been ironed out successfully, neither man had been happy with the other.

"He nearly got you killed," Wolfe muttered, reaching up to absently scratch Bear under his chin. "Besides that, I don't like being lied to."

Eyeing him shrewdly, Storm said, "You haven't been snapping at Max—or me. Neither of us was especially truthful there for a while. Give Jared a break, will you, please?"

"I *am* giving him a break. I'm still speaking to him."

Storm laughed softly, shaking her head. If she had learned anything since meeting him, she had learned that Wolfe's stubbornness equaled her own. "Well, just try to remember that he *is* on our side, after all. He's not the enemy."

"All right."

She sat back in her chair as the computer digested her commands, and smiled up at him. "Besides, there are better ways to focus your energy. Do you realize you haven't thrown me to the floor and had your way with me even once today?"

He frowned. "Wasn't that you this morning? Among all the boxes in the living room?"

"Yes, but that was before breakfast."

He leaned across the desk, meeting her halfway as she straightened in her chair, and kissed her. "And wasn't that you I had lunch with today?" he murmured.

"Yes, but that was in a bed."

Wolfe glanced aside at the minuscule floor space

of the computer room, then eyed her rather cluttered desk. "Well, there's no room in here."

Storm sighed mournfully. "I knew it. Engaged just a few weeks, and already you're getting bored with me."

"If I get any more bored with you, they're going to have to put me in traction."

She laughed. "Complaining?"

"Hell, no." He smiled, and his eyes were like the glowing blue at the base of a flame. "In fact, I'm a bit anxious to get back to that new house of ours and have another go at christening the bed."

They had found and rented a terrific house with an enclosed garden, where Bear could sun himself and chase bugs, and had moved their things there days ago. But with their working hours—and tendency to forget practical matters whenever they were alone—they were still in the process of settling in.

Though they hadn't yet decided where "home" would be in the future, the *Mysteries Past* exhibit would demand that both of them remain in San Francisco for at least the coming months.

"We need to finish unpacking," she pointed out mildly.

"A minute ago you were hot for my body," he said in a wounded tone.

"I still am, but when it comes to love among the boxes—once is enough." Storm grinned at him and began typing in the commands that would get her out of the computer system for the day. "By the way—

even though neither of you has said much about it, it's pretty obvious you and Jared have known each other a long time. Not so surprising, I suppose, given your jobs. Him with Interpol and you with Lloyd's."

"Our paths have crossed in the last ten years," Wolfe admitted.

"So you've learned to respect each other's authority."

Her voice had been placid, but Wolfe realized she wasn't yet prepared to drop the subject.

"Yes," he said, "we respect each other's authority—and ability to do our jobs. That hasn't changed. But Jared crossed a line, Storm. He might not have hung you out like bait on a hook, but he didn't give you information you had every right to know, information that would at least have put you on guard. You deserved better. You know it, I know it, and he knows it."

"I'm an Interpol agent. Risk comes with the job."

"You're a technical specialist for Interpol, not a field agent. It was your own sense and savvy that kept you alive, not any training from Interpol. And Jared had no right to put you in that position without so much as a warning to watch your back."

"What's done is done."

Wolfe drew a breath and released it slowly. "Look, I know he's your boss. I respect that. You want to defend him, I understand; your loyalty is one of the reasons I love you. But if you expect me to forgive him anytime soon for unnecessarily endangering your life, forget it."

"It's not going to do me any good to argue, huh?"

"No. Not about this."

Whatever response Storm might have made became unimportant when the subject of their discussion rapped on the door and pushed it open without waiting for a response.

"We've got trouble," Jared said.

It was early Saturday evening when Morgan's phone rang, and she picked it up hastily since Quinn was sleeping in the next room. "Hello?"

"How is he?" Max asked.

"Getting restless. I had to threaten to tie him to the bed, but he finally agreed to at least try to sleep. He's already been up a couple of times, Max. The doc was right—he does heal fast."

"Probably a necessity for a man in his line of work."

Morgan hesitated, then said, "You don't sound very disapproving of his line of work."

"It isn't my place to judge. Besides, do you honestly think my approval or disapproval would change anything?"

"No. No, it wouldn't. I guess I'm just surprised at how calmly you're taking all this. And how helpful you've been to Quinn."

"Did you expect me to say no when you called?"

Morgan had to laugh. "To be honest, it never crossed my mind that you might. All I was thinking was that you could get a doctor here quietly without the police having to know. But it would probably have been better for both of us if you—or I—had called the police that night."

"Better for the exhibit, you mean?"

"Yeah. Of course that's what I meant. Better for the exhibit." Morgan cleared her throat. "It would be a dandy way to get at your collection, we both know that. Pretend to be after another thief, pretend to be helping the good guys, and—hey, presto—you're on the inside, where all the goodies are. A Trojan horse."

"Do you think that's what Alex is doing?"

"I don't know. And neither do you."

Max sighed. "So far, he's done nothing to threaten the collection. He's at least nominally under Interpol's control, here to work on the right side of the law. I have to believe that. Because the thief he's trying to help Interpol put behind bars is far, far worse than Quinn has ever been."

"I forgot to ask about that the other night. Who is this thief you're risking your collection to trap?"

"Well, unlike Quinn, this one hasn't caught the fancy of the press or public, so there's been almost no publicity about his activities. You probably haven't heard of him. At Interpol, his code name is Nightshade."

Briefly distracted by the name, she said, "Isn't that another name for some plants—like belladonna?"

"Pure poison. And he—or she, I suppose—is definitely that. A far more violent and dangerous personality than Quinn, that much everyone is certain of. There have been eight murders committed during Nightshade's robberies in the past six years, all of them because someone got in his way."

"You're right, I haven't heard of him. Does he work in Europe, or—"

"All over, but the majority of the robberies were committed here in the States. Every law-enforcement agency in the world has tried to identify him, and no one has even come up with a name. No living witnesses, no fingerprints or other forensic evidence conveniently left behind, and the computers can't even find a pattern in the robberies, except that he favors gems and tends toward the more old-fashioned scaling-the-wall-and-breaking-a-window sort of burglaries."

"Low-tech rather than high-tech."

"As far as Interpol can determine, yeah. It's one reason we picked an older museum in which to display the collection. Any thief worth his salt is going to know we're installing better electronic security, but he or she could also be at least reasonably certain that in this huge old building there are bound to be a few chinks in the defenses."

Morgan thought about that for a moment, then asked curiously, "If there's no pattern, then how do you know all the robberies were committed by the same person?"

Max's sigh was a breath of sound. "Because the bastard always leaves a calling card. Which you don't know about, by the way, because Interpol and other police agencies keep it quiet in order to I.D. his crimes. He always leaves a dead rose. On the body if he kills someone in the commission of the robbery, and in place of whatever gem he took if there was no murder."

She shivered. "That's a morbid touch."

"No kidding. You should hear some of the theories advanced by police, FBI, and Interpol behavioral experts. The general consensus is that, aside from his love of gems and his tendency to kill anyone who gets in his way, Nightshade probably has a few more kinks in his nature."

"Sounds like. And since he's been so elusive, you guys decided to stack the deck in your favor. It's likely that a collection as priceless as yours going on public display for the first time in more than thirty years would lure Nightshade here to San Francisco. And if you know he's here and what he's after, you can set a trap to catch him."

"That's the idea."

"Won't he suspect a trap?"

"If he's as smart as everyone agrees he is, he will. But greed tends to undermine common sense, or at least that's the hope in this case. That plus the edge we hope we have: Quinn. Setting a thief to catch a thief. The bait *has* to be something big, something very tempting to someone like Nightshade, to encourage him to perhaps act more recklessly than is normal for him."

"I'd say the Bannister collection is probably making him drool," Morgan said.

"Alex and Jared expect so. It's the only shot they've had at getting their hands on Nightshade, Morgan. In eight years, he hasn't put a foot wrong, and the odds are against him making a serious enough mistake in the future to let the police catch him. And even if he does, God knows how many people will have to die first. So . . . luring him to a trap designed just for him is worth all the risks we're taking."

"Even the risk that the true danger to the collection is Quinn?"

"Even that."

"Okay, if we assume Quinn really is doing what he says he's doing, then what's his motive for putting his own life on the line? Is it like Jared said, just a way to stay out of prison himself?"

"That's not my story, Morgan. You'll have to ask Alex about it."

"And of course he'll tell me the truth."

"You never know."

"Yeah. Well, maybe I'll ask him."

"In the meantime," Max said, "aside from checking on Alex, I also called to warn you."

"Oh, Christ, what now?"

"I got a call earlier from Keane Tyler. The body of

a murdered woman was found a few miles from the museum. They haven't gotten an I.D. yet, but apparently there's some evidence she's connected to the museum."

"Connected how?"

"We don't know. Whatever the evidence is, the police intend to keep it quiet."

"Even from you?"

"Even from me." Unemotionally, Max added, "Ken Dugan and I were called in to take a look at the body. Neither of us knows her." Dugan was the head curator of the Museum of Historical Art.

Morgan swallowed. "Maybe I should—"

"Not yet. Keane and his people are talking to museum employees, but I've told him you won't be available until Monday or Tuesday."

"And he's okay with that?"

"Let's say I called in a favor. He's okay with it. But he will want to speak to you when you get in. Maybe show you a photo of the woman."

"Max, does this have anything to do with the exhibit?"

"I don't know."

"They still haven't found out who murdered that poor Ace employee a few weeks ago—"

"We don't know there's a connection between the two murders. As far as the police have been able to determine, this woman is not and never has been an Ace employee." Ace Security was the company ostensibly handling the installation of the new security system in the museum; Storm was posing as one of their security specialists.

"But she's somehow connected to the museum?"

"That's what Keane says. And because of the exhibit, the police are investigating the possibilities of a connection very thoroughly. In any case, until we know more, it's fairly useless to speculate."

"Yeah. Yeah, I guess so."

"I just wanted to let you know what was going on and warn you to expect the police activity when you go back to the museum."

"Should I tell Alex about this?"

"You can, or Jared will when Alex is back on his feet. I'd wait a couple of days, though. There's nothing he could do about it now anyway. That's assuming there is a connection with the museum."

"I don't really believe in coincidence, Max."

"No. No, neither do I. Take care, Morgan."

"I will. You too."

In the next room, Quinn listened to two soft clicks and then the dial tone.

"Shit," he muttered half under his breath.

He put the bedroom phone back on its base and stared down at his left hand as he flexed it slowly. His shoulder throbbed a protest, and he grimaced. But he didn't stop the slow, deliberate movements.

He had to get back on his feet.

Time was running out.

* * *

She moved through the darkness as though it were a part of her, slipping between the shadows of the buildings with nothing more than a whisper of sound. Even with the heavier-than-usual pack she carried, she was able to be silent. A distant siren caused her to freeze momentarily, but it faded even farther away and she continued on.

It was a familiar path she walked, one she had walked countless times in recent weeks, but even so she didn't let her guard down. Planning and practice, she had discovered, were the keys to success.

She was very successful, very good at what she did.

Less than ten minutes later, she was moving silently through the dungeonlike corridors of the museum's huge basement. Patrols down here were almost nonexistent, but she was forced to avoid one bored guard moving through the main corridor methodically checking doors.

After he'd gone, she looked at her watch, mentally reminded herself she'd have just enough time before his next pass through the corridor, then continued on.

She had to pass through two more doors, both locked and both easily opened with the aid of tools she carried, before she reached her goal. It was dark down here, with no more than dim safety lights burning, but with the aid of the small but powerful flashlight she carried, there was enough light for her to do her work.

She shrugged off the backpack and knelt to open it. The first thing she lifted from the bag was a canvas-wrapped bundle. She placed it on the floor beside her pack and carefully turned back the canvas to reveal a knife. It was about twelve inches long, with a hammered brass blade and carved wooden handle.

It looked old. It was old.

It was also stained with dried blood.

She smiled and got busy.

By Sunday morning Quinn felt well enough to get dressed and move around Morgan's apartment under his own steam. Slowly at first, but steadily gaining strength.

Max had come by with the doctor to check on his progress early in the day, but other than those visitors Quinn and Morgan were alone together. True to his word, Quinn shelved his Don Juan persona, and she wasn't very surprised to find him an excellent companion.

He was a lively and amusing conversationalist, which she had known, never seemed to lose his sense of humor, could talk intelligently on any number of subjects, had seen a respectable chunk of the world, and played a mean game of poker. He even helped her in the kitchen. Skillfully yet.

Morgan didn't mention the murdered woman Max had told her about. She didn't bring up the subject of why Quinn was in San Francisco, ask him exactly what he'd been doing to get himself shot, or castigate him for not telling her the truth—ostensible truth, anyway—about his involvement with the *Mysteries Past* trap.

Quinn also didn't mention anything potentially touchy. She thought both of them avoided the more dangerous subjects, and though she didn't know his reasons she certainly knew hers.

Quite simply, she didn't want him to lie to her—and she was reasonably sure he would.

They were casual with each other, and aside from one heated argument when Quinn wanted to give up her bed and sleep on the couch instead (Morgan won), they got along fine. But there was a growing awareness between them, a building tension that was difficult to ignore. Perhaps it was the inevitable result of spending so much time together, or perhaps something much more complicated, and by Monday night Morgan was clinging to her resolve with both hands.

She was afraid she was on the verge of doing something incredibly stupid, and she had the unnerved feeling he knew it too.

After they'd eaten dinner and cleaned up the kitchen, Morgan left him watching an old movie on television while she went to take a shower. She had gone out of her way to be conservative in her clothes, wearing mostly oversize sweaters and shirts with jeans and, at night, a pair of oriental-style black pajamas and robe that covered her decently by anybody's standards.

It didn't seem to help.

When she returned to the living room, clad in her oriental pajamas and a robe, the television was turned down low, only one lamp burned, and Quinn was standing by the front window—the same one through which he'd entered wounded—gazing out at a chilly, foggy San Francisco night. He was wearing jeans with a button-up white shirt, the collar open and cuffs turned back loosely on his tanned forearms. The bandage on his shoulder didn't show, and he didn't look as if he'd ever been wounded.

"Is something wrong?" she asked immediately, wondering if he'd been alerted by anything he heard or saw.

"No, I was just thinking . . . it's a good night for skulking around out there." He turned, but his face was still in shadow.

Morgan felt oddly breathless and swore at herself silently for it. She was being ridiculous. *And stupid. Let's not forget stupid.* "Oh. Is this the kind of night you like? For—skulking, I mean."

He didn't answer immediately, and when he did there was a thread of tension in his voice. "It's the kind of night I'm used to. The kind of night I've seen a lot of. When the line between black and white blurs in the darkness."

She went slowly toward him, halting no more than an arm's length away. His size always surprised her when she was this close to him, because there was something so lithe and graceful about the way he moved she tended to forget the sheer physical power of broad shoulders and superbly conditioned muscles. She had to tilt her head back to look up at him.

"Is that all you find nights like this good for? What about when you're inside, like this?"

He drew a short breath and let it out roughly. "Something blameless, I suppose. Read a good book, watch television. Play cards."

"Strip poker?"

"A game you wouldn't play," he reminded her.

"Maybe I've changed my mind." She heard herself say it and couldn't believe the words were coming out of her mouth. *I'm out of my mind. Absolutely, unconditionally out of my mind . . .*

Quinn reached up with one hand to brush a strand of her long black hair away from her face, his fingers lingering for just a moment to stroke her cheek. His eyes were heavy-lidded, his mouth sensuous, and she could feel a slight tremor in his long fingers as they touched her.

Then, abruptly, he turned away and crossed the room to the hallway leading to the bedroom. "Good night, Morgana," he said briskly over his shoulder. Seconds later, the bedroom door closed softly.

. . . and not much of a vamp, apparently.

There wasn't much a woman could do when she had been rejected except wrap her pride about herself and try to put the rebuff behind her, so that's what Morgan did. She even managed, after a couple of glasses of wine, to drop off to sleep some-where around dawn.

When she woke up Tuesday morning, Quinn was gone.

It was just after nine when Max met Morgan in the lobby of the museum as she came in.

"Keane's due here in about an hour to talk to you," Max said after greeting her. "How's your houseguest?"

"Gone," Morgan replied succinctly, proud of her matter-of-fact tone. "He was up and dressed most of yesterday, and gone when I got up this morning." She paused, then added dryly, "While I was getting ready to leave, a florist delivered a lovely vase of flowers. No card."

"Well, at least he said thank you."

"He did say it once or twice while he was healing," she admitted. "But the flowers were a nice touch."

Max smiled slightly, but his eyes were grave. "Don't be too hard on yourself for . . . feeling the effects of his charm."

"I think I should be appalled," she muttered.

"Do you? Morgan, have you realized that, even six months ago, you were so fixated on work and so closed off from other people that you would have seen Quinn as pure evil, a completely negative force?"

"You're trying to tell me that would have been a bad thing?"

"Of course it would have. People are far more complex than that; their desires and motives tangled and contradictory. Alex is no more a purely evil man than he is a purely good man—he's just a man. And you've opened up enough, learned to trust your instincts enough, to be able to see that."

"And just complicate the hell out of my life. Oh, goodie."

"You have to admit you're enjoying this complicated new life a lot more than you were your old one."

Morgan did admit that, but silently. What she said was, "He's a thief, Max. Whatever he's doing now with Interpol is because he had to, not because he wanted to."

"Granted. But even good men can make bad choices, Morgan. Keep it in mind."

"You like him," she realized, surprised.

"I like him. I don't harbor any illusions about him, though. He's three parts chameleon, and he'll always find a way to fit himself into whatever role he's playing. So it is a bit difficult to see the man behind the gifted actor."

Morgan thought about that for a moment, absently watching visitors wandering through the lobby. "Didn't you just contradict yourself? He can't be a good man who made a bad choice *and* a chameleon always playing a part and hiding his true self. Can he?"

"Can't he?" Without waiting for her to respond

to that, Max added, "I have a meeting with Ken and the board, but Storm, Wolfe, and Jared are waiting for you in your office. You should all get up to speed on the latest . . . developments."

"Gotcha." Morgan made her way across the lobby and into the administrative area of the museum. She found her relatively small office occupied by two large men and one very small blonde and had to squeeze past Wolfe to get to the chair behind her desk.

"Hi, all."

"We were just discussing your houseguest," Storm offered in her customary drawl. She was in one of the visitor's chairs and Jared was in the other, with Wolfe wedged between the desk and a filing cabinet.

"Yeah? What about him?"

"Well, for one thing, what was he doing to end up getting shot? I mean, the collection isn't in place here yet. The trap isn't set."

Morgan found it perfectly reasonable that Storm knew about Quinn and the trap being set; aside from being Wolfe's fiancée, she was also their computer expert and had written the security program that would protect the Bannister collection. She *had* to know.

"I didn't ask, and he didn't offer any explanations." Morgan looked at Jared, brows lifting. "Shouldn't you know? And should Interpol be such a . . . visible presence in the museum?"

"I'm not known as an agent on this side of the Atlantic; as far as onlookers are concerned, I'm an independent security consultant called in to work with Wolfe."

Morgan found that a bit ironic but repeated her other question. "Shouldn't you know why Quinn was shot?"

The Interpol agent answered readily. "Quinn's convinced that Nightshade is already in the city. That he might even live here. So he's been . . . looking around."

"Breaking into private homes?"

Wincing slightly, Jared said, "I told him not to tell me about it if he did. He claims he's mostly kept an eye on the nightly activities in the city, just to identify the players more than anything else. But, since we're convinced Nightshade is a collector, searching for a secret cache in a private home is probably not a bad idea."

"Was that what he was doing Thursday night?"

"No, he says he was near this museum—and spotted someone apparently casing the building, for at least the third night in a row. On both previous nights, this person slipped away from him in the fog, so Quinn was, naturally, determined not to lose him. What he wanted was to follow him or her back to, presumably, a house, apartment, or hotel. Unfortunately, somewhere near the waterfront, his quarry doubled back and caught him. Shot him with a silenced automatic."

Morgan blocked from her mind the memory of that terrifying night and Quinn bleeding in her living room to say calmly, "Max said the bullet went in at an angle, otherwise it probably would have killed Quinn. But he heals fast."

"Already up and gone, is he?" Jared said.

"This morning." Morgan offered nothing more.

It was Storm who asked, "Couldn't that bullet be used as evidence? I mean—"

Jared said, "I know what you mean. Yeah, if we ever do get our hands on this guy, if he has a gun, and if a ballistics expert can match it to the bullet the doctor dug out of Quinn's shoulder, we could at least hang an attempted-murder charge on him. We're waiting for a ballistics report now. What I'm interested to see is whether that bullet matches the ones taken from four of Nightshade's previous victims."

Wolfe spoke up for the first time to say, "If it does, you'll know that Nightshade is in the city and that Quinn came very close to him that night."

"Too close," Morgan said.

"Too close in more ways than one," Jared said. "If it was Nightshade, it's at least possible that he now knows someone has been shadowing him, following him across rooftops. And the police don't usually work that way."

"But another thief might." Morgan didn't like the hollow sound of her own voice.

"Another thief might," Jared agreed. "So Nightshade has to be wondering who's following him. And why."

"Then there's this new wrinkle," Storm said. "A

murdered woman possibly connected to the museum. Inspector Tyler and his people are being awfully cagey about the connection, but just from their manner I'd say they're pretty damned sure there is one."

"So we have to assume the same thing," Wolfe said. "First the Ace employee being blackmailed and then murdered and now this." He was gazing steadily at Jared. "There's two lives that might have been saved if nobody had planned to display the Bannister collection."

Jared didn't flinch away from that hard stare. "And God knows how many Nightshade will kill if we don't stop him here and now. Just for the record, I'm betting the police will rule out Nightshade in the Jane Doe murder."

"Why?" Morgan asked.

"Because in virtually every case, Nightshade has left his victims where they fell, and they've tended to fall at the scene of one of his robberies. This woman was found near nothing of value to a thief, and no break-in or theft was reported. Plus, according to my sources she was stabbed; Nightshade always uses a gun. And as far as we know, he's always taken credit for his crimes. That dead-rose calling card."

"Which means," Storm said, "we could have yet another player in the game. And this one has his own set of rules. Very nasty rules."

CHAPTER
FOUR

"Any luck?" Keane asked Gillian as they met up near the museum's lobby.

"Not so you'd notice." She sighed, pushing an errant strand of brown hair back off her face. "I just talked to the last of the cleaning crew, and none of them recognizes our Jane Doe."

"And I just talked to the last guard on the list. Same deal. Doesn't know her, never noticed her here."

"It's Wednesday," Gillian pointed out. "We've talked to every soul who's worked for or in the museum during the last six months. Nada. Unless our next step is to start tracking and questioning visitors, I'd say we've hit a dead end."

He scowled. "No luck searching the basement?"

"Have you *been* in the basement?" she asked politely. "Our people can't effectively search down there. A trained archaeologist or historian might spot something out of place—given a few years and a little luck. Seriously, it's like the bargain basement from hell."

"But they looked around down there?"

"Oh, yeah. Checked windows and doors, peered around with flashlights, scared themselves silly turning corners to find Bronze Age warriors staring back at them. One of our rookies nearly shot a marble Greek woman holding an urn."

"Shit."

"Uh-huh. Getting the creeps aside, it's sort of hard to search a place like that, especially when you don't know what you're looking for. And after Pete was lost for nearly half an hour, somebody suggested we leave trails of bread crumbs."

"So we have no connection between Jane Doe and this museum except for the scrap of paper deliberately left on the body."

"Looks that way."

Keane scowled again. "I don't like being pointed in a specific direction. I like it even less when it begins to look like somebody might be leading me around by the nose."

"And in the opposite direction from where you really should be looking?"

"Exactly."

Gillian eyed him, then smiled wryly. "So we keep poking around in the museum, huh?"

"What other choice do we have? Goddammit."

It was the following Friday evening when Morgan came out of her kitchen to find a visitor had arrived. Via the window.

Oddly enough, she wasn't at all surprised to see him standing there, much as he had the night he'd been wounded. Except that he wasn't wounded now, or masked. And his lean, handsome face was, she thought, uncharacteristically strained.

"Good evening," she said politely. "I really do have to do something about that lock, don't I?"

"It might be a good idea."

"On the other hand, I could just hang garlic in the window."

"That only works on vampires, I hear."

"Let's see . . . Vampires appear only at night, they move so fast you'd think they could fly, they're creatures of legend and myth, they can cling to the side of a building like a bat . . . I'm sure I can think of something that doesn't apply to you, but so far—"

"They sleep in coffins and drink the blood of the living."

Morgan raised her eyebrows silently.

"Oh, come on," he said.

Noting that he at least wasn't standing so stiffly

now, Morgan shrugged and said, "Okay, points for that. But I may hang a cross in the window anyway, just—you should pardon the expression—for the hell of it."

He waited until she crossed the room to stand before him, and when he spoke it was quickly. "I never really thanked you for taking care of me, Morgana."

"You thanked me. And you sent flowers. Points for that, too, by the way. Is that why you're here, to thank me more?"

"I thought I would."

"You're welcome."

"You went out on a limb for me. I know that."

"My pleasure."

"I'm serious, Morgana. You could have called the police. Should have. And I'm . . . grateful that you didn't do that."

It was a bit amusing to watch the usually unflappable Quinn grope for words, but Morgan didn't allow herself to smile. "Noted. I appreciate your gratitude."

Quinn eyed her with faint exasperation. "You don't make it easy for me," he told her.

She did smile then. "Oh, I see—you want me to make it *easy* for you. Why should I?"

He cleared his throat. "Do both of us know what we're talking about?"

"Yes. We're talking about the fact that I more or

less offered myself to you Monday night—and you bolted so fast you practically left your boots behind."

A little smile curved his mouth. "The image that conjures, Morgana, is hardly flattering. To either of us."

"I agree. Is that why you really came back here? Because you had second thoughts?"

Quinn hesitated, then shook his head. "No, you were obviously not in your right mind at the time."

"I wasn't?" She put her hands on her hips and stared up at him. "Are you trying to save me from myself, Alex?"

"Something like that," he murmured.

"Then why did you come back here?"

"To thank you, that's all. I just . . . didn't like leaving that way. Without a word."

"I didn't care for it much myself. Especially the walking-away-when-I-offered-you-my-body part. That's sort of hard on a woman's ego."

"You only said maybe you'd changed your mind about strip poker."

"We both know exactly what I meant."

He cleared his throat again. "If it helps, I really—really—wanted to stay."

"Then why didn't you?"

"It would be a mistake, Morgana. Never doubt that."

"Because you're Quinn?" They hadn't talked about this when he'd been recovering here, and she had a peculiar idea that was really why he'd come back—because he wanted her to fully understand who and what he was.

"Isn't that reason enough? Name any major city in the Western world, and the cops there want me behind bars at the very least. And there are a couple of places in the Far East as well. That won't change, no matter how this turns out. I'm too effective to go public, and Interpol knows it. They've got me by the—short hairs." He laughed, honest amusement in the sound. "I can't complain. I had a hell of a dance, and now I have to pay the band."

"Extend the metaphor." She smiled faintly. "The music hasn't stopped, the tune's just changed. You enjoy the dance, Alex. And Interpol knows that. So they changed the music for you."

"And made sure I'd dance for them?" He laughed again. "Probably." His voice and face became abruptly expressionless. "The point is that . . . I'm never going to be respectable, Morgana. I don't want to be. You're right; I *enjoy* this dance. I don't feel a bit of regret about my past."

"But they caught you," she murmured.

He nodded. "They caught me. They could have locked me up; instead, they gave me a choice. And I chose. I'll keep my bargain with them. I'll dance to their tune. As you said—only the music's changed; the dance is just as much fun."

"You won't be able to steal for yourself any-more," she noted, watching him with an expression of mild interest.

He shrugged carelessly. "The proceeds of my past will see me through even a long future in style, sweet."

In a thoughtful tone, she said, "I would have expected them to demand you return those proceeds."

"They tried." He smiled sardonically. "I told them I'd forget how to dance."

"You are a complete villain, aren't you?"

Quinn eyed her a bit warily. "I don't know why on earth it's so," he commented, "but I have the most insane urge to insist that I am, in fact, just that."

"And selfish and egotistical and reckless. Without morals, scruples, compassion, or shame. Lawless, heartless, wicked, and rebellious. How am I doing?"

"Just fine," he answered with a suggestion of gritted teeth.

She nodded seriously. "Let's see . . . you're a thief of world renown, there's no doubt of that. You've quite cheerfully broken a number of the laws of God and man. Without, according to you, one iota of remorse. And you're on the right side of the law now only because it was infinitely preferable to spending the remainder of your life in a prison cell."

"All true," he said grimly.

"Do you also kick puppies and steal candy from children?"

Quinn drew a deep breath. "Only on odd Thursdays."

She smiled a little. "You know . . . I'd have a much easier time believing all these rotten things about you if you didn't try so hard to make me believe them."

With a glint of despair in his vivid eyes, he said, "Morgan, get it through your head—I'm not a nice person."

"I never said you were."

Quinn blinked but recovered quickly. "I get it. You're a danger junkie, that's why you brazenly invited me to be your lover."

"A danger junkie. Well, maybe. I would never have guessed I'd turn into one, mind you, but anything's possible. Meet a world-infamous cat burglar in a dark museum one night and all kinds of doors are suddenly before you." Morgan's tone remained thoughtful. "It's a new path. A less-traveled path. All the best journeys in life are the unexpected ones. So why not?"

"Why are you talking like a fortune cookie?"

Morgan hadn't enjoyed herself so much in years, and it took everything she had to keep from laughing out loud. Instead, she said gravely, "All kinds of doors. I'll say this for you, Alex. They're interesting doors. Very interesting doors. And the one thing I know for sure is that I really do want to find out what's behind those doors."

"Tigers," he warned.

"Somehow I doubt that. But not handsome princes either. You're not that magnanimous.

Adventure, I'd say. Maybe danger. Changes, for sure. I think my life is ready for changes."

"Morgan—"

"I'm a big girl, Alex, all grown up and everything. I think I can make decisions about my life. And who to let into it. I think that's what being a grown-up is all about."

"Morgan, I'm a *thief*. I break the law. I do bad things. Remember? I am not the sort of man you should let into your life."

She lifted an eyebrow at him. "Alex, you can't expect me to believe you're an evil ogre when you won't even let yourself be decently seduced. Any genuine villain would have been in my bed like a shot. Especially a boob man. Which we both know you are."

Quinn bowed his head and muttered a string of soft but heartfelt oaths.

Perfectly aware that he was trying hard not to laugh and trying equally hard to be serious about this, Morgan said gravely, "Look, I'm not an idiot. Yes, you've broken the law, frequently and with a certain amount of panache. Being a law-abiding person myself, I find that hard to understand, much less excuse. I can't even console myself by believing that some tragedy led you into a life of crime in the best melodramatic tradition. You enjoyed your past, and you're enjoying this dangerous shell game now.

"I've told myself all that. I've been very rational about the situation. And if I were looking for a happily-ever-after ending, this conversation wouldn't be taking place. Because I know damned well any woman who gets involved with you is asking for trouble. She's also asking for heartache—not because you're an evil man, but because you aren't."

Quinn raised his head and stared at her.

Her amusement gone, Morgan smiled a bit ruefully. "I've tried. I have tried. But I can't seem to do much about this. You'd be damnably easy to love, Alex. Rogues always are, and you're certainly that. But I'm not fool enough to believe I could catch the wind in my hands, so you don't have to worry about me clinging. I don't want golden rings or bedroom promises. Just . . . an adventure. And I won't make it difficult for you. I won't even ask you to say good-bye when it's over."

"Dammit, would you stop—"

"Being noble?" she interrupted, her dry voice cutting through his rough one. "Isn't that what you've been doing?"

After a moment, he said, "I don't want to hurt you."

"I know. And you certainly get nine out of ten for effort."

The light comment didn't alter his grim expression. "Ten out of ten, because it stops here." Each word was bitten off sharply with the sound of finality. "If you want to play in the danger zone, pick some other rogue to show you how."

Morgan gazed at the spot where he'd stood long after he was gone. Then, gradually, she began smiling. Things were, she decided cheerfully, definitely looking up.

It was nearly midnight as Jared stood restlessly at the window of his hotel room. His suit jacket and tie had long since been discarded, but he still wore his big automatic in its accustomed shoulder holster, and he needed only to pull on a light jacket if he had to leave in a hurry. Which is what he more or less expected.

It was an unusually clear night for the moment, affording an excellent view of the colorful city lights, but he knew fog was forecast and that it would probably be of the pea-soup variety. Not that the view interested him anyway; his work demanded all the caution of walking a knife's edge, and he had taught himself long ago to focus his concentration. Too often, keeping his mind on business had been a simple matter of life or death.

When the phone finally rang, he turned instantly from the window and picked up the receiver. "Hello?"

"I hear things are a little tense between you and Wolfe."

Jared relaxed, but only slightly. "And have you also heard that Morgan talks too much?"

"Yes, I have heard that—but how do you know it was Morgan? It might have been Storm."

"I know Storm. She'll talk to Wolfe about me, but she wouldn't talk to you, Max—not about undercurrents."

Max chuckled. "No, you trained her too well. As a matter of fact, it was Morgan who mentioned it. She said things had been very strained lately."

"Yeah, well—give her two points for observation; it didn't take ESP to see it."

"You want me to talk to him?"

"No, I don't think so." Jared was glancing at his watch as he spoke. "Between his preoccupation with Storm and his hostility toward me, he hasn't had a lot of time to think about what we're doing, and I'd just as soon keep it that way as long as possible. The last thing I want right now is a lot of questions, especially from Wolfe."

Max was silent for a moment, then sighed. "All right, I'll keep out of it. For now."

"Thanks."

"Don't mention it. Have you told Alex about the ballistics report?"

"Not yet. We're supposed to meet tonight."

"How do you think he'll take it?"

"The certain knowledge that Nightshade is in San Francisco and is the one who put a bullet in him? I think he'll do something reckless."

"Like what?"

"I don't know. But the possibilities are making me very nervous. Max, we've still got a few days before the collection is in place and the exhibit ready to open to the public. It's not too late to stop this."

"That isn't an option."

"You're a hardheaded bastard, you know that?"

"As a matter of fact, I do. Look, relax, will you?" Amusement crept into Max's deep voice. "As tense as you are, anybody'd think there was something dangerous going on."

Jared made a rude noise and cradled the receiver without force. His somewhat rueful amusement didn't last long, however. He checked his watch and remained by the phone for some minutes, but when it finally rang it pulled him away from the window for a second time.

And, this time, the conversation was much briefer.

"Yeah?"

"You sound impatient. Am I late?"

Jared checked his watch again. "Yes. I was about to go looking for you."

"You wouldn't have found me."

"Don't bet on it."

A soft laugh. "One of these days, we'll put that to the test, you and I."

"If we live long enough, you're on. Now, do we need to meet tonight?"

"I think so. . . ."

The cold fog drifting over the bay began to obscure the distant, hulking outline of Alcatraz, and

Quinn was glad. Though it was no longer a place where dangerous criminals were held, the defunct prison and its lonely island continued to be a stark, visible reminder of the price demanded of those who chose to be lawless.

Quinn didn't need the reminder.

Still, as he turned the collar of his jacket up and dug his hands into the pockets, he watched the rocky island until the mist enveloped it and rendered it invisible. It was an eerie sight, the fog creeping over the water toward him while, behind Quinn, the moonlight gleamed down on the city. At least for now, some time after midnight. In another hour, Quinn thought, he probably wouldn't be able to see his hand in front of his face.

He was beginning to really like this city.

"Why the hell are we meeting here?"

Quinn had been aware of the presence before he heard or saw anything, so the low voice didn't startle him. "I thought it was rather apt," he murmured in response. "Before the fog rolled in, Alcatraz was shining like a beacon in the moonlight."

Jared sighed. "Are you getting edgy? You, Alex?" His voice held a very slight note of mockery.

Quinn turned his back on the archaic, mist-enshrouded prison and looked at his companion. "No, but I'll be glad when this is over. I'd forgotten how long the nights get."

"Your choice," Jared reminded him.

"Yeah, I know."

Jared had keen eyes, and the moon was still visible hanging low over the city, so he was able to see the lean face of his brother clearly. "Is your shoulder bothering you?" he asked a bit roughly.

Quinn shrugged, the movement easy and showing no sign of the damage a bullet had caused barely more than a week previously. "No. You know I'm a quick healer."

"Even for a quick healer, that was a nasty wound. You probably should have stayed at Morgan's longer than a few days."

"No," Quinn said. "I shouldn't have done that."

After a moment, Jared said, "So, Max was right."

"About what?"

"Don't be deliberately dense, Alex."

Quinn resisted the impulse to ask if he could be accidentally dense. "Max is very perceptive—but he isn't always right. As for Morgan, let's just say that I have enough common sense for both of us."

"And no time for romance?"

"And no time for romance." Quinn wondered, not for the first time, if becoming such an accomplished liar had been a good thing or a bad one. It might have kept his skin intact a bit longer, he thought, but sooner or later it was all going to catch up with him—and a great many people would no doubt be furious at him.

Jared seemed to be thinking along the same lines.

"We've been amazingly lucky so far," he said.

"But you really can't afford to get in any deeper with Morgan."

"I know that."

"She knows too much already."

Quinn drew a deep breath but kept his voice light. "Pardon me for not thinking too clearly when I was bleeding. I'll try to do better next time."

"I'm not blaming you for that."

"Too kind."

Jared swore under his breath. "Look, all I'm saying is that we're running out of time. You really *don't* have the leisure—or the right—to pull any woman into a situation like this, especially when you're dealing with someone as deadly as Nightshade."

Calmer now, Quinn said quietly, "Yes. You're right, I know that. And I am trying."

Deciding that it was time to change the subject, Jared said, "Well, we do have other things to think about. The police have their preliminary reports on the Jane Doe, and the ballistics report on the bullet the doc dug out of your shoulder came in."

"And?"

"Current thinking is that the Jane Doe isn't one of Nightshade's victims. She was stabbed, for one thing. For another, he never bothers to try and delay identification of his victims. Given that and where she was found, it seems unlikely that Nightshade killed her."

"Not his style. And that so-called clue left on the body sounds even less like him."

Jared said, "I just found out about that myself. How did you find out?"

"I often know things I'm not supposed to know. How do you think I was able to keep one jump ahead of the police for so many years?" Quinn shook his head. "Don't worry—there's no leak in the police department here. Or in Interpol, for that matter."

Deciding not to ask, Jared merely said, "Still no I.D. on that body, by the way. No match in the missing-persons database. The forensics specialists are trying to get a viable fingerprint, but so far no luck. Nobody's recognized her photo within blocks of the area where she was found. The only thing the police are certain of is that her killer is pointing them toward the museum. Whether as a distraction or a taunt, not even the police shrinks are willing to guess."

"What's your guess?"

"It's obvious and meant to look obvious. It also points at the museum, but not specifically at the *Mysteries Past* exhibit." Jared paused, then shook his head. "We don't know a thief killed her, so pointing the police toward the museum could be something as simple—and as sick—as a joke. Her death could have absolutely nothing to do with the museum or the exhibit. But the police have to follow the lead, so . . . That's a hell of a big building. Impossible for the police to search completely."

"And they're wasting a lot of time trying."

"Maybe. They've questioned virtually everyone

connected to the museum, showed them a photo of the Jane Doe. So far, nobody admits to having seen her, in the museum or outside it. The police are beginning to think her killer was just trying to throw them off the scent, that she has nothing at all to do with the museum."

Quinn considered that for a moment in silence, then said, "Without more to go on, I'm not surprised the police don't know where to fit that particular puzzle piece."

"You think she fits somewhere, that she's part of someone's plans for the museum or the exhibit?"

"Oh, yes," Quinn replied matter-of-factly. "In a situation like this, there are no coincidences."

"Then we've got another player."

"It's very likely."

"Great. That's just great."

Quinn studied his brother, then said, "Are you going to give me the results of the ballistics report?"

"Do I have to?"

"No. Nightshade shot me."

Jared sighed. "The bullet matched those taken from his previous victims. The question is, did he know who he was shooting."

"He couldn't have *known* anything. He probably suspected another thief, maybe trying to I.D. him or trying to get rid of some of the competition."

"Even if he didn't connect you with the museum, he has to suspect a trap."

"Probably. I would." Without waiting for a response to that, Quinn added, "The collection is being set up in the museum now, so there are armed guards everywhere around the clock; no thief in his right mind would try to go after it until the exhibit opens to the public."

"Can we assume Nightshade is in his right mind?"

"We can assume he's not stupid. I don't believe he'd try for the collection now with all the security so visible. He'll wait, until the museum has to accommodate the public, has to reduce the number of guards and rely on electronic security. That's when it's most vulnerable.

"We have the by-invitation-only private showing next Friday, and then the exhibit opens to the public on Saturday. I think we both agree that the sooner we lure Nightshade into the trap, the better. If we let him, he could well wait for the next two months and make his move when we've relaxed our guard."

"I'd rather not have to haunt the museum for the next two months," Jared said politely. "The sooner we wrap this up, the happier I'll be."

"Yes, I imagine you're pretty fed up with having to be my watchdog."

"It isn't my favorite job, I admit."

Curiously, Quinn asked, "Because you don't like being a watchdog, or because it's me?"

Jared drew a breath and let it out slowly. "Let's not go there, okay?"

Quinn hadn't kept himself alive and at large for ten years without learning when it was safer to back off. So he backed off. "Right. Look, I don't see that I can learn anything more by using the methods I've been using so far. With the collection out of the vaults, the stakes have just shot sky-high."

"Meaning?"

"Meaning I can no longer afford to be cautious."

"You're saying you've been acting cautiously all this time?"

"Of course."

"Could have fooled me."

Quinn could have said that he had, in fact, fooled his brother, but instead said, "Oh, I'm always careful."

That solemn statement was so wide of the mark that Jared could only shake his head. "Sure you are."

"I am. And I plan to be very, very careful during the next step of my plan."

"Which is?" Jared inquired somewhat warily.

"Well, hunting by night hasn't earned me much except a bullet. I think it's time I tried a more direct approach."

Jared sighed. "I've got a feeling I won't like this."

"No, probably not." Quinn's even, white teeth showed in a sudden grin. "But I will."

CHAPTER
FIVE

May I have this dance?"

Morgan West would have known the voice any-where, even here in a Sea Cliff mansion in the middle of an elegant, black-tie party. Rather numbly, she looked up to meet the laughing green eyes of the most famous—and infamous—cat burglar in the world.

Quinn.

He was dressed for the party, a handsome heart-breaker in his stark black dinner jacket. His fair hair gleamed as he bowed very slightly with exqui-site grace before her, and Morgan knew without doubt that at least half the female eyes in the crowded ballroom were fixed on him.

The other half just hadn't seen him yet.

"Oh, Christ," she murmured.

Quinn lifted her drink from her hand and set it

on a nearby table. "As I believe I told you once before, Morgana—not nearly," he said nonchalantly.

As he led her out onto the dance floor, Morgan told herself she certainly didn't want to make a scene. That was why she wasn't resisting him, of course. And it was also why she fixed a pleasantly noncommittal smile on her face despite the fact that her heart was going like a trip-hammer.

"What are you doing here?" she demanded in a low, fierce voice.

"I'm dancing with the most beautiful woman in the room," he replied, suiting action to words as he drew her into his arms and began moving to the music, which was slow and dreamy.

Morgan refused to be flattered, and she kept her arms too stiff to allow him to pull her as close as he obviously wanted to. She was wearing a nearly backless black evening gown, and the sudden remembrance of just how much of her bare skin was showing made her feel self-conscious for the first time.

Not that she wanted *him* to know that, of course.

"Would you please shed your Don Juan suit and get serious?" she requested.

He chuckled softly, dancing with grace and without effort. "That was the bald truth, sweet."

"Yeah, right." Morgan sighed and couldn't help glancing around somewhat nervously, even though she kept the polite smile pasted to her lips and made sure her voice was low enough to escape being overheard. "Look, there are a dozen private guards watching over Leo Cassady's collection, and at least one cop here as a guest. Surely you aren't thinking—"

"You're the one who isn't thinking, Morgana." His voice was low as well, but casual and unconcerned. "I prefer the secrecy of darkness and the anonymity of a mask, remember? Besides that, it would be rude in the extreme; I would never think of relieving our host of his valuables. No, I am simply here as a guest—an invited guest. Alexander Brandon at your service, ma'am. My friends call me Alex."

As she danced automatically and gazed up at him, Morgan reminded herself of several things. First, *Quinn* was only a nickname, a pseudonym for a face-less thief that had been coined years before. Alexander was certainly his real first name—she believed that much since he'd been practically on his deathbed when he'd admitted it—but since he and Jared Chavalier were brothers, the name of Brandon was undoubtedly no more than a cover for whatever he was up to.

Second, if Quinn was here in Leo Cassady's home by invitation, someone must have vouched for him. Max, perhaps? He was really the only one who could have, she thought. Maxim Bannister was probably the only man Leo would trust enough to admit a stranger to his home.

And, third, Morgan reminded herself of just how tangled this entire situation had become. The *Mysteries Past* exhibit had opened to the public today, Saturday, and it had been a rousing success. But the priceless collection was bait for a trap to catch a very dangerous thief, and Quinn was supposedly helping.

Supposedly.

"You dance divinely, Morgana," Quinn said with his usual beguiling charm, smiling down at her. "I knew you would. But if you'd only relax just a bit—" His hand exerted a slight pressure at her waist in an attempt to draw her closer.

"No," she said, resisting successfully without losing the rhythm of the dance.

His smile twisted a bit, though his wicked green eyes were alight with amusement. "So reluctant to trust me? I only want to obey the spirit of this dance and hold you closer."

Morgan refused to be seduced. It was almost impossible, but she refused. "Never mind the spirit. You're holding me close enough."

Those roguish eyes dropped to briefly examine the low-cut neckline of her black evening gown, and he said wistfully, "Not nearly close enough to suit me."

For her entire adult life—and most of her teens— Morgan had fought almost constantly against the tendency of people, especially men, to assume that her generous bust was undoubtedly matched by an I.Q. in the low two digits, and so she tended to bristle whenever any man called attention to her measurements either by word or by look.

Any man except Quinn, that is. He had the peculiar knack of saying things that were utterly outrageous and yet made her want to giggle, and she always felt that his interest was as sincerely admiring of nature's generous beauty as it was—almost comically—lustful.

She even heard herself muttering, "See, I knew you were a boob man."

"I certainly am now," he responded, equally blunt and a little amused.

"Well, you'll just have to suffer," she told him in the most severe tone she could manage.

He sighed. "I've been suffering since the night we met, Morgana."

"Tough," she said.

"You're a hard woman. I've said that before, haven't I?"

He'd been wearing a towel and a bandage at the time. Morgan shoved the memory away. "Look, I just want to know what you're doing here. And *don't* say dancing with me."

"All right, I won't," he said affably. "What I'm doing here is attending a party to celebrate the opening of the *Mysteries Past* exhibit."

Morgan gritted her teeth but kept smiling. "I'm in no mood to fence with you. Did Max get you into the house?"

"I've been on the guest list for this party since the beginning, sweet."

Forgetting to keep smiling, she frowned up at him. "What? You couldn't have been. Leo's always planned to throw a party the night of the *Mysteries Past* opening, and he sent out invitations more than a month ago—in fact, more than two months ago. How could you possibly—"

Quinn shook his head slightly, then guided her away from the center of the room. Not many of the guests seemed to take note of them, but Morgan caught a glimpse of Max Bannister watching from the other side of the room, his gray eyes unreadable.

Now that she knew Quinn was—supposedly, anyway—helping Interpol catch another thief, Morgan didn't feel quite so troubled about her previous encounters with the cat burglar, and after having nursed him back to health when he'd been shot, she could hardly look on him as a stranger. But she didn't trust him.

Yeah, you're willing to take him into your bed, but you don't trust him. That's smart.

That's just smart as hell.

He led her from the crowded ballroom without giving her a chance to protest, finding his way easily down a short hallway and out onto a slightly chilly, deserted terrace. Leo hadn't opened the French doors of the ballroom, probably because it had been raining when the party began; the flagstone terrace was still wet, and a heavy fog was creeping in over the garden. Still, if a guest *did* happen to wander out, the party's host was prepared: There were Japanese-type lanterns hung to provide light for the terrace and garden, along with scattered tables and chairs—very wet at the moment.

Everything gleamed from the rain, and the

incoming fog made the garden an eerie sight. It was very quiet on the terrace, unnaturally so, with the thick mist providing its usual muffling effect; both the music from the ballroom and the sounds of the ocean could only just be heard.

Morgan assumed that Quinn wanted to talk to her without the greater chance of being overheard inside, so she made no effort to protest or to ask him why he'd brought her out here.

Still holding one of her hands, Quinn half sat on the stone balustrade edging the terrace and laughed softly as if some private joke amused him greatly. "Tell me something, Morgana. Have you ever stopped to think that I might be . . . more than Quinn?"

"What do you mean?"

His wide, powerful shoulders lifted in a shrug, and those vivid eyes remained on her face. "Well, Quinn is a creature of the night. His name's a pseudonym, a nickname—"

"An alias," she supplied helpfully.

He let out a low laugh. "All right, an alias. My point is that he moves in the shadows, his face masked to the world—most of the world, anyway—and few know very much about him. But it isn't always night, Morgana. Masks tend to look a bit peculiar in the daylight, and Quinn would hardly have a passport or driver's license—to say nothing of a dinner jacket. So who do you think I am when I'm not Quinn?"

Oddly enough, that question hadn't even occurred to Morgan. "You're . . . Alex," she answered a bit helplessly.

"Yes, but who is Alex?"

"How could I know that?"

"How could you, indeed. After all, Alex Brandon only arrived here yesterday. From England. I'm a collector."

The sheer audacity of him had the usual effect on Morgan; she didn't know whether to laugh or hit him with something. So Alexander Brandon was supposed to be a collector? "Tell me you're kidding," she begged.

He laughed again, the sound still soft. "Afraid not. My daytime persona, you see, is quite well established. Alexander Brandon has a rather nice house in London, which was left to him by his father, as well as apartments in Paris and New York. He has a dual citizenship—British and American—and, in fact, attended college here in the States. He came into a trust fund at twenty-one and manages a number of investments, also inherited, so he doesn't really have to work unless he wants to. And he seldom wants to. However, he travels quite a bit. And he collects artworks—particularly gems."

Morgan had the feeling her mouth was hanging open.

With a smothered sound that might have been another laugh, Quinn went on carelessly. "His family name is quite well respected. So well, in fact, that you might find it on most any list of socially and financially powerful families—on either side of the Atlantic. And Leo Cassady sent him an invitation to this party more than two months ago—which he accepted."

"Of all the gall," Morgan said wonderingly.

Knowing she wasn't talking about Leo, Quinn sighed mournfully. "Yes, I know. I'm beyond redemption."

Frowning at him, she said, "Is that how Max knows you? From this blameless other life you created for yourself, I mean? And Wolfe?"

"We have encountered one another a few times over the years. Though neither of them knew I was Quinn until fairly recently," Quinn murmured.

"That must have been a shock for them," she said.

"You could say that, yes."

Morgan was still frowning. "So . . . now you're openly here in San Francisco, as Alexander Brandon, scion of a noble family and well known as a collector of rare and precious gems."

"Exactly."

"Where are you staying?"

"I have a suite at the Imperial."

It was one of the newer and more luxurious hotels to grace Nob Hill, a fact that shouldn't have surprised Morgan. If Quinn was playing the part of a rich collector, then he'd naturally stay at the best hotel in town. But she couldn't help wondering . . .

"Is Interpol paying the bills?" she asked bluntly.

"No. I am."

"You are? Wait a minute, now. You're spending your own money—quite probably ill-gotten gains—to maintain this cover of yours so that you can help Interpol catch a thief so they won't put you in prison?"

Quinn tugged at her hand slightly so that she took a step closer to him; she was standing almost between his knees. "You put things so colorfully— but, yes, that's the gist of it. I don't know why that should surprise you, Morgana."

"Well, it does." She brooded over the question, hardly aware of their closeness. "It's an awfully elaborate situation for someone who's supposedly just trying to keep his ass out of prison. Unless . . . Has this other thief done something to you? You personally?"

Quinn's voice was dry. "Aside from putting a bullet in me, you mean?"

Morgan had a flash of memory—Quinn lying in her bed unconscious, that awful wound high on his chest—and something inside her tightened in remembered pain. With an effort, she managed to push the memory away. It reminded her, though, that here was another question she should have asked—and *hadn't*—simply because she'd been so preoccupied with the vexing reality of Quinn's effect on her.

"So he is the one who shot you? Is that why you're doing this? Because he shot you?"

Quinn was holding her hand against his thigh and looked down at it for a moment before he met her eyes. In the soft glow of the lanterns, the light diffused by the mist curling around them, he looked unusually serious. "That would be reason enough for most people."

"What else?"

"Does there have to be another reason?"

Morgan nodded. "For you? Yes, I think so. You've tried your best to convince me you're out for nobody except Quinn—but some of what I'm seeing doesn't add up. If you're as selfish and self-involved as you say, why not just go through the motions to satisfy Interpol? Why put yourself—and your own money—on the line if you don't have to?"

"Who says I don't have to? Interpol can be a harsh taskmaster, sweet."

"Maybe so, but I have a feeling you have better motives than just saving your own skin."

"Don't paint me with noble colors, Morgana," he said softly. "In the first storm, they'll wash off. And you'll be disappointed at what's underneath."

It held echoes of something he'd tried to tell her before, a warning not to get involved with him on an intimate level, and though Morgan appreciated the spirit of the warning, she was not a woman prepared to allow others to make up her mind for her. She had come to certain conclusions about Quinn's character, and those conclusions would be confirmed—or disproved—by his own actions and behavior.

Some of those actions, particularly before she had met him, certainly painted him in a bad light. He was a criminal, there seemed no doubt of that. He had, as his own brother had said bitterly, looted

Europe for the better part of ten years. And he was on the side of the angels now only because the choice was preferable to going to prison.

She *knew* that, all of it. But from the night they had met weeks ago, Morgan had been conscious of a nagging certainty that there was much, much more to the man than he allowed the world to see. She had told herself more than once it was only her own attraction to him that made her feel that, but instincts she had learned to trust told her that wasn't it.

So what was it? What really went on behind those vivid eyes, that charming smile?

The real question, she thought, wasn't who Quinn was when he wasn't being a cat burglar; the question was, who was this man with the dual identity, brilliant mind, and a reputation that was both internationally infamous and highly respected? Who was he really, at the core of himself?

She thought that was a mystery well worth pondering.

"Morgana?"

She blinked, realizing only then that her silence had spanned several minutes. "Hmm?"

"Did you hear what I said?"

Morgan found herself smiling a little, because he sounded so aggrieved. "Yes, I heard what you said."

"And?"

"And—I'm not painting you with noble colors. Or gilding you, for that matter. I just happen to believe you aren't after this other thief only because he shot you, or only because Interpol thinks you're the ace up their sleeve."

"Morgan—"

"What do you know about Nightshade that I haven't already been told?"

He paused before he answered, this time for several minutes, and when he finally did speak his voice was unusually flat and clipped. "I don't know how much you've been told. But Nightshade has been active about eight years—maybe more, but that long at least. Mostly here in the States, a few times in Europe. He's very, very good. And if somebody gets in his way, they're dead."

Morgan didn't realize she had shivered until Quinn released her hand to take his jacket off and drape it around her shoulders. She didn't protest, but said softly, "It isn't that cold out here. But the way you sounded . . ."

His hands remained on her shoulders, long fingers flexing just a bit. "You'll have to forgive me, Morgana. I don't care too much for murderers."

Enveloped in the warmth of his jacket, surrounded by the familiar scent of him, and very aware of his touch, Morgan struggled to keep her attention on the conversation. "Especially when one of them shoots you?"

"Especially then."

She shook her head a little, baffled and intrigued by a man who could cheerfully admit to having been the world's most infamous thief for a decade and yet speak of another thief's penchant for violence with chilling loathing in his voice. No wonder she couldn't convince herself Quinn was an evil man; how could she, when his own words had, more than once, shown him to possess very definite principles— even if she hadn't quite figured out what they were.

"Who are you, Alex?" she asked quietly.

His hands tightened on her shoulders, drawing her a step closer, and his sensual mouth curved in a slight, curiously self-mocking smile. "I'm Quinn. No matter who else, or what else, I'm Quinn. Never forget that, Morgana."

She watched her hands lift to his broad chest, her fingers probing to feel him through the crisp white shirt. They were very close, so close she felt enclosed by him.

He had kissed her before, once as a teasing ploy to distract her so that he could filch her necklace and again in the hulk of an abandoned building when they had narrowly escaped with their lives. After that, even during the days and nights he'd spent in her apartment recovering from his wound, he had been careful not to allow desire to spark something between them, and when she had indicated her own willingness he had simply left, removing himself and the problem of his response to her.

She thought he honestly believed he would be bad for her, and that was why he turned mocking or re-minded her of just who and what he was whenever she got too close. And he was probably right, she reminded herself. He would no doubt be *very* bad for her, and she'd have only herself to blame if she was crazy enough to let herself fall for a thief.

She thought she was crazy enough. And knowing that did nothing to prevent her from responding when he pulled her suddenly into his arms. When his hard, warm mouth closed over hers, she gave a little purr of guileless pleasure and let herself enjoy it.

Quinn hadn't planned on this when he brought Morgan out here to talk—but then, his plans never seemed to turn out the way he intended when she was around. She had the knack of making him forget all his good intentions.

The road to hell is paved with good intentions.

An apt proverb, he thought, and then he forgot to think at all, because she was warm and responsive, and he had wanted to hold her like this for a long, long time.

He also wanted more, a lot more, and if there'd been a bed—hell, even a thin rug—nearby, he very likely would have forgotten everything else except the woman in his arms. But there was no bed or rug, just a wet, foggy terrace outside a ballroom where a party was in full swing, and where he was supposed to be looking for a ruthless thief—

"Excuse me." The voice was brusque rather than apologetic, and too determined to ignore.

Quinn lifted his head slowly, gazing down at Morgan's sleepy eyes and dazed expression, and if he hadn't been related by blood to the man who'd interrupted them, he probably would have committed a very satisfying murder.

"Go away," Quinn said, his rough voice not yet under control.

"No," Jared replied with wonderful simplicity. He stood as if rooted to the terrace.

"You're a sorry bastard, you know that?"

"I'm sure you think so. Especially right now."

"What I think is that the goddamned leash is getting a bit tight, Jared."

"It can get tighter."

"And I can break the chain. I have before."

The tense exchange recalled Morgan to a sense of her surroundings. She pushed herself back away from him, blinking, absolutely appalled to realize that she had totally forgotten the presence of a hundred people partying just yards away.

Her only solace was the knowledge that Quinn had been as involved as she—but that was little comfort.

"I—I'll just go back inside," she murmured, startled by the husky sound of her voice. "Oh—your jacket." She swung the dinner jacket from around her shoulders and handed it to Quinn, then more or less fled into the house.

He didn't follow her.

Morgan automatically began to make her way back to the ballroom, but she was met in the short hallway by a petite blonde with fierce green eyes, who immediately took her arm and led her toward the powder room instead.

"A bit damp out, I guess," Storm Tremaine drawled.

"It's stopped raining," Morgan said, experimenting with her voice and relieved to find it nearly normal.

"Really? I never would have known."

Morgan was baffled by that lazy comment until she got a look at herself in the powder-room mirror. "Oh, God," she moaned.

"Yeah, I thought you might like to pull yourself together before the cream of San Francisco society got an eyeful," Storm said, sitting down in a boudoir chair before the tile vanity while her friend claimed the other chair. They were, thankfully, alone in the spacious room. "Where's your purse?"

"I don't know. I think it was on that little table just inside the ballroom. I think." Morgan was attempting to tuck unruly strands of her long black hair back into its former elegant style, unsure if it had been the dampness outside or Quinn's fingers that had wrought such damage.

"Here, then." Storm handed over a small hairbrush and several pins. "Your makeup looks okay. Except for—"

"I know," Morgan muttered, all too aware that her lipstick was a bit smeared. Nobody looking at her could doubt she had just been thoroughly kissed. "Dammit, this stuff wasn't supposed to smear. For *any* reason."

Propping an elbow on the vanity as she watched

her friend, Storm said, "I guess the manufacturers never tested it against passionate cat burglars."

"How did you know who he was? I mean—" Morgan stopped herself with a sigh as she realized. "Wolfe, of course." Since Storm was engaged to Wolfe Nickerson, there were likely few secrets between them.

"Of course. He introduced us just before you got waltzed out onto the terrace. So your Quinn is Alexander Brandon, huh?"

"So he says." Having done what she could with her hair, Morgan used a tissue and Storm's lipstick to repair the rest of the damage to her pride.

"And he's gone public, so to speak. It's an interesting ploy, I admit, especially if he's so sure the thief he's after also wears a blameless public face."

Morgan returned the lipstick and, very carefully, said, "Tell me something, friend. Is there anybody who *doesn't* know what Quinn's up to?"

"Outside our own little circle, I certainly hope so." Storm smiled slightly. "Wolfe said you'd probably hit me with something when I told you just how much I do know, but I'm counting on your sweet disposition."

"Oh, yeah? I wouldn't count on that if I were you. I'm not in a real good mood right now."

Solemnly, Storm said, "Then I'll have to risk your wrath, I suppose."

"Just spit it out, will you?"

"I don't really work for Ace Security," Storm told her in that solemn voice. "I'm with Interpol."

Morgan didn't have to look in the mirror to

know her mouth had fallen open in shock. "Interpol? Like Jared?"

"Uh-huh. He's more or less my boss, at least on this assignment. I hope this room isn't bugged," she added thoughtfully, glancing around.

"Why would it be bugged?"

"No reason I can think of." Apologetically, Storm added, "They teach us to be paranoid."

Morgan was torn between fascination and irritation; fascination because her rather ordinary world had grown in the last few months to include internationally famous cat burglars and Interpol agents, and irritated because those around her had taken their own sweet time letting her in on their plans.

Amused, Storm said, "Don't blow up, now. If it makes you feel any better, I didn't know Quinn was in on this until just before he was shot, and I had no idea that all the guys knew him."

Suddenly curious, Morgan said, "Quinn told me that Max and Wolfe didn't know about his burgling until recently. Did Wolfe tell you how he found out?"

"Umm. Caught him with his hand in a safe in London about a year ago."

Morgan winced. "That must have been quite an encounter."

"The word Wolfe used was *tense*."

"I can imagine." Morgan sighed. "I wonder how Max found out."

"No idea. And Jared's so furious on the subject I haven't dared ask him. Can't really blame him, I suppose. Nice thing, for an international cop to find out his own brother's an international thief. A bit awkward."

"To say the least," Morgan murmured, remembering how Jared had told her not to "get any fool romantic notions about nobility" into her head concerning Quinn's current association with Interpol.

"A bit awkward for you too," Storm said quietly.

Awkward? Morgan considered the word and found that her friend had picked a good one.

As the director of the exhibit of an utterly priceless collection of gems and artworks that had just gone on public display, Morgan had access to something that any thief would have sold more than his soul to possess. Any thief.

It was easy enough to say the collection was safe from Quinn, that he was walking the straight and narrow now, bound to help catch a thief he clearly despised. Easy enough to let his charm sway her, his desire ignite hers. Easy enough to gaze into his beguiling green eyes and convince herself that she saw something in him the world would find surprising—if not downright inconceivable.

Easy enough to tell herself she wasn't a fool.

Morgan looked at her reflection in the mirror, seeing a woman who was once again elegant but whose lips still bore the faintly smudged appearance of someone who had been kissed with hungry passion.

"Awkward," she said. "Yes, you could say that."

CHAPTER
SIX

"Did anybody ever tell you your timing is lousy?" Quinn asked, shrugging into his jacket. His voice was back to normal, light and rather careless. The earlier biting tone was completely gone.

"Only you," Jared replied, his own voice calm now. "But I could say the same thing about your timing. Alex, there are a hundred people in that house, and if your theory is correct one of them is Nightshade. So what the hell are you doing necking on the terrace?"

"We weren't necking," Quinn replied somewhat indignantly. "We hadn't gotten that far—thanks to you."

Jared let out a short laugh, but it didn't sound very amused. "For once in your life, will you get serious?"

"I'm completely serious." Quinn stood up and

smoothed his jacket, buttoning it neatly. When he spoke again, his voice was more sober. "I had to talk to Morgan, you know that. This is the first time she's seen me socially, and if I hadn't told her who I was supposed to be, God only knows what might have happened. She tends to be a bit impulsive, you know."

"Yes, I do know that."

Quinn shrugged. "So, since I didn't know how she'd react, it seemed more prudent to bring her out here."

Jared didn't bother to point out that they hadn't been talking very much when he'd interrupted them. "Well, do you think you could put your love life on hold long enough to get some work done? You can't really study all the guests if you're out here on the terrace."

"The night is young," Quinn reminded him lightly.

He wouldn't have willingly admitted it, but Jared knew only too well that he had about as much hope of controlling Quinn as any man had of controlling the wind. That did not, however, stop him from trying. "You aren't planning on doing a little night hunting after the party, are you?"

"That depends on what I find here."

"Alex, it's too risky for you to play both parts all the time, and you know it." Jared's voice had roughened.

Quinn's voice remained light. "I know my limits—and the risks. I also have burned in my mind that one good glimpse I got of Nightshade just before he shot me, and if I see anyone tonight who even *seems* to move the same way he did, I won't let him out of my sight."

Jared didn't speak immediately, and when he did it was to make a serious comment. "We did have a few women on the list; if you're so sure Nightshade's a man, at least that narrows the possibilities."

"I'm sure, though I couldn't tell you exactly why. His posture, the way he moved, something. Hell, maybe I caught a whiff of aftershave just before he fired. Anyway, all I can do for the moment is look for anything familiar and listen in case the bastard gives himself away somehow."

"The chances of that have to be slim to none."

"Think positive," Quinn advised. "It's always worked for me. Now, don't you think we'd better return to the party before the wrong person notices something odd?"

Jared waited until Quinn took several steps away from him before saying, "Alex?"

Quinn half turned to look back at him. "Yeah?"

"That's a snappy shade of lipstick you're wearing. Better suited to a brunette, though."

With a low laugh, Quinn produced a snowy handkerchief and removed the evidence of his interlude with Morgan. Then he half saluted Jared and went back into the house.

Jared waited for several minutes just so they wouldn't reappear inside at the same time. And if anyone had been on the damp, chilly terrace to hear him speak, they might have been surprised at what he muttered to himself.

"I wonder when all this is going to blow up in my face."

Morgan caught glimpses of Quinn throughout the next couple of hours, but she took care to keep herself too busy to watch him. Since she never lacked for dancing partners and was well known to most of the guests, it was easy enough to look and act as if she was enjoying the party and had nothing more serious on her mind than who to dance with next or whether or not she wanted to try a champagne cocktail.

The appearance was, to say the least, deceptive. Morgan did quite a lot of thinking while she danced and smiled. Ever since she had faced up to a few unnerving things in the powder room, she had been thinking more seriously than she could ever remember doing in her life.

And it occurred to her at some point during the evening that the interlude with Quinn out on the terrace might have more than one explanation. Yes, he had wanted to talk to her privately, no doubt because he had to make certain she understood why he'd suddenly appeared in public. But there might have been another motive in his devious mind.

As a collector, he could be expected to visit the *Mysteries Past* exhibit, but it would certainly look a bit odd if he began haunting the museum—something he probably wanted to do in order to remain close to the trap's bait. However, if he made it obvious that he was drawn to the museum by something other than the lure of the Bannister collection—her, for instance—then no one would be very surprised to find him there, even frequently or at odd hours.

Morgan didn't want to accept that possibility, but it fit too logically to be denied.

The son of a bitch intended to use her.

And choosing a damp, foggy terrace as the setting for his first move had also been part of the plan. He'd been safe in starting something when and where he had. No matter how passionate the interlude had become, it was highly unlikely that anything serious would have happened; the surroundings had been too cold, far too wet, and hideously uncomfortable, as well as lacking in privacy.

He'd known they would be interrupted—could easily have arranged it beforehand with Jared, even down to the taut exchange of hostilities.

Morgan told herself that it was just speculation, there was no proof he meant to make her a part of his cover—but when he cut in neatly to take her away from the gallery owner she'd been dancing with, her suspicions grew. And they grew even more when he managed to hold her far closer than she had allowed during their first dance, so that her hands were on his shoulders and his were on her back.

"You've been ignoring me, Morgana," he reproved, smiling down at her.

He was an intriguing, charming, conniving *scoundrel,* Morgan decided with a building anger that was welcome. Worse, he was a heartless thief who would steal a necklace right off a woman's neck while he kissed her—and if there was anything lower than that, she didn't know what it could be.

The anger felt so good that Morgan wrapped herself in it, and it was such strong armor that she was able to return his smile with perfect ease, undisturbed by their closeness or by the touch of his warm hands on her bare back. "Oh, since I haven't been told how well I'm supposed to know you, I thought it best. We *have* just met tonight, right?"

"Yes—but it must have been love at first sight," he said soulfully.

"I see." Morgan allowed her arms to slip up around his neck, turning the dance into something far more intimate than even he had intended. She veiled her eyes with her lashes, fixing them on his neat tie, and made her smile seductive. "You should have told me." She thought her voice was seductive as well, but there must have been something there to give her away, because Quinn didn't buy the act.

He was silent for a moment or so while they danced, then cleared his throat and said in a matter-of-fact voice, "You're mad as hell, aren't you?"

Her lashes lifted as she met his wary eyes, and she knew her own were probably, as he'd once observed, spitting rage just like a cat's. In a silken tone, she said, "I passed mad as hell about an hour ago. You don't want to know what I am now."

"I'm rather glad you aren't armed, I know that much," he murmured.

She let him feel several long fingernails gently caress the sensitive nape of his neck. "Don't be too sure I'm not armed."

"I've said it before, I know, but you look magnificent when you're angry, Morgana." He smiled at her, this one seemingly genuine, amused—and a bit sheepish. And his deep voice was unusually sincere when he went on. "If you like, I'll stop right here in front of God and San Francisco and apologize on bended knee. I'm a cad and a louse, and I should have asked for your help instead of trying to use you. I'm sorry."

It was a totally disarming apology, and Morgan wasn't surprised to feel her rage begin to drain away. Irritably, she said, "Well, why didn't you?"

"I thought you'd say no," he replied simply.

Still angry and glad of it, she said, "Being asked is a damned sight better than being used."

"Yes. I know."

"Good. Then you'll know why I'm pissed." Quite deliberately, Morgan freed herself from his embrace and walked off the dance floor.

This time Storm met her in the powder room, and the blonde was obviously highly entertained. "Okay, you clearly won that round," she said with a laugh. "Public rejection, and with flair too."

Morgan laughed despite herself as she sat down before the vanity. "He deserved it, the rotten louse. He thinks he can pull *my* strings, I'll be happy to prove him wrong."

Storm, whom no one had ever accused of being slow on the uptake, pursed her lips as she sat down beside her friend and said, "So the earlier scene out on the terrace was more . . . um . . . contrived than it seemed?"

"A lot more contrived. Guess who's just fallen head-over-heels in love with the director of the *Mysteries Past* exhibit?"

"Ah. To give him an excuse to hang around the museum, I gather."

"That was his plan."

Storm grinned. "Which you've now derailed."

Morgan smiled slowly. "Not necessarily."

It only took a moment for Storm to get it, and she began to laugh. "You're going to make him work for it."

"Let's just say he can play the lovelorn swain if he wants an excuse to hang around the museum in the daytime. I just don't plan to be too terribly receptive."

Still smiling, Storm said, "Nice way to make your point without interfering while he keeps an eye on the museum."

"I thought so."

Storm eyed her thoughtfully. "Uh-huh. Just doing your job while not getting in the way of his?"

"Exactly."

"Manipulating the master manipulator?"

"You don't think it can be done?"

"I think," Storm replied slowly, "that you'd better be careful, Morgan. Very, very careful."

She studied the photograph briefly before handing it back to him. "So, that's all you want? That one piece?"

"That's all."

"The entire Bannister collection to choose from, and you pick this?"

"Is it a problem?"

Amused, she shook her head. "No, it isn't a problem. I don't usually get hired to penetrate layers of sophisticated security for something like this, but what the hell. You want, I deliver. That's the deal. Provided you agree to the price, of course."

"The price is fine. Half now and half on delivery is also fine. Your reputation precedes you; my research indicates you're trustworthy and that you can be counted on to have complete loyalty to your employer. For the duration, and for a price."

Unoffended, she smiled. "That's right."

"I'll expect to hear from you as soon as possible."

"You will. I'd just as soon do what I came here to do and get out of this city. There are far too many thieves skulking around for my taste."

"The pot calling the kettle black."

She laughed. "I'm no thief. I'm an artist."

"As far as I'm concerned, that remains to be seen."

"You'll see," she said. "Everyone will see."

Morgan quite deliberately stayed away from the museum on Sunday, then came to work on Monday morning as usual. She chided herself for it later, but the truth was that she looked for Quinn at the museum for most of the day. It wasn't easy, considering the crush of people eager to view the *Mysteries Past* exhibit, which to no one's surprise was proving to be very popular and highly profitable for the museum, but she looked for him nevertheless.

And never mind that she was being an idiot.

She wanted to believe in him, that was the problem. Maybe as a salve to her conscience, or maybe just because she needed to believe she saw something in him that most others would have found surprising if not impossible.

Something good.

If he'd been dark, Morgan thought vaguely, brooding or sardonic, it might have been easier to believe the worst of him. But he was fair and handsome, even his voice was beautiful, and how was a woman supposed to *know*?

All she had were her instincts, and they told her there was much more to Quinn than met the eye.

So she looked for him and didn't pretend to herself that she wasn't eager to see him again. She had even dressed with more care than usual, choosing a slim, calf-length black skirt that she wore with a full-sleeved white blouse and a really beautiful, hand-beaded vest done in opulent gold, black, and hints of rust. The outfit was completed with black pumps, and she wore her long black hair swept up in an elegant French twist.

Morgan had told herself that she had dressed so carefully only because, now that *Mysteries Past* was open, the director of the exhibit had a responsibility to look her best—but she didn't believe herself. She had dressed with Quinn in mind, and she knew it.

She wanted to look . . . sophisticated and cultured. And tall.

And if it occurred to her that *sexy* might have been added to a description of the appearance she was trying to achieve, she ignored the realization. She looked for Quinn all day, searching the crowd of faces for the one imprinted in her mind. She thought she was being subtle about it, a happy delusion shattered when Storm emerged from the computer room somewhere around three in the afternoon.

"You know, I really wouldn't expect to see him here for at least another hour or so," the petite blonde drawled as she joined Morgan near the guards' desk in the museum's lobby. Her little blond cat, Bear, rode her shoulder as usual, so exact a feline replica of Storm that he seemed an eerie familiar.

"See who?" Morgan hugged her clipboard and tried to look innocent. It wasn't her best expression.

Storm pursed her lips slightly, and her green eyes danced. "Alex Brandon."

"Dammit, was I that obvious?"

"Afraid so. The way you keep staring at tall blond men is a little hard to miss. I picked it up on my monitor, as a matter of fact."

Morgan sighed and said *dammit* again without heat and without self-consciousness. "Well, in that case—why wouldn't you expect to see him for at least another hour?"

Storm glanced casually around to make certain they couldn't be overheard before she replied. "He has to sleep sometime, doesn't he? I imagine he's on watch or on the move most of the night, and since the collection is safest during the day with the museum filled with people, that'd be a good time to sleep."

"I knew that." Morgan frowned at herself.

Storm chuckled. "He probably wasn't in bed before seven or eight this morning, so he likely hasn't been up more than an hour, if that long. I'd give him time for a shave and shower, as well as breakfast, if I were you."

"You've made your point." Morgan sighed. "If this keeps up, I'm never going to see him in the daylight. I mean, he was at my apartment for a couple of days when he was healing, but we didn't go outside, so I haven't actually *seen* him in the sunshine."

"One of your ambitions?"

"Don't laugh, but yes."

"Why on earth would I laugh? It seems a

reasonable enough aim to me. Especially if you've the suspicion he's a vampire."

Morgan looked at her friend seriously. "No, because I've seen his reflection in a mirror."

"Oh. Well, that does seem to prove he isn't a creature of the night. Not that kind of creature, anyway. I don't suppose he could be another kind?"

"Only vampires are famous for their seductive but deadly charm," Morgan reminded her, still solemn.

Storm nodded gravely. "That's what I thought. You could wear a cross, I guess, and find out for sure."

Silently, Morgan hooked a finger inside the open collar of her blouse and held out a fine golden chain from which dangled a polished gold cross. Storm studied the cross seriously, then met Morgan's earnest gaze. Then they both burst out laughing.

A bit unsteadily, Storm said, "Lord, this man must have quite an effect on you if he's got you half-seriously contemplating the undead."

"Let's put it this way. I wouldn't be surprised to find he's three parts sorcerer at the very least." Morgan got hold of herself. She looked at her clipboard and tried to remember that she was being paid to do a job. "Umm . . . I have to go do another walk-through of the exhibit and make sure everything's going all right. If anyone should ask—"

"I'll tell him right where you are," Storm assured her.

"If you were a true friend, you'd lash me to the nearest mast before I make an utter fool of myself,"

Morgan said somewhat mournfully. "All that crafty devil has to do is smile and say something—anything—and I forget all my good intentions."

With a faint smile, Storm said, "I'd be glad to lash you to a mast *if* I thought that was what you really wanted."

"I'm not fooling anybody today, am I?"

"No. But don't let that worry you. We're all entitled to at least one bit of reckless folly in our lives, Morgan. My daddy taught me that. It's something to remember."

"Have you had yours?" Morgan asked curiously.

The small blonde smiled. "Of course I have. I fell for Wolfe in the middle of a very tricky situation when I couldn't tell him the truth about myself. It was reckless and foolish—but it turned out all right in the end. Something else for you to remember: Often the definition of a foolish act is just . . . bad timing."

Morgan nodded thoughtfully and left her friend, beginning to make her way through the crowded museum toward the *Mysteries Past* exhibit, housed on the second floor and in the west wing of the huge building.

Reckless folly. A good description, Morgan thought. After all, nobody in their right mind would consider this fascination with an internationally notorious cat burglar anything *but* reckless folly. Bad timing? Oh, yes, it was that too.

And knowing all that did absolutely nothing to

knock some sense into her normally sensible head, she reflected wryly.

"It's impressive as hell," Keane Tyler commented to his partner as they wandered through the exhibit.

"I'll say," Gillian Newman agreed. "Whoever designed these display cases is a real artist; all the pieces look wonderful. And if we ever have time, I want to go through and read all the information cards on each piece. Looks like most of this stuff has a very colorful history."

"I'm a bit more worried about its future than its past."

"Still no valid connection to our Jane Doe," Gillian reminded him. "So I'm still wondering why we're here."

"I told you. I don't like it when a killer points me in a specific direction with a very obvious *clue*. Bugs the hell out of me."

"Uh-huh. And so we're here. Again."

Keane shrugged irritably. "I want to eliminate this place from our line of investigation."

"I thought we pretty much had. Been here, done this. We haven't been able to find a soul who recognizes our Jane Doe, or any evidence that she was ever here."

"I know. So why the hell did her killer want us looking in this direction?"

"Maybe sleight of hand," Max offered as he joined them, accompanied by a thin, rather mousy-looking young woman with huge black-rimmed glasses and a solemn expression. "He could want you looking away from his real target."

Sighing, Keane said, "With your collection out of the vaults and on exhibit, Max, it is the prime target for any thief in the city. Hell, maybe in the world. But, yeah, it could also be a distraction from something else."

"Anything you need from us, just ask. Speaking of which, I wanted to introduce the museum's new assistant curator. Chloe Webster—Inspector Keane Tyler and Inspector Gillian Newman. Chloe just started today."

They all made happy-to-meet-you noises, and then Chloe said, "Inspector Tyler, Mr. Dugan asked me to tell you that we'll have that list of contributors to the museum for you by the end of the day."

"Thanks, Ms. Webster."

Max said, "Reaching a bit, aren't you, Keane?"

"I'm reaching a mile. But until we I.D. our Jane Doe or eliminate any connection to the museum or this exhibit, we'll be checking every possibility." Keane smiled wryly. "You have powerful friends, Max, and they all want to make absolutely certain everything possible is being done to protect your collection."

"Sorry to make your job harder."

"You aren't making it harder." The words were

barely out of his mouth when the alarms were set off for the third time that afternoon. Keane winced. "But this fancy security system Storm designed is giving me a hell of a headache."

The alarms were swiftly silenced, and they all heard a nearby guard's walkie-talkie mutter, "Clear. All clear."

"We're still making adjustments," Max admitted, smiling faintly.

"I better go check on . . . Excuse me—" Chloe left them rather hurriedly.

"She's more nervous than you are," Keane observed to Max.

"She's young and it's her first important job." Max paused before adding, "She may quit when she finds out about our latest . . . wrinkle."

Keane was immediately alert. "What is it?"

"I know we agreed that searching the storage areas in a building this size and complexity was a fairly useless exercise and that you pulled your people out of the basement, but I asked Wolfe and some of the extra guards to take a look around anyway. A few minutes ago they found something."

"What?" Gillian asked.

"A message," Max said.

CHAPTER
SEVEN

Morgan strolled through the exhibit wing, casual but watchful, studying visitor reactions to the various displays as well as noting potential traffic bottlenecks as particular pieces of the Bannister collection drew more interest than others. The display cases had been designed specifically for the individual pieces or groups of similarly themed pieces and were very carefully lighted, so each case showed off its contents beautifully.

The exhibit was actually made up of four connected rooms within the wing, with the display cases—freestanding and lining the walls—helping to direct the flow of people smoothly through the expansive space. There were a few benches scattered about, but the idea was to keep people moving, and the careful design appeared to be doing its job well.

Morgan jotted several notes to herself, reminders to see about more lighting for one corner; an extra velvet rope to redirect traffic through a particular room; and to have an inconveniently placed bench moved from its present location.

She answered a few questions from people who knew she was the director of the exhibit, returned a few lost children to their parents, and coped with a couple more accidentally triggered alarms.

Earlier in the day she had spoken to Max and Wolfe, but both seemed to have disappeared by late afternoon. She hadn't seen any sign of Jared, which didn't surprise her. Jared, like Quinn, would undoubtedly spend more nights than days in the vicinity of the museum, since the thief they were intent on luring was virtually guaranteed to make his move during the dark hours.

Morgan had thought about that only fleetingly during the day, partly because she kept herself busy and partly because the deadly danger Nightshade was famous for was something she didn't like to think about. She did her job briskly and professionally and tried to avoid looking for tall blond cat burglars.

It wasn't until nearly six o'clock, when the museum's visitors were beginning to make their way toward the exits and she was doing a final walkthrough of the exhibit for the day, that she saw Quinn.

He was standing alone at the central and most elaborate display case the exhibit could boast, the one holding the clear star of the show, the spectacular Bolling diamond. He was dressed casually in dark slacks and a cream-colored turtleneck sweater, with a black leather jacket worn open. Hands in his pockets, head bent, he stood gazing intently at the priceless seventy-five-carat teardrop canary diamond in the display case. And maybe it was the special lighting of the case that made his face look shadowed, as if it were hollowed with hunger—or avarice.

Then again, maybe the lighting had nothing to do with it.

Morgan paused in the doorway of the room and watched him silently, uneasy. The last few visitors in this area wandered past her, talking, and she nodded automatically at one of the guards who was following his usual patrol past the room, but she could hardly take her eyes off Quinn.

Max Bannister, certainly nobody's fool and a notable judge of character, believed this man saw his unique collection only as bait set out to lure a far more deadly thief. Wolfe was risking his job and sterling reputation because he believed the same thing—or, at least, because he trusted Max's judgment. Even Jared, despite the bitter anger he'd shown about his brother's life of crime, seemed to have no doubt that Quinn had no designs on the Bannister collection.

But now, watching him as he stared at the Bolling diamond, Morgan felt her throat close up and her hands were suddenly cold. His face was so still, his eyes oddly intent, and she couldn't help wondering . . .

Was the enigmatic Quinn making fools of them all?

Drawing a deep breath and then holding her clipboard rather like a shield, she moved slowly toward him. And it was obvious he knew he'd been under observation, because he spoke rather absent-mindedly as soon as she reached him.

"Hello, Morgana. Do you know the history?"

"Of the Bolling?" She was pleased by her own calm voice. "No, not really, other than that it's supposed to be cursed. As director of the exhibit, my responsibilities are all administrative. I know, of course, all the facts about the pieces—carat weight and the grades of each stone, for instance—but I don't believe in curses, and gems were never my favorite subject."

"You don't believe in curses?"

"Of course not. Myth and legend."

"It's all just myth and legend," Quinn said. "Until it isn't." With barely a pause, he went on. "So, as an archaeologist you prefer relics? Bits of pottery and fossils?"

"Something like that."

He turned his head suddenly and smiled at her. "I thought diamonds were a girl's best friend."

"Not this girl. To be honest, I don't even like diamonds. Rubies, yes; sapphires and emeralds, definitely—but not diamonds, even the colored ones."

"Too hard? Too cold?" He seemed honestly curious.

"I don't know why; I've never thought about it."

She shrugged off the subject, wondering irritably if he even remembered that she had rather publicly rejected him hardly forty-eight hours before.

He looked at the room around them, his expression critically assessing. "The design of the exhibit is excellent; my compliments."

"Being a connoisseur of such things?"

"I have closely studied a number of gem exhibits over the years," he reminded her modestly.

He had skillfully plundered a few as well. Morgan sighed. "Yeah. Well, I can't take all the credit for this one. Max and I designed the layout, but Wolfe and Storm had input because of security considerations and we had additional professional help with the lighting and display angles."

"A very efficient team. What's going on in the basement?"

Morgan blinked. "The basement?"

"There were two police inspectors here earlier talking to Max, and all three headed toward the basement with rather grim looks on their faces. I believe there are several guards down there as well. And Wolfe."

"How long have you been here?"

"An hour or so. What's going on in the basement, Morgana?"

"I have no idea," she replied frankly. "Shall we go and find out?"

Before he could answer, a serene and polite recording announced over the public-address system that the museum would be closing in fifteen minutes. Quinn waited for the end of the announcement, then said, "I'd rather not make myself memorable to the police, if it's all the same to you."

"But you have this blameless daytime persona," she said innocently. "Why would Alexander Brandon hide his face from the police?"

"Not his face. But the police are hardly idiots, and excessive interest from me in the basement of a museum might strike even the casual observer as odd." He sighed. "Why don't I wait for you in the lobby, Morgana? I'm sure you can think of some way of updating me as to what's happening without giving the guards the mistaken impression that you have any personal interest in me whatsoever."

"I think I can manage that," she said coolly.

"Then I'll wait for you in the lobby."

It wasn't until they parted company in one of the corridors, Quinn headed for the lobby, and Morgan toward the basement, that she allowed herself to smile, if a bit wryly. Her annoying thief didn't seem all that dismayed by her public rejection and cool attitude.

Dammit.

Once in the cavernous basement of the huge museum, Morgan had to ask one of the guards she saw to tell her where the others were. Even with directions it took her several minutes to reach the central storage room and another few to wind her way through the maze of crates and shelves before she located Max, Wolfe, and the two police inspectors.

"What's up?" she asked Max.

It was Wolfe who answered, his tone grim. "We found a little token, apparently from the killer of that unidentified woman."

"We don't know that," Keane Tyler objected. "The forensics team isn't here yet, Wolfe."

"And I'll bet my reputation they'll find that the blood is hers and the knife is the murder weapon."

"Blood? Knife?" Morgan looked again to Max.

He pointed to a rather roughly carved marble statue a few feet away, and Morgan studied it warily. It was in a line of several life-size statues, all down here in storage because they were damaged or had been rotated out of exhibit to make way for other displays. The indicated figure dated from the Middle Ages and depicted a warrior.

Morgan took a couple of steps toward the statue and looked more closely. The figure's raised fist, she realized, had once held a marble knife or dagger that had at some point been broken off or removed. Now it held a dully gleaming hammered-brass hunting knife with a carved wooden handle.

The knife was stained a rusty brown for more than half its length.

"Jesus," Morgan said. She turned back to the others. "What's the point? I mean, you don't think she was killed down here, do you?"

"No signs so far," Keane said, adding disgustedly, "but now, of course, we'll have to search the entire goddamned building, at least on this level, for forensic evidence. No more wandering around with flashlights; this time we get serious." He stared around at the confusion of crates and shelves. "Everything dusty as hell, packed away God only knows how long. And this is just the central storage room; Wolfe tells me there are dozens of rooms nearly as large as this one, all of them crammed with more shit like this."

"Thirty-two rooms, according to the plans." Morgan was frowning. "And that doesn't count what's probably miles of corridor. So either he killed her down here, or else he's trying to make you waste time looking to find out if he killed her down here?"

Wolfe said, "If he killed her down here—whenever he got down here—it had to be before the new security system went on-line." He was staring at Keane.

The inspector hesitated, then said, "She could have been killed weeks ago. The M.E. believes the body was refrigerated almost to the point of being frozen."

"So he could have planted the knife weeks ago," Max said. "Got down here long before there was decent electronic security protecting this area."

"At least we can hope it was that long ago," Wolfe muttered.

"But why?" Morgan shook her head. "Just so you'd have to search the place now? That doesn't make sense. Pointing the investigation in this direction, so specifically—why?"

"Trying to divert our attention," Wolfe said.

"Keep us and the police from looking wherever it is we need to be looking."

"Or make us look so hard we don't see the forest for the trees," Gillian suggested.

Keane looked once more at the forest of storage surrounding them and sighed. "Both viable theories."

Morgan said, "Well, all I can contribute to the investigation is the fact that he had to have time down here, and he had to have at least some equipment."

"Why?" Keane asked.

"Because drilling a round hole through marble takes time and a drill," Morgan replied. "And cutting marble takes a saw or chisel. Guys, I know that piece, and the knife it originally held was part of the fist, carved from the same slab of marble. I can check to make sure, but I think the knife was undamaged when the figure was brought down here for storage. So that means somebody cut away the original marble knife and then drilled a round hole through the fist so the handle of that hunting knife would slide right in but be held tightly enough not to drop out again."

"How much time are we talking?" Keane asked.

"An hour at least, probably longer."

"And a noisy hour at that," Max said.

Morgan nodded. "Yeah. Problem is, you could be standing on the floor above this room and never hear a thing, especially during the day with visitors wandering around. And we never had guards really patrol down here, just do routine checks of the exterior doors and main corridors."

"Great," Gillian said. "That's just great. So we have no way of even establishing a window of opportunity—except the one we already have. *Sometime* in the last few weeks."

"And we're still working from a couple of giant assumptions," Keane said. "That this is the knife that killed Jane Doe, and that she or her murder is really connected to the museum or the exhibit."

"Assumptions somebody obviously wants us to make," Wolfe said. "I don't believe in coincidence."

"No," Morgan said, unknowingly echoing the cat burglar awaiting her upstairs, "that all this is connected is a lot more likely than not. Somebody has gone to a great deal of trouble to give us some nice, clear clues—and a whole bunch of puzzle pieces. Anybody else getting the feeling we're being led around by our noses?"

She found Quinn waiting patiently for her in the lobby, standing several feet from the watchful guard. The last of the day's visitors had gone, and the huge room had that hollow, stark feeling of too much cold marble and stone and too few warm bodies.

It was hardly an ideal place to talk, so when she reached him Morgan wasn't surprised to find that he didn't even bring up the subject of what was going on in the basement.

"Morgana, I'm in the mood for Italian food, I think, and I know of a great restaurant near the bay with the best cook this side of Naples. Will you join me?"

Bluntly, she asked, "Business or pleasure?"

He answered that readily and with a smile. "Your company is always a pleasure, sweet." Then he lowered his voice. "However, I'll admit there is a possibility that someone I'd like to keep an eye on will also be at the restaurant."

"Who?"

"That, I'd rather not say." When she frowned at him, Quinn added, "Suspicions are not facts, Morgana, and they're a long way from evidence. I'd prefer not to name names—to anyone—until I'm sure."

"You mean not even Max or Jared—or Wolfe— knows that you have an idea who Nightshade really is?" She kept her own voice very low.

"They know I have an idea," Quinn conceded, "but they don't know who I'm watching."

There were a number of questions Morgan wanted to ask, but she knew this was not the time or place for a long discussion.

"Italian food sounds great," she said. "I'll just go check on a couple of things and get my jacket."

"I'll wait here for you."

Since she was a responsible and efficient woman, Morgan made two brief stops before reaching her office, checking with the guards in the security room and then with Storm in the computer room to make certain all was well as the museum went into a night-security mode. One of the guards watching the security monitors asked her if the blond man in the lobby was supposed to be on his "sheet"—meaning the list of persons with special clearance to enter the museum at will—and Morgan had to pause for thought before answering.

"No," she said finally out of a sense of caution, but then qualified the reply by adding, "Not unless Max or Wolfe says so. But he'll probably be around most days. His name is Alex Brandon, and he's a collector. Ask Wolfe what his clearance is, will you?"

"Gotcha," the guard replied, writing himself a note.

When Morgan stopped at the computer room where Storm spent her working hours, it was to find the petite blonde leaning back in her chair, booted feet propped on her desk and her little cat asleep in her lap as she studied a video monitor hanging in the corner of the crowded room. She could use the computer console on her desk to direct the museum's security program to show her any part of the museum under video surveillance, and at the moment she was looking at the lobby. At, specifically, a tall, blond man waiting patiently.

"Hi," Morgan said, deciding not to comment. "Any problems before I go?"

"Nah, nothing to speak of. I've fixed that glitch in the system, so I doubt we'll have any more accidental alarms." Storm's bright green eyes returned to their study of the monitor, and she smiled when Quinn turned his own gaze to look directly into the video pickup he wasn't supposed to be able to see. "Look at that. When he got here a couple of hours ago, I watched him all through the museum, and he always knew where the cameras were—even the ones we've so cleverly hidden. Wolfe says he has a sixth sense when it comes to any kind of a camera being pointed at him, that he feels it somehow. No wonder the police have never been able to capture him on tape or film."

Morgan followed her friend's gaze, and though she couldn't help a rueful smile when Quinn winked cheerily at the camera, her voice held a certain amount of frustration. "Damn him. Just when I think I've got him figured out, I start having second thoughts. Is he on the right side of the law this time, or isn't he?"

Storm looked at her, one brow on the rise. "Maybe the operative phrase in that question is *this time*. Even if you give him the benefit of the doubt and assume Max, Wolfe, and Jared are all right to trust him to keep his hands off the collection—and none of them is a fool, we both know that—then what's he going to do afterward? Let's say our little trap works and Nightshade winds up behind bars—what then? Does Quinn slip Interpol's leash and fade back into the misty night? Does he go to prison for past crimes? Or is the plan for him to be a . . . consultant or something like that for the cops?"

Remembering an earlier discussion with Quinn, Morgan said, "He told me he was too effective to go public—which would mean a trial and possibly prison—and more or less said he enjoyed dancing to Interpol's tune. Which is probably the only answer I'll get."

Storm pursed her lips thoughtfully and stroked the sleeping Bear with a light touch. "Shrewd of Interpol if they plan to make good use of his talents."

"Yeah. He's sure to be worth more to them outside a jail than in. Even if they never recover a thing he stole, I'll bet they'd rather use him than prosecute." Morgan sighed. "Which only tells me one thing. Interpol operates mostly in Paris and other parts of Europe—and so would he."

"How's your French?" Storm asked solemnly.

"Better than my Latin."

"I could give you lessons," the blonde offered.

Morgan eyed her. "Do you speak French with a Southern accent?"

"According to Jared I do, but I've never had any trouble being understood."

"Well, I may take you up on the offer," Morgan said. "Then again—the only French word I'm likely to need to know is the one for good-bye. And I already know that one." She shook her head before her friend could respond. "Never mind. I'm going to eat Italian food and try my best to remember all the logical, rational, sensible reasons why I shouldn't lose my head."

"Good luck," Storm murmured.

Morgan went on to her office, where she deposited her clipboard on her desk and put on the stylish gold blazer she had worn that morning. Then she locked up her office and returned to where Quinn waited in the lobby.

Wolfe was there and talking to him as she approached; she couldn't hear what the security expert was saying, but he was frowning a bit. Quinn was wearing a pleasant but noncommittal half smile; that seemed his only response to whatever he was being told. When he caught sight of Morgan, Quinn looked past Wolfe to watch her coming toward them, and Wolfe turned to address her rather abruptly.

"Will you be here tomorrow?"

"With the exhibit open? Sure. From now until we close up shop, I work six days a week."

Wolfe lifted an eyebrow at her. "Does Max know about that?"

"We've discussed the matter." Morgan smiled. "He wasn't happy, but when I pointed out that I'd be here whether I was getting paid or not, he gave in. I'm under orders to take long lunches and knock off early whenever possible, and I'm forbidden to darken the doors on Sunday. Why, do you need me for something tomorrow?"

"I'll let you know."

"Okay," she murmured, wondering if Wolfe felt uncomfortable discussing security business with her in the presence of Quinn. If so, it was certainly understandable.

Wolfe glanced at Quinn, then at Morgan, seemed about to say something, but finally shook his head in the gesture of a man who was acknowledging that a situation was out of his hands. "Have a nice evening," he said, and left them to head for the hall of offices.

Gazing after the darker man, Quinn said meditatively, "Do you get the feeling Wolfe isn't entirely happy with any of us?"

"Yes, and I can't blame him. Anything happens to the Bannister collection and Lloyd's is on the hook for more millions than I even want to think about."

Quinn took her arm and began guiding her toward the front doors. "True. Have I mentioned, by the way, that you look like a few million yourself today?"

It caught her off guard—*damn* the man for sounding unnervingly sincere without warning—but Morgan recovered quickly and was able to reply with commendable calm as they walked across the pavement outside the museum. "No, you haven't mentioned that."

"Well, you certainly do. You look ravishing in jeans, mind you, but this is very elegant." He guided her toward the low-slung black sports car waiting at the curb.

"Thank you." Wondering if he did this kind of thing deliberately just to keep her off balance, Morgan remained silent while he installed her in the passenger side. She waited for him to join her and spoke only when the little car pulled away from the curb with a muted roar.

"Answer a question for me?"

He sent her a quick smile. "I'll have to hear it first."

"Umm . . . Do you know the security layout of the museum—and the exhibit?" She had wondered about that only after Storm had made the observation that he "sensed"—or knew—the placement of all the security video cameras.

"Do you really think Jared would be so trusting?"

"That," she commented thoughtfully, "is not an answer."

Quinn chuckled softly. "Morgana, I get the distinct feeling I've somehow roused your suspicions."

"That isn't an answer either. Look, Alex, we've agreed that the truth seems to be a slippery commodity between the two of us." She half turned on the seat to study his profile. It was a good profile, which was inspiring—but not as regards clarity of thought. "So I'd appreciate it if you give me a direct answer whenever possible. If you'd rather not say, then tell me so—this habit you have of neatly evading various subjects is not calculated to persuade me to trust you."

"Yeah, I was afraid of that." Stopping the car at a traffic light, he glanced at her a bit more seriously. "I'll try not to do that so often."

She noticed he didn't promise to stop doing it. "So . . . do you or don't you know the security setup of the exhibit?"

"I don't. I probably could have gotten it from Max—who does trust me, by the way—but I decided not to. I have a better chance of anticipating Nightshade if I have to study the museum and exhibit just the way he does. The only advantage I have is that I *know* there's a weakness in the defenses."

"The trap? Is it Storm's security program?"

"You don't know?"

Morgan sighed. "I'm ashamed to admit it, but I haven't even asked."

In an understanding tone, Quinn said, "The situation *is* a bit complicated."

"Never mind. Do you know where the trap is?"

"Yes, I do. I told Wolfe in the lobby just before you joined us, and he confirmed my deductions."

"No wonder he was frowning."

"As I said, he isn't very happy with any of us. I did point out to him that the trap only *looks* like a hole in the defenses, expressly designed to lure Nightshade in and snare him before he can get anywhere near the collection."

"And was he mollified by this reminder?"

Quinn smiled. "No. He seemed to feel that Nightshade might be suspicious enough to avoid the trap and find his own way in."

"Why would he be suspicious?"

"Because of me, I'm afraid." He sighed. "Morgana, thieves don't normally follow one another in the dead of night. But I followed him the night he was casing the museum, the night he shot me. He has to wonder about that. He knows he didn't kill me, because no unexplained shootings have been reported in the city, so he knows I may still be a potential problem."

"But he doesn't know who you are," Morgan said slowly.

"I'm an unanswered question all the way around—and a man like Nightshade hates unanswered questions."

She frowned a little as she studied his face. "You know, every time you talk about Nightshade, I get the feeling there's more to this. You say you don't know much about him . . . but I think you do."

"Morgana, you are full of questions today."

"Is that a warning?"

"It's an observation."

It may have been only that, but Morgan decided to drop the subject anyway. Quinn had already been more forthcoming than she had expected, and she preferred to quit while she was ahead. In any case, they arrived at the restaurant just then, and a number of speculations filled her mind.

She didn't comment until he had parked the car and come around to open her door. "So Tony's is the best restaurant this side of Naples, huh?"

"I think so," Quinn replied innocently as he closed her car door and took her arm.

"And I suppose the fact that it tends to be a kind of hangout for art collectors and dealers as well as museum people is a coincidence?"

He sent her a glance, amusement in his green eyes. "No, is it? Fancy that."

"You can be maddening, you know that?"

"Watch your step, Morgana," he murmured, probably referring to the uneven flagstone steps leading up to the restaurant's front door.

Though it was just after seven in the evening, the place was already three-quarters full; many of the museums in the area closed at six, and this was, as Morgan had said, a favorite place to unwind as well as dine. The food was not only excellent, it was also served generously and priced reasonably, and the casual but efficient waitresses knew your name by the third visit.

Or, in Quinn's case, the second.

"I ate lunch here Saturday," he told Morgan, after the friendly waitress had conducted them to a window booth and asked "Mr. Brandon" if he wanted coffee as usual.

Morgan—who was also known to the waitress

and who had ordered coffee as well—accepted that somewhat ruefully with a nod and then glanced around casually, curious to see if she could spot whoever it was that Quinn wanted to keep an eye on.

The one glance told her it would be impossible. There were more than a dozen people scattered about the room who were in some way involved in the art world either as collectors, patrons, or employees of the various museums, galleries, and shops in the area. Even Leo Cassady, their host for the party the other night, and Ken Dugan, head curator of the museum housing the *Mysteries Past* exhibit, were present, both with attractive female companions.

"Give up?" Quinn murmured.

Morgan unfolded her napkin and placed it over her lap, making a production out of it. "I don't know what you're talking about," she told him politely.

"You mean you weren't trying to guess who it is I'm keeping an eye on?" He smiled wickedly. "Nice try, sweet, but you should never try to play poker with a cardsharp."

C H A P T E R
EIGHT

She scowled at him. "Thanks for yet another warning. Obviously, you could look as innocent as a lamb with both sleeves full of aces."

Leaning back to allow the waitress to place his coffee before him, Quinn said, "I didn't know lambs had sleeves."

"You know what I mean. *Your* sleeves full of aces." Morgan reached for the sugar and poured a liberal amount into her coffee, then added a generous measure of cream.

Quinn watched her with a slightly pained expression on his handsome face. "American coffee is filled with flavor; why do you want to turn it into dessert?"

Since he'd stayed at her apartment, Morgan knew how he took his coffee. "Look, just because you macho types think drinking something incredibly bitter is a gourmet experience doesn't make it so."

"Is the coffee bitter?" the waitress asked anxiously. "I'm so sorry."

Morgan looked up at her rather blankly, then realized the attractive redhead was hovering, pad in hand and pencil poised, to take their orders for the meal.

"I can make a fresh pot—"

"No, it's fine." Morgan glanced at Quinn, who was studying the menu with one of those maddening little smiles of his, then returned her gaze to the distressed waitress. "Really, it is. I was just . . . trying to make a point." She hastily picked up her menu.

A couple of minutes later, their meal ordered and the waitress departed for the kitchen, Morgan frowned at her companion. "It didn't work."

"What didn't work?"

"Trying to lead me off on a tangent. Maybe I should start guessing who it is you're watching."

"So I can tell you if you're hot or cold?" Quinn shook his head. "Sorry, Morgana—no deal."

She felt frustrated but not terribly surprised, and since he *was* a much better poker player than she was, she knew there was no use in hoping he'd tell her anything he didn't want her to know. "Well, hell," she said in disgust.

Quinn smiled, but his eyes were suddenly grave. "Suppose you found out that I believed someone you knew was an international thief and murderer. Could you look at them, speak to them, with the ease you had yesterday? Could you be sure that you wouldn't inadvertently give away your knowledge or somehow put them on their guard—which would certainly ruin our plans and likely put you in danger? Could you, Morgana?"

After a moment, she sighed. "No, I don't think I could. I'm not that good an actress."

"If it makes you feel any better, that's the major reason I haven't told any of the others. Because it takes a certain kind of nerve—or a devious nature, I suppose—to lie convincingly even under the stress of facing a killer. I know myself; I know that I *can* do that. And since I can't be so sure of anyone else, I prefer not to take the risk."

"But it is someone I know? Nightshade is?"

"Someone you know—if I'm right."

Morgan gazed at him soberly. "I get the feeling that no matter what you say—you don't have any doubts."

Quinn's humorous mouth quirked in an oddly self-mocking little smile. "Which ought to teach me a lesson. I'm obviously not the poker player I thought I was."

"Your face didn't give it away. Or even what you said," Morgan answered absently. "Just something I felt. But you are sure, aren't you? You know who Nightshade is."

"I can't answer that."

"You mean you won't."

"All right, I won't."

"Well, that's clear enough." Morgan sighed.

"You're better off not knowing, believe me."

"If you say so."

Quinn didn't comment on her reservations; he merely nodded, still grave. "Good. Then why don't we enjoy the meal, and you can fill me in on whatever was going on in the museum's basement."

"Ah." Morgan nodded. "Then tonight is definitely more business than pleasure."

"I thought that was the way you wanted it."

"Oh, stop pretending. You know exactly why I walked off that dance floor."

He didn't hesitate. "Because I was an idiot and you decided to teach me a lesson."

"Did it work?" Her tone was rueful.

Quinn smiled slowly. "It worked. Probably even better than you could have hoped."

"Meaning?"

"Let's just say I've reconsidered my options."

Morgan wasn't at all sure she liked the sound of that. "And?"

"And I need you on my side, Morgan. So whichever way you want to play it is fine with me."

"*Play* it?" She could have sworn there was a gleam in his eye at her tart response. It made her even more wary.

"Well . . . our public relationship. If showing little or no interest in me publicly is the way you'd rather go, that's fine. I can play the lovelorn swain."

"Did you have the powder room at Leo's bugged?" she demanded.

"Excuse me?" He appeared honestly baffled.

"Never mind." Morgan got a grip on herself. "So your plan is to hang around the museum looking wistful while I play hard to get?"

"It seems to be your plan."

Morgan trusted his solemn tone about as much as she trusted her own ability to fly without a plane. "Uh-huh. So if that takes care of the public show, what about the private one?"

"Morgana, I'm surprised at you. As if I would put on any kind of *show* with you in private."

"So you're going to be completely honest with me in private?"

"I'm going to be . . . completely Alex."

Morgan stared at him for a long moment, silently admitting just which of them was the master manipulator. Then she said mildly, "Well, it ought to be interesting. I guess I get you until midnight, huh? Until you turn into Quinn?"

"Actually, that's pretty literal," he admitted. "Jared and I split the duty. I go on at midnight."

"Back into the darkness. Skulking."

"It could be much worse, you know," he said in a soothing tone. "I could be dull." He reached across the table and touched the back of her hand very lightly, his index finger tracing an intricate pattern.

Morgan watched what he was doing for a moment, using every ounce of her self-control to preserve a detached expression even though she had the suspicion all her bones were melting. She had to slide her hand away from him before she dared to meet his eyes, and she was rather proud when her voice emerged dryly.

"Alex, do you know the definition of *scoundrel*?"

His green eyes were brightly amused. "A villain with a smile?"

"Close enough," Morgan replied with a sigh, and leaned back to allow the waitress to deliver their meal.

It was nearly two in the morning when Quinn moved ghostlike along the dark, silent building until he reached a side door. There was no lock to bar his way, and within seconds he was passing along a dim hallway, still making no more noise than a shadow. He paused outside a heavily carved set of doors and studied the faint strip of light visible at the floor, then smiled to himself and entered the room.

The faint light came from only two sources: a cheerful fire burning in the rock fireplace and a reading lamp on the opposite side of the study. Still, it was easy for Quinn to see the room's waiting occupant.

"You're late." His host turned away from a tall window to frown at him.

Quinn removed his black ski mask and the supple black gloves he wore and tucked them into his belt.

"There's quite a bit of security in this neighborhood, so I had to be careful," he responded calmly.

The other man didn't cross the room or even move away from the window; he merely stood there, one hand on the back of the chair beside him, and looked at Quinn. "Did you get it?"

Silently, Quinn opened a chamois pouch at his belt and removed a smaller velvet bag, which he tossed to his host. "As you Yanks say—it was a piece of cake." Subtly different from what Morgan was accustomed to hearing from him, his voice was more rapid than lazy, the words a bit more clipped, the pronunciation more British than American.

A brilliant cascade of diamonds flowed into the other man's hand as he upended the velvet bag, and he stared down at the necklace without blinking for a long moment. Then, softly, he said, "The Carstairs diamonds."

"Get out your loupe and satisfy yourself the necklace is genuine," Quinn advised him. "I don't want there to be any question."

His host left the window finally to cross the room to an antique desk, and he removed a jeweler's loupe from the center drawer. He turned on the desk lamp to provide more light, and under that studied the necklace thoroughly.

"Well?" Quinn asked when the other man straightened.

"It's genuine."

"Terrific." Quinn's deep voice held a faint trace

of mockery, as if the other man's taciturnity amused him. "So, are we ready to talk about the Bannister collection now?"

"I told you, I don't like the setup."

"Neither do I." Quinn sat casually on the arm of a leather wingback chair and gave his host a very direct look. "The exhibit has the best security money can buy—which shouldn't surprise either one of us. But we both know that even the best security is little more than an illusion to help owners and insurance companies sleep at night. No system is foolproof."

The other man's eyes were suddenly hard and bright. "Have you found a way in?"

Quinn smiled. "I've found two ways in."

". . . and then he took me home," Morgan told Storm, finishing a rather lengthy description of her date the previous night. "And he didn't even ask to come in for coffee."

"That cad," Storm said solemnly.

Morgan stared at her friend for a moment, then giggled. "Did I sound aggrieved?"

"Just a little bit."

"Well, I guess I am a little bit." Sitting on the edge of Storm's desk, Morgan frowned as she absently scratched Bear under his lifted chin. "After I'd finally come to the conclusion that I really would be stupid to trust him, he was a perfect gentleman all evening. I mean . . . we talked business.

We talked about what Wolfe and the guards found in the basement and debated possibilities, but it was all very casual—as casual as it can be when you're discussing a murder."

"Did either one of you come up with a theory or possibility we haven't considered?" Storm was in her usual pose, leaning back in her chair with her boots propped up on the desk.

"I didn't. If he did, he kept it to himself." Morgan sighed. "That's the thing about Alex. Everything's under the surface, hidden, guarded."

"Do you think he doesn't trust you? Or is it that he knows you don't trust him?"

"Either. Both. Hell, I don't know. But I do trust him. Sort of. Part of him. Up to a point."

Storm began to laugh. "You want to qualify that a bit more?"

"You begin to see my problem."

"I saw your problem a long time ago," Storm replied, sobering. "Did he ask you out again?"

Morgan nodded. "For tonight, as a matter of fact. When I told him I'd decided weeks ago not to go to that fund-raiser Ken's organized, he asked if I'd change my mind and go with him. I heard myself saying yes before I had a chance to think it through." She shook her head. "You know, for someone who's officially been in San Francisco only a little while, he sure has all the hot tickets."

"A man who plans ahead, obviously."

"Yeah—and it makes me very nervous." Morgan

sighed and got off the desk. She went to the door but paused there to look at her friend somewhat bemusedly. "It really is like he's two different men."

"And you feel ambivalent about one of them?"

"Oh, no, that isn't the problem." Morgan's voice was certain. "I find both of them too fascinating for my peace of mind. What really bothers me is that the one I trust the most . . . is the man who wears a ski mask."

"That," Storm said, "is very interesting."

"It's unnerving, that's what it is." Sighing, Morgan added, "I've got to go and check on the exhibit. See you later."

The remainder of that morning was fairly calm, with no unexpected crises and only one minor problem—which was easily solved by another slight adjustment of the flow of traffic through the exhibit. After that, Morgan had little to do except be on hand and answer the occasional question from a visitor.

She returned to her office and left her clipboard there just before noon, planning to take a long lunch as she'd promised Max she would. She stopped at the door of the computer room when she went back down the hall, finding Wolfe there talking to Storm.

"Hi." Morgan frowned slightly at Wolfe. "Did you want to talk to me about something? Yesterday in the lobby, I thought maybe you did."

Wolfe shook his head. "No, I was just going to suggest that we post a few more signs about touching the glass of the display cases, but when you redirected the traffic flow this morning that seemed to put a little extra space between the people and the cases."

Morgan nodded, but her gaze went from his face to Storm's and then back again. "Okay—so what else is wrong? You two look a bit grim."

"I never look grim," Storm objected. "Just . . . concerned."

"Why?" Morgan repeated.

It was Wolfe who answered. "Keane Tyler just called. The Carstairs diamonds were stolen last night."

Morgan leaned against the doorjamb and crossed her arms beneath her breasts. She was still frowning at Wolfe. "That's a shame, but why did he call you?"

"He thought we should know, and the theft won't be made public because that's the way the Carstairs family wants it. The necklace was in a safe at the family home, but the security system was top of the line, maybe better than what we have here around the exhibit—and the thief waltzed through without tripping a single alarm. There were even guard dogs patrolling outside, and they never let out a whimper."

"Sound familiar?" Storm murmured.

"You don't think it was Quinn?" Morgan said.

"No," Wolfe responded immediately. But he wasn't looking at her when he said it, and he was frowning.

In a dispassionate tone, Storm said, "We all know there are plenty of thieves in San Francisco. Especially right now. Just because this particular thief beat a dandy security system doesn't mean it was Quinn."

"Of course not," Morgan said, but she heard a hollow note in her own voice.

Wolfe did look at her then, still frowning. "Let's not jump to conclusions, any of us. That necklace has been a prime target for years, and the security system is months old—long enough for someone to have gotten their hands on the diagrams and found a weak spot."

"That's true," Storm agreed.

Morgan looked at them both, then said, "Yeah. Okay, well, let me know if Keane finds out anything. I have my cell phone with me, and I'll be back in a couple of hours."

Wolfe started to say something, but Storm caught his eye and shook her head warningly. When they were alone a minute later, he said, "I was going to ask her to join us for lunch."

"I know." Storm smiled at him. "Excellent intentions, but bad timing." She nodded toward the monitor in the room, and when Wolfe turned to stare at it he saw what she meant.

Quinn was standing in the lobby.

Morgan was so surprised when she saw him there that for a moment she forgot the disturbing news she'd just learned. "What're you doing here? It's barely noon."

Eerily burglarlike in a dark sweater and black slacks, he smiled and shrugged. "I couldn't sleep, so I decided to come and find out if I could take you to lunch."

Just once, I want to be able to say no to him. Just once.

"Sure," she said.

A couple of minutes later Morgan found herself in his little sports car, and by then she'd remembered Wolfe's troubling news. She didn't want to admit to the twinge of doubt she'd felt, but she couldn't help turning in the seat to study Quinn's face as she spoke in a deliberately casual tone.

"Ever heard of the Carstairs necklace?"

Somewhat dryly, he replied, "The same way I've heard of the Hope diamond; who hasn't? Why?"

"It was stolen last night."

He let out a low whistle, and the only emotion his face showed was mild interest. "I'd like to know who managed that."

"It . . . wasn't you," she said, trying not to make it a question even though it was.

Quinn turned his head to look at her briefly, then returned his gaze to the road. "No. It wasn't me."

Morgan had the upsetting idea that she had hurt him. "I had to ask."

"I know."

"I'm sorry."

He glanced at her again, this time with a crooked smile. "Why? We both know what I am. You'd have to be an idiot not to suspect me, Morgana—and you are far from an idiot."

"I just wish . . ."

"What?"

"Well, I just wish Nightshade would make his move and get it over with. I don't think I can stand waiting for the next two months."

"Somehow I doubt he'll wait so long. The Bannister collection will be impossible for him to resist, believe me. I'd be very surprised if he waits as much as two weeks before making an attempt."

"Intuition? Or experience?"

"A bit of both, I suppose." Quinn sent her another quick smile. "That is why I'm here, remember? To provide an expert's point of view. Set a thief to catch a thief?"

She sighed. "I wish you didn't sound so damned pleased about that."

"Never mind," he said with a chuckle. "You'll feel better after lunch."

Morgan nodded and then looked around to see where they were going. "Tony's?"

"I thought so, unless you have another preference."

"No, that's fine. Alex?"

"Hmm?"

"The night we met—you stole a dagger from that museum."

"Yes, I did," he agreed calmly.

"I don't suppose you returned it later?"

"No."

He sounded a little amused, Morgan thought, and wondered if she seemed to him incredibly naive. But she had to ask.

"And since then? If you *had* stolen anything else . . . would you tell me about it?"

Quinn turned the car into the parking lot at Tony's restaurant as he spoke, and his voice was very matter-of-fact. "No, Morgana, I wouldn't tell you." He pulled into a parking space but paused before turning off the engine to look at her with a slight smile. "Still willing to have lunch with me?"

Looking into those vibrant green eyes, Morgan heard herself sigh and then heard herself say, "Sure."

She wasn't surprised. Neither was Quinn.

Damn him.

Since Storm had to deal with a worried call from Ken Dugan—who was understandably anxious about museum security since the discovery in the basement—Wolfe took the opportunity to go down and check on the progress of the police forensics team. They had slipped into the museum as quietly and anonymously as possible, working under an official order not to disturb the museum or the *Mysteries Past* exhibit, and Wolfe doubted that any of today's visitors had even noticed.

He found Inspector Gillian Newman supervising the removal of the knife from the statue's marble fist.

"Keane isn't back yet?"

"Our boss wanted him to check out the Carstairs house," she replied readily. "Everybody's getting paranoid, looking for connections to this museum or the exhibit, and since Keane is the expert on thieves in this town . . ."

"They want his take."

"Exactly."

Wolfe frowned as he watched technicians easing the knife from the statue's grip. "Do we know anything else about that?"

"Not much more. It's blood on the blade, we know that, but it'll take a while to compare it to Jane Doe's. No fingerprints on the handle, which figures. Forensics found some marble dust, but whoever did this cleaned up after himself."

"So Morgan was right about the statue being undamaged when it was brought down here for storage."

"According to the museum records, yeah. Sean, drill marks?"

The technician, who was on a stepladder peering down into the warrior's fist with a flashlight and a magnifying glass, nodded. "Definitely. And saw marks where the original marble knife was."

"Morgan was right about that too," Wolfe said.

"Looks like. He brought a nice little bag of tools

with him. Which, to my mind, says he didn't kill anybody down here. He just planted that knife."

"How do you figure? Because he came prepared?"

"It makes sense. He had what looks like a murder weapon he wanted to plant, and he wanted to be . . . really creative about it."

Still frowning, Wolfe said, "The only thing I don't get is, why here? You cops had no reason to do a more thorough search down here, it just wasn't practical. If Max hadn't asked some of the guards and me to look around, this might not have been found for months. If ever."

"There has to be a reason," Gillian said. "A piece of the puzzle we don't yet have."

"You mean another one?"

Reasonably, she said, "It's a picture we're meant to see—sooner or later. Otherwise, there wouldn't be so many blatant clues left for us to find. We're following a trail."

"Or maybe Morgan was right about something else. Maybe we're all being led around by the nose."

In the past, Morgan had found that the fund-raisers she'd attended were either pleasant or incredibly boring; since the entire purpose was to raise money for some worthy cause (in this case to help out one of the private museums that had been burgled during the past weeks), a logical aim was to keep costs down. Ergo, the food tended to be banquet-bland and the entertainment adequate rather than inspiring. So to have a pleasant evening was to consider the event a success.

This particular fund-raiser had been organized by several museum curators—gentlemen not known for their adventurous spirits or love of the absurd—and their choice of entertainment was, to say the least, singular.

"It has a certain something," Quinn commented, leaning close to Morgan so she could hear him over the noise filling the large room. His expression was grave.

She winced at a discordant clash of notes from a band that seemed to have come from some twilight zone of amateur nights. "Oh, yeah, it has something. It has a beat and you can dance to it. But please don't ask me to."

He chuckled. "Well, we've done our duty. We listened to the speeches, ate the meal, and conversed intelligently with our table companions." He glanced around their table, which, like all the others in the room, seated twelve people—and was now deserted except for them and a very young couple on the other side who were totally wrapped up in each other.

"Most of whom bailed half an hour ago," Morgan pointed out, half closing her eyes as the enthusiastic drummer showed off his talents.

Quinn leaned even closer to her and, his breath warm against her neck, said, "I think they all showed good sense. Why don't we follow suit? It's a beautiful night, and I happen to know of a coffee shop about two blocks from here; what do you say? We can walk off that mystery chicken dish and get some fresh air—and a decent cup of coffee."

Morgan was in complete agreement, though she did feel a bit guilty in joining the exodus from the building. "I should find Ken and tell him he did a good job," she said to Quinn.

"Tell him tomorrow at the museum," he suggested. "It'll give you time to construct a really sincere face."

She couldn't help laughing as they got up. "Is nothing sacred to you?"

Guiding her through the jungle of pushed-back chairs and the occasional—and inexplicable—dancers, Quinn said, "In the area of manners and mores, you mean? Sure. I just happen to believe we should all be completely honest with ourselves—especially when we have to lie to be polite to others."

Morgan thought about that while they made their way from the hotel that was hosting the fund-raiser. She thought about lies. And she wondered which man had told her the most lies, Alex or Quinn.

As long as she followed her instincts and emotions, she had little hesitation in trusting Quinn. She wasn't so sure about Alex Brandon, partly, she suspected, because she hadn't quite convinced herself he was a real person. A psychologist would no doubt have found that as interesting as Storm had, but the truth was that after hearing about him for years and having several rather dramatic nighttime encounters with him, Quinn was the most real man she had ever known.

CHAPTER
NINE

You're very quiet, Morgana. Something wrong?"

She looked at her hand resting lightly on his arm, then drew in a breath of the clear night air and turned her gaze ahead of them again as they strolled along the sidewalk toward the coffee shop. "No. I was just thinking. Are you always honest with yourself, Alex?"

"Anyone who plays . . . identity games has to be."

"Identity games," she repeated slowly. "Is that what you do?"

He was silent for a moment, then spoke in an unusually serious tone. "I could say that when I was a boy I could never decide what I wanted to be when I grew up, but that wouldn't be true. What is true is that I had certain . . . talents that were not exactly suitable for your average career."

"Such as?" She thought he would say something about opening locks or blending into the night, but his answer was far more complex.

"The ability to reinvent myself whenever I had to. The ability to function well under . . . unusual kinds of pressure. The ability to work completely alone—and a liking for it." He shrugged. "I don't know what I might have done, but in college a friend dared me to . . . liberate something from the dean's house one night. I did it. And I liked it."

Morgan looked up at him curiously. "A college prank is a long way from professional burglary."

He smiled. "True."

"Was there any one thing that . . . bridged that distance? Something that happened to you, I mean."

"A tragedy that propelled me into a life of crime?"

She couldn't help but smile. "I said something like that once, didn't I?"

"Yes. And you were right to be doubtful of it." They had reached the coffee shop by then, and Quinn stopped on the sidewalk and turned to look down at her with a faint, rueful smile. "It was nothing so . . . romantic or quixotic, sweet, not a decision made in the heat of some painful emotion. I made a conscious, carefully thought-out, cold-blooded choice. No apologies. No regrets."

Morgan sighed and let go of his arm. "I need a cup of coffee."

His smile went even more crooked. "I'm not making it easy for you, am I?"

"No. But then—you never said you would." She tried to sound humorous about it.

Quinn gazed at her upturned face for a moment, then bent his head and kissed her. It was a brief kiss but by no means light, and Morgan would have melted against him except that his hands were on her shoulders holding her still. When he lifted his head rather abruptly, she had the dazed impression that he said something a bit profane under his breath, but she didn't quite catch it.

He turned her briskly toward the door of the coffee shop and said, "You may not have realized, but it's nearly eleven."

Morgan allowed herself to be steered, but she heard the telltale frustration in her voice when she said, "Can't you take a night off?"

"Not this night—but I'll see what I can do about the future."

Once they were inside and seated at a small table in the crowded shop, Morgan wasn't quite sure which way the conversation would go, but Quinn was definite. To her surprise, he wanted to talk about her.

"My family?" She looked at him bemusedly. "Why do you ask?"

"It's all a part of the boy-meets-girl stuff," he told her in a grave tone. "I just realized I know practically nothing about your background."

So, still a little mystified, Morgan briefly described a life that, to her, had always seemed quite ordinary. A middle-class upbringing as an only child; her parents' deaths in a car accident when she was eighteen and the modest inheritance that had put her through college; summer archaeological digs in various parts of the world; the jobs and positions she'd taken over the years.

"You've been alone a long time," he noted.

She nodded. "I guess—six years since college." Gazing at him steadily, she added in a deliberate tone, "I was briefly engaged once, the summer before graduation."

"What happened?"

Morgan had never told anyone about this, but she found the words coming easily now, so easily that it startled her. "He was another archaeology student, we seemed to have everything in common. I thought so, anyway. But there were warning signs—and I should have paid attention."

"Warning signs?"

"Mmm. He liked to see me dress a certain way—in clingy sweaters, for instance, and short skirts. His thoughts and opinions seemed to be more important than mine. In fact, he never wanted to talk to me about anything that mattered to me—even archaeology. He was always telling me I should wear my hair up or use more eye makeup or a different perfume."

Morgan shook her head and managed a smile. "Eventually I realized that who I was didn't matter to him—just what I looked like. And how I looked on his arm. He thought all his friends envied him because I looked . . ."

"Sexy?" Quinn supplied quietly.

"I guess. It was something I didn't want to believe about him, that he could be so . . . superficial. But, when we went back to school in the fall for our senior year, they gave us an I.Q. test."

"And you scored higher than he did?" Quinn guessed.

Morgan looked down at her coffee cup, frowning a little as she remembered. "Twenty points higher. At first, he didn't believe it. He kept saying somebody must have screwed up the test. I finally lost my temper and told him I'd scored high before and that the results were accurate. Then he—he just looked at me in shock. His eyes moved up and down over me in total incredulity, and he couldn't seem to say a word. So I did. I gave him back his ring and said good-bye."

"Morgana?"

She looked across the table at Quinn.

"Any man who could look at you and not see the intelligence and vitality in your eyes would have to be either blind or incredibly stupid." His own eyes laughed suddenly. "Of course, he'd also have to be blind or made of stone not to notice that you do look splendid in clingy sweaters."

Morgan couldn't help laughing, but she responded seriously to what she sensed was a serious point of his. "That experience made me wary—but not especially bitter. Noticing someone's looks is an automatic thing, after all, so I can hardly blame people for noticing mine. Obviously it's a problem only when they can't get past appearances." She paused, then added, "But you must admit that in me the . . . inner and outer woman are more contradictory than usual."

Quinn looked thoughtful. "As far as first impressions go, that may be true. But—trust me—it's a fleeting moment. Once you begin speaking, your wit and intelligence are obvious."

"If you say so."

Smiling, he said, "I'm sure at least a few of the men you've known in the years since college have proven me right."

"A few, I guess. Max is one. And Wolfe. Neither one of them has ever made me feel like an ornament."

"And me? Have I ever made you feel that way?"

"No." Wryly, she added, "Neither one of you. Although Alex has come closer than Quinn. The Don Juan bit."

"Sorry about that. If it helps, it was only . . ."

"You playing a part?"

"More or less."

"Yeah, I got that. Do us both a favor and quit it, okay?"

"I'll see what I can do."

She doubted him, but Morgan was a bit surprised, over the next few days, to find that Alex really did seem to have shed his Don Juan persona. He turned up at the museum every day, usually in late afternoon, and somehow always ended up taking her for drinks and dinner, once to a movie. He

continued to be a pleasant, amusing companion—
and a perfect gentleman.

The question was, what was he up to?

It wasn't until late Friday evening that Morgan began to get an inkling. Her evening with Alex had
ended a bit earlier than usual because he'd had "a few
chores to take care of." So she was home, brooding.

She sat there on her comfortable couch, still
wearing her work outfit of skirt and sweater but
shoeless, her feet drawn up on the cushions, and
scowled at the muted television. Slowly but inex-
orably, a fine, pure fury grew to fill her. It felt wonderful. Her mind was clear, her senses sharp, and
for the first time in several days she knew she was
looking directly at something he'd done his level
best to distract her from seeing.

Damn him! That lousy, rotten, no-good thief
had done it to her again. With all the skilled leg-
erdemain of a master magician, he had convinced
her that an illusion was real; she had been so intrigued—and seduced—by *Alex* that she had paid
little attention to the nighttime activities of *Quinn*.

Oh, she'd asked the occasional mild question,
but she hadn't really thought about the matter. And
she should have. She really should have.

Characteristically, once anger took hold of her,
Morgan didn't stop to think about what she was
doing. She found a pair of black Reeboks and laced

them swiftly onto her stockinged feet, caught up her purse, and left the apartment without even remembering to turn off the television.

Instead of rushing openly to the museum, she crossed the street and kept to the shadows, moving with all the stealth she could summon. She hung the strap of her shoulder bag to cross her chest so she was able to keep her hands free, but she was so intent on finding Quinn that she didn't follow her usual custom of keeping one cautious hand on her can of pepper spray.

It was easy enough to approach the museum without making her presence known, but once there she had to figure out where Quinn would be keeping watch. None of her archaeological or administrative skills covered the problem of possible vantage points for cat burglars, so all she could depend on was her common sense—and that extra sense she could occasionally tap into in order to feel him.

He was certainly close, she knew that much. Because she could feel him. Perhaps oddly, concentrating harder made the sensation more elusive. The trick, she quickly discovered, was to relax and simply ask herself where he was, because when she did that, the sense of his presence grew stronger.

He'd have to be high up, of course, with a clear view of the museum—but not so high that he couldn't get down in a hurry if he needed to, Morgan decided. She studied the buildings all around the museum, allowing that extra sense to open up.

There. He was there. It was a building that was only a couple of stories taller than the museum and less than half a block away.

Once she reached the building, she realized it was a perfect choice from a common-sense point of view. An apartment building with a handy fire escape, it was in the process of being renovated and was obviously empty of tenants and curious doormen.

Five floors. Morgan gritted her teeth and climbed, trying to be quiet and silently cursing herself because she'd forgotten to bring a flashlight. The moon provided some light, but the angle of the fire escape kept her in total darkness most of the time. Which was, she decided later, the main reason he was able to catch her off guard.

It happened so quickly that Morgan had no time to yell. All of a sudden she was grabbed and yanked against a hard body, her arms pinned, and a cloth that smelled sickly-sweet covered her nose and mouth. She tried to struggle even as she fought to hold her breath, and she was vaguely aware that her heavy purse struck the metal of the fire escape with a sound that seemed to her incredibly loud.

By then her lungs were screaming for air, her nails clawing for any part of her attacker she could reach, and a sudden jolt of pain in one ankle told her she'd kicked the fire escape and had been punished for it. Dizziness swept over her, and as the strength began to drain from her body she was conscious of a last, purely annoyed thought.

In all those old gothic romances, she remembered, the heroine always went charging off into the night, alone and unarmed, because she heard a suspicious sound or had a realization. Not only did she always land in trouble for it, but inevitably she was dressed in either a filmy nightgown or something equally unsuitable for nighttime wandering.

Morgan had always sneered at those heroines, promising herself that *she* would never venture into danger with such a stupid lack of preparation. And, until now, she could say she'd been at least partially successful. After all, when she had gone charging (alone and mostly unarmed) to Quinn's rescue some time back when the bad guys had captured him, at least she had been sensibly dressed. And it really hadn't been her fault that neither her cell phone nor can of pepper spray had been helpful.

This time, she reflected irritably, she'd not only blundered out without the means to defend herself, but she hadn't even had the sense to put on a pair of jeans first.

She could feel her attacker's body behind her, impressively hard, feel the ruthless strength of an arm that seemed to be cutting her in half, and she had the dim realization—a strange but comforting certainty—that it wasn't Quinn doing this to her. Then the chloroform did its work, and as she slumped against him she could feel her short skirt riding up her thighs.

Dammit, I should have put on some jeans. . . .

* * *

She heard voices. Two of them, both male and both familiar to her. She was lying on something very hard and cold and uncomfortable, but she seemed to be wrapped in something like a blanket, and she felt peculiarly safe. She couldn't seem to open her eyes or even stir, but her hearing was excellent.

"Will she be all right?"

"Yeah, I think so. It was chloroform; the cloth was lying on the fire escape beside her."

"What the hell was she doing here?"

"Since she's been unconscious since I found her and before I called you, I've hardly been able to ask her."

"All right—then try this. What happened?"

"Look, I can only guess. Maybe he got suspicious of me and showed up tonight looking for me—either to watch me or else to get rid of me. He had the chloroform with him, and I doubt he carries the stuff whenever he goes out; he was obviously planning to put somebody to sleep. Morgan must have surprised him coming up the fire escape. He couldn't get out of her way, so he had to get rid of her. If I hadn't felt—heard—something and gone down there to check it out, he might have had time to finish the job. She's damned lucky he didn't dump her over the railing and into the alley."

"All right, all right—calm down."

"I am perfectly calm," Quinn said in a voice so sharp it had edges.

Jared sort of sighed. "Yeah. Okay, we'll talk about this later. I gather I'm here to relieve you?"

"If you don't mind." Quinn sighed as well—though his sounded a bit ragged. "I'm not expecting anything else to happen tonight, but I'm not sure enough to leave the place unwatched. I need to take Morgan back to her apartment and make sure she's going to be all right."

"No problem."

"Thanks."

"Sure." Abruptly, Jared sounded amused. "How're you going to get her home?"

"Carry her."

"Down five floors, across four blocks, and up another three floors?"

"She's not very big," Quinn replied a bit absently, his voice even clearer now because he had knelt beside her.

By that point, even if Morgan could have opened her eyes she wouldn't have. Completely aware but utterly boneless, she felt herself gathered up and held in arms her body recognized instantly—simply by the touch of them. She heard an odd little noise escape her, something that sounded embarrassingly sensual, even primitive, and wondered uneasily if Jared heard her. Bad enough if Quinn heard . . .

She had the sensation of descending, even though she heard nothing, and realized that Quinn managed to move almost silently even down a fire escape and carrying her. It made her feel very strange to be carried so effortlessly by him, and that probably delayed her recovery from the chloroform a good five minutes or more.

When Morgan finally managed to force her heavy eyelids up, the fire escape was behind them and Quinn was striding down the sidewalk right out in the open. She concentrated fiercely and managed to raise her head from his shoulder, and though the nausea was horrible, she managed not to get sick.

"I—I think I can walk," she told him, sounding decidedly weak to her own ears.

Quinn looked at her without breaking stride. His face was completely expressionless in the illumination of the streetlights, and his voice was unusually flat. "I doubt it. Your right ankle's badly bruised."

Since she was wrapped in a blanket, Morgan couldn't see her feet. She tried to move the right one experimentally and bit back a sound of pain. Remembering, she realized she must have banged that ankle hard against the fire escape in her struggles to escape her attacker.

Cradled in Quinn's arms, she gazed at his profile and wished miserably that she hadn't let her reckless anger make her go charging out after him. She'd had every right to be mad as hell, dammit, but now *this* had happened, and with him carrying her home—on her shield, so to speak—she felt ridiculously defensive and at fault. But then, even as the feelings surfaced, another realization made her feel a little better. If she *hadn't* blundered into whoever that was on the fire escape, he might have been able to sneak up on Quinn—and he might not have simply put the cat burglar to sleep.

. . . either to watch me or else to get rid of me.

Morgan shivered and felt his arms tighten around her.

"Almost there," he said.

She let her head rest on his shoulder once more and closed her eyes against the waves of nausea. And, apparently, feeling sick wasn't the only after-effect of chloroform, because she dozed off again. Only a few minutes this time; when she opened her eyes again, Quinn was unlocking her apartment door. He must have at some point gotten her keys from her shoulder bag, she mused vaguely.

Inside the apartment, he lowered her to the couch so that she was sitting sideways, her feet up on the cushions. He was gentle enough, but she still caught her breath when her bruised ankle touched the firm cushions. The pain wasn't really horrible, but it was abrupt whenever she tried to move her foot or it touched anything.

Quinn straightened up and stared down at her, his face still curiously hard. In the subdued lighting of the living-room lamps, his green eyes were shuttered. He was dressed in his Quinn costume, black material from neck to toe, and as she looked up at him he dropped her keys onto the coffee table, then unbuckled his compact tool belt from around his waist and dropped it there as well.

He glanced at the television, which was still on and turned low, then looked at her again and said merely, "I'll get some ice for your ankle."

Alone in the quiet living room, Morgan managed to unwrap herself from the blanket so that her arms were free. She found her shoulder bag still attached to her and wrestled the strap off over her head; from the weight, she knew the only thing missing from it was her keys, so her attacker had obviously not attempted to rob her. She sort of slung the bag onto the coffee table, and it landed on top of Quinn's tool belt.

A glance at the clock on her VCR told her it was just after one A.M., which surprised her. How could so much happen in so little time?

Listening to the rattle of ice cubes in her kitchen, she cautiously leaned forward and opened the blanket the rest of the way to expose her legs, and winced at the sight of her right ankle. Even through her (somewhat mangled) hose, the swelling and discoloration were obvious. When she very gingerly moved it, the pain was hot and swift, but at least she *could* move it, so nothing was permanently harmed. Her head was clear once more, and she wasn't so queasy now, which was definitely a relief.

When Quinn returned to the room, he had her ice bag in one hand and a coffee cup in the other. "You left the coffee on," he told her as he handed the cup to her.

"I was in a temper," she admitted, avoiding his

eyes. Her voice was her own again, another thing to be thankful for. She hated sounding like a wimp.

Without immediately commenting on what she said, he got one of the decorative pillows from the other end of the couch and gently lifted her leg so that her foot and ankle were propped up. He eased the ice bag down on her swollen ankle, then left the room again, but only long enough to get a second cup of coffee from the kitchen.

When he came back, he startled her by sitting on the edge of the cushion at her thigh so that they were facing each other. He was sort of leaning sideways over her legs, one elbow and forearm resting on the back of the couch—either deliberately or accidentally blocking her in. The pressure of his hip against her leg distracted her from the heavenly relief of the ice bag on her ankle, and she wondered what spell he had used to make her body respond to him with such instant hunger.

Quinn took a sip of his coffee, then set the cup on the table and looked at her with those veiled eyes. In a carefully measured tone, he said, "Do you mind telling me what the hell you were doing out there tonight? And do you realize how close you came to getting yourself killed?"

"That wasn't the plan."

"Oh, you had a plan?"

"Don't be sarcastic, Alex—it doesn't suit you."

"And lying in a crumpled heap on a fire escape doesn't suit you." His voice was losing its measured precision; it was rougher now, harder. "What made you do it, Morgana? Why the hell were you on that fire escape?"

"I was looking for you, obviously. I don't know anyone else who might be found on the roof of a deserted building in the middle of the night."

Quinn refused to recognize her stab at self-mocking humor. "Why were you looking for me?"

"I told you, I was in a temper."

"About what?"

"About you."

The hard immobility of his face changed when he frowned. "About me? Why? What had I done?"

Morgan took refuge in her coffee. She couldn't hide, but at least it gave her a moment to think. Not that it helped; when she answered him, the words were blurted out with little grace and far too much pain.

"You said wouldn't use me again. That you needed me on your side. Remember?"

He was still frowning at her. "Morgana, I haven't tried to use you."

"Oh, no? Can you look me in the eye and tell me you haven't been very deliberately distracting me since the night at Leo's party when you went public as Alex Brandon? That you haven't used your Alex persona—all charm and gentlemanly attention—to make sure I didn't ask too many questions about what Quinn was up to every night?"

"You talk as if I really am two men." His tone was odd, almost hesitant.

"You as good as say you are," she retorted instantly. "With some nice, neat dividing line separating you two. Night and day, black and white, Quinn and Alex. Two distinctly different men. Except that it's not that simple. You don't have a split personality, and you *aren't* two men—what you are is a hell of a natural actor." Exactly what Max had tried to warn her about, Morgan recalled.

"Am I?"

She nodded. "Oh, yes. A gifted one. Do you want me to tell you how I think your reasoning went?"

"Go ahead." His voice was a bit wry.

"I sat here tonight thinking about it, trying to understand what you were doing—and I finally got it."

He waited, silent and expressionless, his gaze fixed on her face.

"I think that when you decided to go public, there was one small problem you really hadn't planned on. Me." She held his gaze, determined to get this out. "There *was* something between us, something you couldn't ignore or pretend didn't exist. Something real."

Quinn might have heard the very faint question there; he nodded and said gravely, "Yes. There was."

Morgan tried not to let her relief show; she'd been almost sure he did feel something for her. Almost. Going on steadily, she said, "Because of that, because you knew we'd be together often, you were afraid I'd figure out some things you didn't want me to know. For whatever reason."

"For your own good, maybe?" he suggested, more or less telling her she was on the right track.

"We'll talk about *that* later," she told him, ruthlessly keeping them on the subject. "The point is, you decided it would be a good idea to keep me distracted so I wouldn't think too much about the part Quinn was playing at night."

"Morgana—"

"Wait. The defense can argue later."

He smiled slightly and nodded.

Morgan sighed. "Maybe you honestly don't think of it as using me and what I feel, but that's what you've been doing. I don't know if the reasons matter. I don't know if your reasons are good enough to excuse what you did. All I do know is that you used my feelings to help you hide what you were really doing here."

CHAPTER
TEN

What I'm *really* doing?"

"You said something once—that there were times you had to lie to everyone. This is one of those times, I think. All this isn't nearly as straightforward as you'd have us believe, this clever plan to catch Nightshade. You've been lying about it somehow. Maybe to Jared, probably to Max and Wolfe—and certainly to me."

"You think I'm after the collection," he said flatly.

"No."

"No?"

She smiled faintly at his disbelief. "No. Despite everything, including my own common sense, I don't believe you are. I can't know for certain what it is you're trying to do and how you're trying to do it—but I'm willing to bet the ultimate aim *is* to get Nightshade. It's in your voice every time you talk about him. You *do* really want him, and very badly, I think. So much so that you aren't going to let anyone or anything get in the way of catching him."

"That's what you think?"

"That's what I *feel*. Maybe Interpol thought you could catch Nightshade, but that isn't why you're here. You may be dancing to their tune, but only because it's your choice. And nobody's pulling your strings, Alex. Nobody. This—all this, this whole plan to set a trap—was your idea, wasn't it?"

Quinn stared at her for a long moment, then drew a breath and let it out slowly. "You think too much," he murmured, then smiled and added, "and you think too well."

"I'm right about this."

He hesitated, then nodded just a little. "The trap was my idea. Jared wasn't happy about it, but the chance to catch Nightshade was something he couldn't pass up. His . . . superiors at Interpol know we're after Nightshade but don't know how we're planning to catch him."

That was a surprise, and Morgan knew it showed. "They don't know? You mean all this is unofficial?"

Quinn rubbed the back of his neck with one hand and looked at her wryly. "Morgana, Interpol doesn't have a policy of baiting traps with priceless gem collections. In fact, both Jared and I would likely land in jail if it got out that's what we're doing. Unless we're successful, of course. Because, if we're successful, no one, except those of us directly involved, will ever know it was a trap."

"And Interpol was willing to give you that much freedom, let you loose on this side of the Atlantic with only one . . . handler, I guess he's called, holding the leash?"

"Let's just say . . . Jared gambled on his little brother. His superiors believe we're over here gathering information, trying to track Nightshade and figure out a way to catch him. Jared's responsible for me."

Morgan eyed him thoughtfully. "I got the impression that you two were barely on speaking terms. I gather it was a deliberate impression?"

Quinn had the grace to look a little sheepish. "I told you that a lot of what I do is pretense. Jared was understandably furious when he found out who Quinn really is, but he's a man who looks forward—not back. He believes I can . . . redeem myself by helping Interpol now. He's willing to be part of that. But he really *is* mad at me about half the time—he thinks I'm reckless and take too many dumb chances."

"You don't say."

"Sarcasm doesn't suit you either, Morgana."

She frowned at him. "Mmm. So you're the one who went to Max and asked him to risk his collection."

"I'm the one."

"Well, I must say I'm impressed. I knew he'd climb out on a fairly long limb for a friend, but you must be something pretty special."

He assumed a hurt expression. "You don't think so?"

"Stop that. You know what I mean."

Quinn smiled. "Yes, I know. And the truth is . . . Max and I go way back. Besides, once he heard about Nightshade's past activities, he thought catching the bastard sounded like an excellent idea."

Morgan was still frowning. She was reasonably sure that Quinn was being honest with her now, but that didn't mean he'd told her everything. He had an uncanny ability to tell just enough of the truth to make it all sound *right* without giving away anything he really didn't want someone else to know.

It was an unsettling talent—and it didn't help her to understand him the way she needed to. The problem was, she had yet to figure out what drove this man, what made him who he was. Everyone had some core motivation, some inner force propelling them through life as it shaped decisions and choices; what was his? She thought everything would make sense if she could only figure out what it was.

Slowly, probing for the answer to that question, she said, "I think I said once that I thought you had a personal reason for going after Nightshade—now I'm sure. And it isn't because he shot you. Why, Alex? What did he do to make you so determined? How did his path cross yours?"

Quinn didn't say a word for a moment. His face was still, wiped clean of all expression, and when he spoke, his voice was low and strained. "Two years ago, Nightshade killed someone who just happened to be in the wrong place at the wrong time—a not uncommon occurrence during one of his robberies. Only this time his victim was someone I cared about."

From a window in a building several floors taller than the Museum of Historical Art, she studied first the museum and then the nearby building where the Interpol agent watched.

Bad night to skulk around, at least in this area, she acknowledged silently.

The place really was thick with thieves.

And cops.

Quinn had nearly caught her, damn him.

She lowered the binoculars and frowned, conscious of time passing too rapidly for her peace of mind. And her bank account. Almost everything was in place, her plan unfolding nicely so far. There were still a few minor details to take care of, of course, before she was ready to move.

And then there was him.

Quinn.

After tonight, she was more certain than ever that Morgan West was his weakness, his point of vulnerability. On the one hand, that was good: With his attention mostly focused on her, he was more apt to make a mistake—or at the very least be less attentive, less aware.

It could cripple him, that distraction.

On the other hand, his interest in her kept him close to the exhibit and those involved with it. He was on the inside, keenly aware of what was going on.

You had to admire the son of a bitch. He was having his cake and sleeping with her too.

What she had assumed was an unlucky break—encountering Morgan on that fire escape—had instead confirmed something she had guessed weeks ago. Those two could somehow sense each other, and after tonight it was doubtful that Quinn would let Morgan get too far away from him.

Good. That was good.

The more he was distracted from his work, the better for her. Sort of disappointing, not going up against Quinn at his best, but there would be other chances for that.

Lots of other chances.

She turned away from the window and put the binoculars away in her backpack. For now, this was the job she'd been hired to do, and anything that made it easier or simpler for her was all to the good.

Even love.

She heard herself laughing, and wasn't surprised.

"Who did he kill?" Morgan asked slowly.

"Her name was Joanne. Joanne Brent. She was attending a party at a house in London and, apparently, wandered into her host's library very late looking for something to read. She surprised Nightshade at work—and he killed her. Left a dead rose on her body."

"That's awful," Morgan whispered.

"Yes." His voice was stony. "She was twenty-two."

Morgan searched his hard, handsome features, suddenly afraid of a ghost. "You . . . loved her." It wasn't a question.

He shook his head slightly, that look of rigid control softening a bit. "Not the way you mean. I never had a sister, but Joanne was the nearest thing. Until I came here to the States to attend college, we lived near each other in England. She was still a kid when I graduated—eight years younger—and after that I traveled quite a bit, so we didn't see each other often. When she was killed, I hadn't seen her in nearly six months."

"Did she know you were Quinn?"

"No. I trusted her, but . . ."

Perceptively, Morgan said, "You didn't tell her because she would have worried?"

"Something like that."

After a moment, Morgan nodded and said slowly, "You don't need me to point out that revenge tends to punish the one looking for it more than the target."

Quinn smiled, but his eyes were suddenly as hard and cold as emeralds. "I don't want revenge, Morgana. I want justice."

"What kind of justice?"

"The best kind. A man like Nightshade has spent his life collecting beautiful things, most of which he's secreted away so that his are the only eyes to see them. He sits in the middle of his treasures and gloats because he owns what no other man can claim." Quinn smiled again. "So I'm going to take all that away from him. I'm going to put him in prison, surrounded by bare concrete walls and men who have very little appreciation for beauty. And I'm going to make damned sure he rots there."

Morgan couldn't help shivering a little, but she tried to lighten the moment. "Sounds like a plan."

He looked at her for a moment, then smiled a much more genuine smile. "So it does."

She glanced down at the coffee cup she was cradling between her hands, absently aware that it was cooling, then returned her gaze to his face. "Your plan. You decided you could catch Nightshade, and you talked everybody else—Jared, Max, and Wolfe—into going along."

Thoughtfully, Quinn said, "I think Max convinced Wolfe. I was never very good with him. We always had . . . communications problems."

"He doesn't like thieves," Morgan reminded dryly.

"There is that, of course. And he's a bit hidebound about people who bend the law now and then. I always thought Max was as well, but he surprised me."

"You," Morgan said, "are a dangerous man. You have this weird ability to say the most outrageous things and make them sound perfectly reasonable."

Solemnly, Quinn said, "A certain inborn talent and a hell of a lot of practice."

"Mmm. That isn't your only talent. You also have a very devious nature. Answer a question? Truthfully?"

"I'll have to hear it first."

"Okay. Interpol caught up with you—what?—sometime last year?"

"Yes. Not a question I'd lie about, Morgana."

"And not the question I want answered. But this is: They caught you because you let them. Didn't they?"

"Morgana—"

"You needed the resources of Interpol. All your own resources are in Europe, and they told you that Nightshade was probably operating out of the States. So you needed help in finding him. You needed to be inside an international police organization that could legitimately call upon U.S. authorities for information and help."

"So I allowed the police to capture me, possibly lock me away? Morgana—"

"You gambled. You said earlier that Jared gambled on his little brother, but he wasn't the only one doing that. You gambled that you could talk him over to your side, persuade him that setting a thief to catch a thief was a good idea. Gambled that he could persuade his superiors it would be better to use your knowledge and talents than lock you away. You gambled your freedom. Maybe even your life."

He was silent.

"Not a question you can answer truthfully?"

"You think too much," he said again.

"And too well? You let them catch you. It was the first step of your plan. This plan. To catch Nightshade."

He drew a breath and let it out slowly. "You make it sound more dramatic than it was."

"Do I?"

"Yes."

Morgan didn't argue. Instead, she said, "It must be nearly two by now. Will Jared expect you back tonight?"

"We both have cell phones; he'll call if he needs me."

"Will he expect you back tonight?" she repeated steadily.

"No, probably not. He knew I was concerned about you, that I wouldn't want to leave you alone."

In a mild tone, she said, "I'll be all right."

"Yes. Still."

She nodded, unwilling to question him further at the moment. "Okay. Right now, I could use a hot shower to wash away a layer of grime from that fire escape and the last effects of the chloroform."

If he hesitated, it was only for an instant. "Then I'll make a fresh pot of coffee while you take your shower." He took her cup and set it on the coffee table, then got to his feet. "How's the ankle?"

"Ask me when I'm standing."

Quinn helped her to her feet, keeping a firm grip on her arms until it became obvious that her injured ankle could bear weight, then he released her—but remained watchful.

Morgan hobbled toward her bedroom, relieved to find that the pain wasn't as bad as it had been. Over her shoulder, she said to him, "Back in a few minutes."

"I'll be here," he replied.

About that, at least, she knew he was telling the truth.

* * *

When Jared's cell phone vibrated a summons, he was a little surprised to see that the call came from Keane Tyler. He answered with a guarded, "Yeah?"

"Working late, huh?"

"You too. What's up?"

"Still no I.D. on Jane Doe, but the labwork came back on that knife we found in the museum. It's her blood, and the M.E.'s report says it's the murder weapon. No real surprises there."

"Then why're you calling me at two in the morning?"

"Because whoever is leading us around by the nose has left another signpost for us to follow. The M.E., at my request, did a more thorough tox screen on Jane Doe. And found something unexpected. A small amount of venom, injected via a hypodermic and postmortem. Since she was already dead, it obviously wasn't meant to kill her. Wouldn't have anyway."

"So a sign for us."

"Looks like."

"What kind of venom?"

"A spider's. Black widow."

By the time Morgan returned to the living room a little more than half an hour later, she felt much better physically. She'd washed away the dirt of the fire escape and the memory of chloroform, carefully rubbed liniment on her sore ankle (the skin wasn't broken, but there was a nasty bruise), and thought about all he'd told her tonight.

The only certainty she had reached when she returned to him was the rueful knowledge that she had fallen for an extremely complex man she might never fully understand even after a lifetime of knowing him. On the other hand, he was also the most intriguing, baffling, maddening, exciting man she'd ever known, and impossibly sexy to boot.

None of that was a revelation, of course, except for her acceptance of her own feelings. And, being Morgan, once she accepted them, that particular struggle was over. After all, what was the use of kicking and screaming about something beyond one's power to change? She might be the last woman in the world who should have fallen for a famous cat burglar, but the fact remained that she *had*.

Dealing with it was the issue now.

After careful thought, Morgan very deliberately dressed in a loose and comfortable outfit consisting of baggy sweatpants and sweatshirt, with her only pair of bedroom slippers (ridiculously fuzzy things) on her feet. Hardly sexy attire. She had no intention of throwing herself at him yet again and trusted that he would get the point.

Being Quinn, of course, he did.

"Where did you get the blanket?" she asked calmly as she limped back into the living room. The blanket had been folded up and placed over the back of a chair, catching her attention when she came in.

He had been on the couch, looking rather broodingly at an old black-and-white movie on television, and got to his feet as soon as she spoke. His gaze scanned her from head to toe, and a faint gleam was born in the green eyes.

"Jared brought it when I called him to come relieve me on watch," he answered.

"Ah. I wondered."

"Feeling better?"

"Heaps. Don't I look it?"

"Fishing, Morgana?"

"Curious."

He smiled. "I get the point, if that's what you're wondering. But I think I should tell you that you'd look sexy draped in sackcloth."

She eased down on the other end of the couch and looked up at him expressionlessly. "I always wondered what that was. Sackcloth, I mean."

"A very rough, coarse cloth."

"That was what I thought. But I wasn't sure. Did you happen to earn a college degree in the history of fashion?"

"No."

Morgan waited, one eyebrow rising, and Quinn suddenly uttered a low laugh.

"Actually, I have a law degree."

For an instant she wanted to laugh but managed

to control the impulse. "I see. Well, at least you completely understood the laws you were breaking."

"I'll get the coffee," Quinn said, retreating.

Morgan smiled to herself, then searched among the pillows on the couch for the remote and turned the television off. When he returned, she accepted her cup and sipped the hot liquid cautiously. "I won't be worth shooting tomorrow," she commented as he sat down a foot or so away from her.

"You mean today." He glanced at her, then said, "I talked to Jared while you were in the shower and asked him to fill in the others in the morning. So they probably won't expect you to show up on time. If at all."

"I guess they had to know, huh?"

"I think so." Quinn gazed into his coffee cup as if it held the secrets of the universe. "If that *was* Nightshade who put you to sleep, he's getting either nervous or suspicious—and either way could mean it's likely that he'll make his move soon."

There were still several questions Morgan wanted to ask about all this—things that bothered her in a sort of vague, indeterminate way—but she chose not to ask them right now for two reasons: first, because she was more than ready to focus on their relationship and, second, because she had a hunch he would tell her more if allowed to do so in his own way.

While all that was floating through her mind, he

leaned forward to set his cup on the coffee table and then half turned toward her as he sat back.

"Morgana?"

She looked at him, finding his expression very serious.

"I wasn't trying to use your feelings to distract you. At least . . . not consciously. I didn't particularly want you to ask questions about what I was doing at night, but we both know I'm capable of lying if I have to."

"So you would have lied to me."

"Yes," he replied without hesitation. "If I believed it was something you didn't need to know about or, worse, would put you in danger if you knew." He drew a breath. "It seemed safest to keep you occupied during the day, and since it was definitely not a hardship—"

"You must have lost sleep doing it. Being Quinn every night and Alex during the day."

"Some, but nothing I can't handle. Morgan, I hope you understand. There are things I didn't want to have to explain—not yet anyway—and I knew damned well that if you concentrated that sharp mind of yours on what I was doing at night, you'd figure out more than I wanted you to know."

"Thanks for the compliment," she said. "But I've a feeling your little plan is so twisty I wouldn't be able to find my way through it with a road map."

He smiled slightly. "Maybe not. I think I've

taken a few turns blindly myself. That happens when you have to improvise without warning."

"Is that what you've been doing? Improvising?"

"As you said—I hadn't counted on you. I hadn't counted on being . . . distracted. Still, I thought I could handle it. Then when I came to you after I was shot, not out of reason or logic but just because . . . because I had an overwhelming need to be with you, I knew I was in trouble. And I knew I didn't have a hope in hell of keeping you in a nice, safe little compartment of my life—even to protect you."

Morgan resisted the urge to ask him to define his feelings for her a bit more clearly; she was determined not to prod him to say anything he wasn't ready to divulge on his own. "Protect me from what?"

"From all the risks involved in what I'm doing." He sounded frustrated. "Goddammit, Nightshade *kills* people, don't you understand that? Without a second thought or even an instant's hesitation, he kills anyone who gets in his way. I don't want you in his way, Morgana. I don't want him to even imagine you could be a problem. It's bad enough that you're publicly linked with me at all; the closer you are to me, the closer you are to *him*—visible to him and drawing his attention. Besides that, considering how many times you've already charged into dangerous situations—"

"Just that one time, when I followed those men

who had you," she objected. "You can't count the first time, because I was there by accident; my date took me to that museum in all innocence." Then she frowned. "Well, maybe not innocence—but you know what I mean."

"What about tonight?"

"That hadn't happened yet, so don't use it as an excuse."

He almost—but not quite—laughed. It was actually more a sound of despair.

"All right, but even then it's been obvious all along that you're too impulsive for your own good. And I could hardly count on *my* good sense where you're concerned; I knew that I wouldn't be able to stay away from you. Seeing you openly as Alex Brandon seemed the best way. But it meant Nightshade would have to know I was interested in you, and his awareness of that was enough of a risk. I didn't want you getting involved with my—my nighttime activities. So I thought that being Alex during the day and being openly interested in you would both make you seem unthreatening to Nightshade and distract your attention from what I was doing at night."

Morgan blinked. There were several things bothering her about all that, but one realization was uppermost in her mind. "Wait a minute. Are you saying that you went public just because of me? It wasn't part of your plan to find Nightshade?"

"I'd already found Nightshade," he admitted

reluctantly. "And for God's sake, don't tell Jared—he'd shoot me."

She felt a bit dazed. "You had already found Nightshade. And being Alex won't help lure him into the trap?"

"As a matter of fact, being Alex was one of those improvised turns I mentioned—and it's complicated the situation in more ways than I want to discuss."

Morgan stared at him. Almost idly, she said, "You know, if I find out your name isn't really Alex, I'll—"

He didn't wait to hear what she'd do. "I give you my word of honor that my mother named me Alexander. Satisfied?"

"On that point. But I'm very puzzled about the rest of this," she admitted. "And I've got this weird feeling that you've distracted me again."

Gravely, he said, "We always seem to cover a remarkable amount of ground when we talk, don't we?"

"Seems like. But it always comes back to this. What's between us."

"Morgana, if you want to continue to be aloof in public—"

"No, I don't mean public. I mean private. I mean this, between us. The reason you're distracted, the reason I'm distracted. What we both keep dancing around. What are we going to do about this, Alex?"

After a moment, he said slowly, "It would be a bad idea, you know that. Without trust between lovers—"

She was mildly incredulous. "Trust? Alex, stop and think a minute. I am a sensible, rational, law-abiding woman who never so much as cheated on a parking meter before I met you. So what happened the night we met? I lied to the police when I didn't tell them you stole that dagger. And what happened the night those thugs grabbed you? Not only did I risk life and limb to try to help you, but then I more or less betrayed my good friend and employer, Max—I thought—by warning you that *Mysteries Past* was a trap. And I didn't call the cops when you lay bleeding on my floor. Does any of this suggest something to you? Like maybe that I seem to have a certain lack of good judgment where you're concerned?"

His eyes were even more vivid than usual, and his mouth curved in a slight smile. "But do you trust me?"

Morgan sighed and abandoned her last shred of dignity. "I love you, and that'll have to be good enough."

She had the satisfaction of knowing she had surprised him at least, but she couldn't read anything else in his suddenly still face and brilliant eyes.

"Say that again," he murmured.

"I love you." She said it quietly and without drama, but with utter certainty. "I've known that for weeks."

C H A P T E R
ELEVEN

I t isn't safe to love me," he said.

"Do you think that matters?"

"Morgana, I don't want to be something you regret."

"You won't be. I promise you, Alex. You won't be."

Quinn leaned forward slowly, releasing her hands so that his arms could encircle her, pulling her toward him as his head bent and his warm, hard mouth found hers. Morgan made a little sound, much as she had when he'd picked her up, and her arms slid up around his neck eagerly. She could no more temper her instant, fiery response to him than she could voluntarily stop the runaway beating of her heart.

Her body seemed attuned to him, to his touch, in a way she'd never felt before. It was nothing so simple as passion; what he ignited in her was a craving so elemental and absolute it was akin to the need of her body for sustenance. She had the dim realization that some part of her would starve to death without him.

He lifted his head at last and looked at her with eyes so dark there was only a hint of green visible. Huskily, he said, "I promised myself I wouldn't let anything . . . irrevocable happen between us until I could be completely honest with you. Until you could know the truth, all the truth. Morgana—"

She slid her fingers into his thick golden hair and pulled him down so that she could kiss him, and against his mouth she murmured, "Alex, I want you—and that's the only truth I care about right now."

Quinn hesitated for another moment, his entire body tense, but then he made a rough sound and kissed her hungrily. His hands moved down her back, probing through the material of her sweatshirt, while the tip of his tongue teased the sensitive inner surface of her lips. Morgan heard herself utter another of those primitive little whimpers, wordless but urgent with wanting, and then all her senses went haywire.

Just like before, the relentless need Morgan felt for him was stunning—but this time she was aware that he was every bit as involved in what was happening as she was. He wasn't holding back, wasn't detached, and wasn't trying to distract her. And he didn't have to try to make her want him.

Morgan hadn't intended this to happen tonight,

she really hadn't, but the only emotional hesitation she felt about it was a need to be reassured that he wouldn't walk away from her as he had before. "Stay with me," she invited unsteadily when his lips trailed across her cheek and traced her jawline. "Stay with me tonight."

"Are you sure, sweetheart?" he demanded hoarsely, drawing away just far enough to make her look at him. His handsome face was taut, his features drawn with a sharpened look of hunger. "I didn't come here prepared for this."

She understood what he was saying, but since she'd never been able to be practical about him anyway, Morgan didn't see any reason to break with tradition at this late date. "I'm sure. I want you to stay."

Quinn looked at her for a moment longer, then kissed her again, more deeply still, almost as if that alone were an act of possession. It sent her senses spinning once more, stealing her breath and increasing the feverish heat of her desire until Morgan wasn't thinking about anything except how he made her feel. Then he was shifting his hold on her, lifting her, and she realized he was carrying her as easily as he had before.

Since he'd spent several days there, he was familiar with her apartment and was able to find his way to her bedroom almost blindly. She blinked up at him a bit dazedly when he set her on her feet beside the bed.

He framed her face in his hands and looked down at her with an odd intensity, as if memorizing her features, his own still strained. "That first night in the museum," he murmured, "when you looked up at me with your cat's eyes, so indignant to find yourself in the company of a thief, I knew this would happen. Even then, I knew."

She managed a smile. "All I knew was how much you annoyed me. And how empty that room seemed when you left."

His thumb brushed her bottom lip in a rhythmic little caress. "I didn't go far that night. I watched the police come, and when they brought you back here I followed them."

"You did?"

"Mmm. And I was at the museum during the day a couple of times after that. So I could see you."

"Before I knew what you looked like . . . but I had that feeling you were somewhere around."

"Something else I didn't bargain on. This connection between us."

"What happened tonight on the fire escape—you didn't hear anything to alert you, did you? You felt it."

"You were in trouble," he murmured. "Someone was trying to hurt you. That's what I felt."

Morgan tried to steady her breathing. "Do you believe in fate, Alex?"

"I do now," he said, and his mouth was hard on hers, the pent-up need of weeks fire inside him.

Inside her.

She pushed the hem of his sweater up blindly because she had to touch his skin, half opening her eyes when he let go of her long enough to yank the garment off and toss it aside. Her eyes went immediately to his left shoulder, and her fingers gently touched the scar there. He'd been right, she realized; he did heal quickly. It was difficult to believe he'd been shot just a few weeks before.

But the scar *was* a reminder, a sign of the danger of what he was doing. Were there more scars, other marks of violence and risk on his body? On his soul?

"Morgan?"

She looked up at him, knowing that he felt her instant's hesitation, that he understood the reason behind it. Just the way he would understand if she stopped this here and now.

Her arms slid up around his neck and she pressed her body against his. "What are you waiting for?" she murmured.

"You. I've always been waiting for you." His arms tightened around her, and when his mouth touched hers again the moment for stopping vanished as though it had never been.

Morgan made a soft, disgruntled sound when he jostled her a bit while he was getting them under the covers, but she didn't open her eyes even when he chuckled. She felt utterly limp and sated, and when he pulled her close to his side again once they were both under the covers, she pillowed her head on his shoulder with a sigh of pure bliss.

"Morgana?"

"Hmm?"

"Am I forgiven?"

She still didn't want to open her eyes, but she was very much awake even though dawn wasn't too far off. After a moment, she said, "Don't spread the word around, but I can't stay mad at you no matter what you do."

His arm tightened around her, and one hand began smoothing her long hair. "I know you aren't still mad—but am I forgiven?"

Morgan lifted her head then and looked down at him. He was serious, she realized. She pushed herself up on one elbow to see him better, and answered seriously. "You're forgiven. But don't ever do that to me again, Alex. I think I can stand being lied to easier than being manipulated."

He was still toying with her hair, and a slight frown drew his brows together. Softly, he said, "I don't want to lie to you."

"No—but you aren't ready to tell me the whole truth." She gave him a rueful smile.

"I have my reasons, sweetheart. I think they're good reasons. Can you accept that?"

She hesitated. "I want to. But it's driving me crazy wondering how many lies you've told me. Can you at least promise that you'll tell me the truth eventually?"

Quinn nodded immediately. "Once the trap is sprung, I swear I'll tell you everything."

"Then I'll accept that." She kept her voice light.

"Just . . . don't lie about this, all right? About us. I don't want any bedroom promises, Alex."

His hand slid to the nape of her neck, and he pulled her down far enough to kiss her slowly. Against her mouth, he murmured, "No bedroom promises."

Morgan had thought herself exhausted, but as his warm mouth moved against hers, she felt a surge of energy—and desire. Quinn seemed equally refreshed; his kisses deepened into hunger, and then he was pressing her back against the pillows and pushing the covers back so he could see her.

For a moment—even after all that had gone before—Morgan felt a little shy. The way he was looking at her, so direct and intent, was a bit unnerving. But then he leaned down to press a soft kiss on her stomach, then another and another in a slow trail up between her breasts, and his low words added a sensual vibration and another kind of seduction to the caresses.

"No bedroom promises—just the truth. Have you any idea what you do to me? What you've been doing to me since the night I reached out and caught you? There hasn't been a day you haven't been on my mind, and the nights . . . the nights. The nights never seemed long before, but now they do, long and cold."

"Even this night?" she asked huskily.

"No." He lifted his head and looked down at her with darkening eyes. "Not this night."

Morgan had had no idea that she was even capable of such a swift and total response, but she soared toward the brink so quickly it was like yielding to an elemental force. He was inside her, filling her, and her newly awakened body was electrified by the sensations.

"You're beautiful," he said huskily, his eyes narrowed on her taut face. "Especially like this, so alive, wanting me."

She couldn't have said anything to that if her life had depended on it. The coiling tension inside her held her in a blissful state of pleasure so acute it bordered on pain, and she couldn't even catch her breath enough to moan.

Quinn's eyes narrowed even more as he slowly, torturously began to move, subtle undulations becoming deep, lazy thrusts, and Morgan couldn't bear it another second. It felt as if every nerve ending she possessed throbbed in rhythmic surges of pleasure, and her wild cry was caught in his mouth as he kissed her fiercely.

He followed her over the brink, his powerful body shuddering and a hoarse sound wrenched from him, and this time, sated and utterly drained, they both slept.

The sky was just beginning to lighten toward gray when Quinn slipped from the bed, careful not to wake Morgan, and went to gaze out the bedroom window. As Morgan had noted, he was accustomed to working nights, and it had reached a point where he found it difficult to sleep when it was dark.

If this kept up much longer, he reflected wryly, he really *would* turn into a vampire.

He stood there at the window, looking out on the quiet street in front of this apartment building, acutely aware of the soft breathing of the woman in the bed behind him. How to keep her safe? That was his greatest worry now. He had tried not to let her see how shaken he'd been over what happened on the fire escape, but the truth was that every time he thought of the danger she'd been in it was like a knife in his heart.

Had it been Nightshade? Or someone else?

Who had been the real target tonight, him—or Morgan?

That was the question he couldn't answer, whether Morgan's attacker had grabbed her only because she'd been in the way or because she had been the real target all along. That was the question that left him cold. Because if she had been the target, he could think of only two reasons why: Someone wanted to get their hands on the director of the *Mysteries Past* exhibit, or someone knew or had guessed how important she was to a thief named Quinn.

And now what? He was running out of time, dammit, he could feel it. After tonight, he was going to be walking a high wire without a net, and he wasn't sure he could maintain his balance. Not now. Not anymore.

He was no longer on that high wire alone.

"Alex?"

He turned immediately, crossing the dim room to return to the bed. Sliding under the covers, he pulled her into his arms and held her without force, fighting the instincts urging him to hold her with all his strength. "Sorry I woke you," he murmured.

"Is something wrong?" she asked softly, her warm body pressed to his.

"No, sweetheart, nothing's wrong," he lied. "Go back to sleep."

Within minutes, he knew she had, her breath soft against his skin. Very gently, careful not to wake her, he stroked her back, enjoying the satiny feel of her skin and the radiant warmth of her body.

She loved him. That was what she'd said, and said with quiet conviction. Knowing him for a liar and a thief, she loved him. It was remarkable. *She* was remarkable.

Staring up at the lightening ceiling of her bedroom, Quinn wondered if Morgan would love him when she knew the truth.

"I thought you weren't supposed to work weekends," Jared said as he came into the computer room.

Sipping her third cup of coffee that morning, Storm shrugged and said, "Wolfe and I are both too restless to stay home with all this going on. The exhibit, the trap, this mysterious other player in the game. We both came in hours ago."

"Where is Wolfe?"

"If he's not prowling around the exhibit, he's down in the basement. Prowling around."

"The police searched the basement."

"Yeah, but we all know it's a huge space. And since he's spent months finding all the corners and hidey-holes—even down there—he won't feel at ease until he's finished his own search."

Jared grunted and sat down in her visitor's chair. She eyed him. "You look beat. Long night?"

"Yeah."

"I thought Alex was taking the midnight-to-dawn duty."

Jared explained briefly what had happened the night before, including the phone call from Keane.

"Morgan's all right?"

"According to Alex, yeah. At the moment, I'm more concerned by what the M.E. found in Jane Doe's body."

"Spider venom. Black widow spider venom. Have you run that little detail through NCIC?"

He nodded. "No matches. Far as the Crime Information Center is concerned, finding spider venom of any kind in an already dead murder victim isn't part of any active killer's M.O. Or any inactive killer's, for that matter."

"I guess you checked with Interpol?"

"Yeah, same results."

Storm leaned back in her chair and propped her boots on the desk. "I'm still stuck wondering why all the signposts. They've gotta be leading us somewhere, but you'd think it would be away from the museum instead of to it. I mean, there are other valuables in the city, but nothing so well protected that a thief would need to go to all this trouble to distract us from them. The Bannister collection has to be a prime target. So why keep leading us back here?"

"The question of the hour."

"We're missing something."

"Yeah, I got that feeling."

"You haven't told Wolfe about Keane's call last night, have you?"

"Keane was planning to call him first thing this morning. Probably has by now."

"Why didn't one of you call last night?"

Jared shrugged. "Didn't see any reason to disturb you two with another seemingly useless puzzle piece."

"I appreciate that." Storm smiled. "Wolfe also appreciates it."

"Wolfe wouldn't appreciate it if I handed him winning lottery numbers."

"Actually, I would," Wolfe said as he came into the room. "Nothing personal, you understand, but money is money." He closed the door behind him.

"Right," Jared murmured.

"Find anything?" Storm asked her fiancé.

"Nah. Keane called. I guess Jared filled you in?"

"Just now. And there's more."

Jared told Wolfe about Morgan's ordeal the night before, and the news immediately brought a scowl to Wolfe's face.

"I don't like this," he announced.

"Morgan's all right. This time, anyway." Jared frowned. "But something Alex said last night has been bugging me. It didn't hit me until hours later. He said that maybe Nightshade had gotten suspicious of him and was watching him."

The three of them looked at one another for a moment, then Wolfe said slowly, "Which means not only that Alex knows who Nightshade is, but that Nightshade may well know that Alex Brandon and Quinn are one and the same."

"Anybody else just feel the bottom drop out of their stomach?" Storm asked.

Completely in sync for once, both Wolfe and Jared raised a hand.

The room was bright when Morgan finally opened her eyes, and for a moment or so she lay there on her stomach in the middle of the bed, her body warm beneath the covers, just blinking drowsily. She felt wonderful. Different, though. So relaxed and content she wanted to purr like a cat sprawled in the sunlight. Every inch of her skin seemed heated in a strange new way, and she had the odd notion that she could feel her heart beating throughout her entire body.

She didn't want to move, reluctant to do anything that might change the blissful sense of fulfillment she felt. But she wasn't a woman who could be still for long unless she was sleeping, and the drowsiness left her. Gradually, she focused on the clock on her nightstand. Twelve. Twelve noon.

Frowning, she pushed herself up onto her elbows, staring at the clock. Noon? She hadn't slept this late in years, why on earth would she— Then she remembered.

It all came back to her in a rush, and she twisted quickly to look around her bedroom, ignoring a few twinges from muscles protesting the sudden movement. The room was empty except for her. But . . . those clothes on the storage chest at the foot of her bed; weren't they his? Black sweater and pants, folded neatly . . . Yes, she thought they were his.

Morgan pushed herself upright and only then heard quiet music from the other side of the apartment. She didn't hear a sign of Quinn, but she was certain he was still here. She could feel his nearness, as usual. After a moment, she slid to the edge of the bed, another twinge in her ankle reminding her of last night's injury. It didn't look too bad, she decided, just a bit puffy and wearing spectacular colors; when she stood up cautiously, it held her weight with only slight pain.

When she went into the bathroom, she realized Quinn had recently taken a shower; the air was still damp, and so was a towel he had draped over the shower-curtain rod. She thought he'd probably used the electric razor she had provided for him when he'd stayed here before.

She took her own shower, letting the hot water clear her mind even as it soothed her sore body. She'd noticed a few more (faint) bruises that had resulted from her struggle on the fire escape, and between that and her unusually active night, she was definitely a little stiff.

The hot water certainly helped, so she lingered there, washing her hair and smiling to herself when she remembered his fingers tangled in it. When she finally got out of the tub and wrapped her hair in a towel, she felt much better. She rummaged in the vanity cabinets underneath the sink and found a bottle of body lotion in the scent of the perfume she usually wore, and rubbed some of that into her skin. She knew it was the rubbing rather than the lotion that made her muscles feel looser and less strained—but soft, scented skin was an added benefit that any woman with a lover could easily appreciate.

Morgan wrapped a towel around herself and unwrapped her hair to begin drying it, and as her blow-dryer roared she thought about that. A lover. Was that what Quinn would be? She didn't know, she really didn't. The timing of all this, considering the circumstances, was hardly the best, and even if it had been, Quinn was not what anyone would choose to call predictable.

Or conventional. Given who and what he was, it was entirely possible that this interlude with her was no more than that—a respite in the middle of a tense situation to let him unwind and seek a purely sexual release of stress.

That was a depressing possibility, she decided, but one she had to consider at least logical and perhaps likely. He was, after all, an unusually handsome and charming man somewhere in his thirties—and though the mysterious Quinn might not have wished to risk possible exposure of his identity with a sex life, his daytime persona of Alex had undoubtedly enjoyed the company of eager females over the years. The evidence of that was clear; he'd been a skilled and sensitive lover, and that required both experience and a thorough knowledge of a woman's body and what would please her.

Morgan was hardly shocked by these realizations. In fact, she wasn't particularly surprised by them. She was a rational woman, and she'd had weeks since meeting Quinn to consider the matter. She had, in fact, thought about him and what involvement with him might mean to the point that she was reasonably sure she had considered every possibility.

Not that it helped, really. It might have been

possible in the last weeks to detach her emotions enough to contemplate the possible consequences of taking a very famous and very enigmatic cat burglar into her bed, but once it had happened, her detachment was gone. Only emotions were left, and all those told her was what she *felt*.

She loved him. Beyond reason or rationality, beyond common sense or consequences, she loved him.

And that was what she had to endure, no matter what the future brought.

By the time her hair was dry, Morgan had more or less decided to play this new turn in their relationship by ear. What other choice did she have? Her life was clearly defined and spread out before him; there were no mysteries, no hidden facts, no false names—no lies. Who and what she was were obvious to him. Who and what *he* was, on the other hand, were still somewhat nebulous. The only thing she knew for certain was that what he was doing was dangerous.

So, at least until Quinn's trap for Nightshade was sprung, her instincts told her to accept whatever he offered and be as patient as she could. Once that was over and he could tell her the truth, then perhaps there would be a discussion about some kind of future for them. Or perhaps not.

Perhaps Quinn would return to Europe and the life he enjoyed and knew so well. Without her.

There was, in any case, absolutely nothing she

could do to either make him love her or make him stay with her. She had a better chance of catching lightning in a bottle than she had of capturing him and, besides that, the last thing she would have chosen would be to see him trapped. Whatever he did in the end had to be his own decision, without pressure from her.

She returned to the bedroom, still thoughtful, and briefly debated before pulling a gold silk robe from her closet. It was one of those garments a single woman might buy for herself but then not wear simply because it was designed for a man to look at, something rich and elegant that caressed the body in a touch of pure sensuality.

Well, she acknowledged silently, there was pressure . . . and then there was *pressure*. After all, no woman worth the name would just stand by and let the man she loved make up his mind about things without at least reminding him of a few advantages a sensible and rational woman could provide. That was certainly fair.

Even Quinn would probably agree.

CHAPTER
TWELVE

Without vanity, Morgan knew she looked good in the deceptively simple robe. The color suited her, and the shimmering material clung to her body in all the right places. She couldn't help smiling a little as she tied the belt at her waist, remembering last night's sweatshirt and pants—and the fuzzy slippers. Talk about from the ridiculous to the sublime!

Barefoot, she padded out into the living room. Empty, with music videos playing quietly on the television. She continued on to the kitchen and there found Quinn, his back to her, busy preparing what looked like an appetizing brunch of pancakes with fruit. Since he'd helped in the kitchen while recovering from his wound, Morgan wasn't surprised by his skill. And he was wearing jeans and a white shirt, some of his own clothes that had been left behind here weeks ago.

She knew very well that his still being here today was a good sign; she had half expected him to leave before she awakened. But Morgan refused to let herself attach too much importance to that. *One step at a time, that's the way to go.*

"Hi," she greeted him casually.

He looked over his shoulder at her, mouth opening to say something that never got said. Instead, he stared at her for a moment, brilliant green eyes scanning her from bare toes to gleaming hair, then turned a dial on the griddle, set the spatula on the counter beside it, and came to her.

Somewhat breathlessly a few moments later, she said, "I always forget how big you are until I'm standing close to you. Why is that?"

"I have no idea." He nuzzled the side of her neck, inhaling slowly. "You smell wonderful."

Her arms up around his neck—and her feet off the floor since he'd lifted her—Morgan murmured something wordless in response and wondered vaguely how his body could feel so hard and yet so pleasurable against hers. He had both his arms tightly wrapped around her so that she was certain there wasn't a square inch of her front not pressed to his, and since her silk robe was whisper-thin, it felt like only the slight barrier of his clothing separated them.

Then he lifted his head suddenly and frowned, and Morgan felt herself being lowered back to her feet.

"I was enjoying myself," she protested.

He smiled slightly, but the frown remained in his eyes. One hand gently brushed her hair back away from her neck. "Sweetheart, did I do this?"

She didn't feel pain when he touched her very lightly just below her ear, but she knew he was looking at a faint bruise because she'd seen it in the mirror. "No, I think our friend on the fire escape did it. If he hadn't been wearing gloves, you could probably get his thumbprint off me. It was when he was holding that cloth over my face."

Quinn nodded slightly, an expression she couldn't read flaring in his eyes. He lowered his head and kissed her, still as hungry as before but brief. "I heard the shower, so I thought you'd be ready for breakfast."

Morgan smiled at him. "I'm starving. But you turned the griddle up instead of down, and the pancakes are burning."

Swearing rather creatively, he released her and hastily went back to the counter to pry smoldering pancakes off the griddle. Morgan turned on the exhaust fan over the stove, hoping to avoid having the smoke detector outside her bedroom door go off, then opened the kitchen window for good measure. A cool breeze wafted in obediently, and the smoke dissipated before it could do any harm.

"I'm glad I made extra batter," he commented ruefully as he dumped blackened pancakes into the trash can. "I must have known you'd come in here looking like Helen of Troy when she launched all those ships."

"You sweet-talker, you," Morgan said.

Stirring his batter, Quinn sent her a smile. "Tell me something, Morgana. Do you believe anything I say?"

"'Bout half," she conceded mildly as she poured herself a cup of coffee. "I'd consider myself in serious need of therapy if I believed more than that."

He chuckled, but then sent her another glance, this one more sober. "Regrets?"

Remembering what he'd said about what could happen if they became lovers without trust, she shook her head and smiled at him. "No, no regrets. I knew what I was doing."

For a moment he concentrated on his cooking, expertly flipping the golden pancakes. Then, softly, he said, "We were both reckless."

Having realized this discussion would take place, Morgan was ready for it and responded calmly. "If you mean birth control, it's all right. My doctor put me on the pill a couple of years ago for an irregular cycle."

He looked at her, very direct. "You don't have to worry about anything else."

"Neither do you." Leaning back against the counter, she conjured a rather regretful smile. "It's become a dangerous world, hasn't it? Even in the bedroom."

Quinn leaned over and kissed her, gently this time. "It always was, sweetheart. The only difference is that now the dangers aren't so obvious—and too often tend to be potentially fatal."

"Yeah. Sometimes it's the pits being a grown-up," Morgan observed. But then, being a naturally optimistic woman, her absent attention fixed on him as he turned the pancakes onto two plates, and her gaze wandered over his broad shoulders, down his back to his lean waist, and then to his narrow hips and long legs. He looked awfully good in jeans, she reflected. Only half aware of making the sound, she sighed. "Then again . . . sometimes it's not bad at all."

Her thoughts must have been obvious from her voice, because he smiled without looking at her and murmured, "You're a wicked woman, Morgana."

Somewhat dryly, she said, "No, just human." Then she refilled their coffee cups and helped him transfer the food to her small kitchen table.

It wasn't until later, when they were finished with the meal and had cleaned up the kitchen, that Morgan somewhat cautiously turned their casual conversation in a more serious direction. "Alex . . . you aren't going to tell me who Nightshade is?"

He had followed her into the living room, and when she asked the question he put his hands on her shoulders and turned her to face him. "We've talked about this, Morgana. If you came face-to-face with a man you knew was Nightshade, could you trust yourself not to react to that knowledge?"

"I suppose not." She looked up at him steadily.

"But I would like to know how badly I screwed things up by climbing that fire escape last night."

He hesitated only an instant. "Hardly at all—*if* I can persuade Nightshade that you were going up there to visit Alex Brandon, with no idea I'm also Quinn."

"Why would I think I could find Alex on a rooftop somewhere around midnight?"

"Help me think of a reason, will you? The last thing I want is for Nightshade to start wondering if you know I'm Quinn. Because, once he does that, he might also wonder why a woman of well-known honesty and integrity such as yourself would be keeping quiet about that."

"And smell a trap?"

"I would, in his place."

Morgan bit her bottom lip for a moment, then eased back away from him and went to sit down—in the chair rather than on the couch. She had trouble thinking clearly when he touched her, and she wanted to think about this.

Quinn sat down at the end of the couch nearest her chair, watching her gravely.

"Alex . . . *he* knows you're Quinn. I mean, he knows that Alex Brandon is Quinn." There was a faint question in her voice, even though she was sure she was right about this.

"He knows."

"Then I don't understand. He knows you're Quinn, and you know he's Nightshade—and you're both wanted by the police in several countries. You're both eyeing *Mysteries Past* because the Bannister collection is something any thief would want—and each of you knows about the other's interest in it. How does that add up to a trap?"

Quinn hesitated, then sighed. "Actually, it's more like a sting. I knew that Nightshade would be at least a little reluctant to go after the Bannister collection on his own, no matter how badly he wants it."

"Why?"

"For one thing, he isn't technically adept. At least not at the level required to breach a cutting-edge security system."

Morgan was beginning to feel a little queasy. "Which you knew going in."

"Yes."

"Alex, are you telling me that you—that Nightshade needs a partner in order to go after the Bannister collection? And that you're it?"

"Yes."

Morgan put her elbows on her knees and covered her face with both hands.

Quinn cleared his throat. "Needless to say, the others don't know about that part. Not even Jared."

"Oh, needless to say," she mumbled through her fingers. She dropped her hands and stared at him. "Because if they *did* know, they'd kill you."

"That was why I didn't tell them."

"Jesus, Alex."

"Morgana, it'll work. It's already working. It's

well known that state-of-the-art electronic security systems are favorites of mine. My specialty, as it were. Nightshade might be able to get inside the museum—but not inside the exhibit. Not without me and the knowledge and skills I can provide. I've spent quite a bit of time and considerable effort convincing him of that fact."

Morgan tried to keep her mind on the logistics of the situation and off her anxiety. "Okay. But why couldn't Quinn go after the collection alone? I mean, why would Quinn need Nightshade?"

"Several reasons," he answered willingly enough. "As you pointed out yourself, the States are . . . unfamiliar ground to Quinn. Even a thief who apparently acts alone has to have contacts: inside sources or informants with reliable information, trustworthy people to provide supplies and equipment, some quick and safe means of transportation once the job is done. All my contacts are in Europe—and I'd have a hell of a time transporting the collection back there. But I came here anyway because, as you say, the Bannister collection is irresistible.

"So . . . when I stumble across another thief while casing the museum, I make it a point to follow him until I know who he is. He's naturally upset that I was able to find him, but I make it clear I don't particularly care who he is and that I have no intention of either exposing him or horning in on his territory. No, I'm going to go back to Europe—

but I want very badly to take one piece of the Bannister collection with me."

"The Bolling?" she guessed.

Quinn smiled slightly. "Are you kidding? That bloody thing's got a curse on it. Every time it's been stolen in its long and colorful history, it's brought disaster to the thief."

Startled, she said, "I didn't know that was the curse."

"Oh, yes, and it's well documented. The diamond came into the hands of the Bannisters somewhere around 1500—legitimately. A gentleman named Edward Bannister found the uncut and unpolished stone lying in a streambed in India. Just lying right out in the open."

"Talk about luck," Morgan said, perfectly aware that Quinn was deliberately trying to distract her. What she wasn't certain of was whether she was going to let him get away with it.

"Yeah. Anyway, he had the stone polished—not faceted—and gave it as a betrothal present to his bride. The first attempt to steal it actually occurred during their honeymoon, and the would-be thief broke his neck trying to escape out a window. Rumor has it that Edward stood over the body wearing nothing but a sheet grabbed in haste from the connubial bed and promptly declared to all present that the diamond was obviously fated to belong to his family and would henceforth be considered an amulet. Then he christened the stone the Bolling diamond."

"Why Bolling?"

Quinn smiled. "Well, Edward couldn't call it the Bannister diamond, because he already had one with that moniker. So he had to think of something else. And it seems he possessed a somewhat ironic sense of humor. The thief who broke his neck trying to steal the stone went by the name of Thomas Bolling."

"And the stone he couldn't steal would forever wear his name. That is ironic. And it's a strange kind of fame."

"Thomas Bolling would probably be pleased; from all accounts, he was both stupid and somewhat depraved and likely would have passed through history unknown if not for his encounter with that pretty yellow diamond."

Morgan eyed Quinn. "Are you *sure* you aren't making this up? It spins very readily off your silver tongue."

"I swear. Ask Max."

"Mmm. Okay, so then what happened?"

"Well, by uttering what he most likely thought would be a warning that would ward off superstitious thieves at least, old Edward appears to have laid a solid foundation for the curse. Maybe fate was listening. Or maybe there simply followed a very long string of amazingly unlucky thieves. In any case, the Bolling diamond began to build quite a reputation. In those days, the stone probably weighed at least a hundred carats and likely more, so it was quite a target. And later on, when it was faceted and eventually set into the pendant, it was so breathtaking that few could resist the lure of it.

"During the next four hundred years, there were dozens of attempts to steal it, some of them remarkably ingenious. But nobody could successfully get it away from the Bannister family. Without exception, all the thieves died—most in decidedly painful ways. A few were caught and died in prison, but all of them died because of that stone."

Morgan shivered a little. She had never been a superstitious woman, but the story definitely unnerved her. No doubt because she was in love with a jewel thief. She cleared her throat and said a bit fiercely, "You stay away from that thing."

He smiled and moved suddenly, sliding off the couch and onto his knees in front of her chair. Before she could do anything, his hands were on her knees, easing them apart. She caught her breath as warm fingers stroked her outer thighs, then slid upward very slowly, under the silk of her robe, until they could cup her bottom and pull her toward him.

"I'm not going to steal the Bolling, Morgana," he murmured, his eyes heavy-lidded and intense. He kissed the side of her neck, then her throat when her head fell back against the chair cushion. His lips trailed slowly down along the V of silky flesh exposed by the robe's lapels, and his voice grew hoarse. "It's the Talisman emerald I'm after."

Morgan slid her fingers into his thick pale-gold hair and tugged gently, frowning at him a bit dazedly when he looked at her. He was distracting her, dammit. "You're *after*?"

"I mean—it's the Talisman emerald that Nightshade *thinks* I'm after. Can we talk about this later?" He caught her lower lip delicately between his teeth, nibbling, then he was kissing her with unhidden hunger.

He got one hand between them long enough to tug at the belt of her robe, and she felt the garment open up as if it had been designed to slip over heated flesh. Her breasts were crushed against his chest, and the feeling of his clothing against her naked skin maddened her.

She wanted him now, right now, that primitive need overwhelming everything else with a suddenness that was dimly terrifying. She didn't realize her hands were tugging at his shirt until she had to lean back a bit to cope with his buttons, and then the tautness of his face and the blazing need in his eyes told her that he was as impatient for her as she was for him.

Quinn helped her to get his shirt off and tossed it aside. He unfastened his jeans and pushed them and his shorts down only as far as necessary, and Morgan heard herself cry out in an incoherent sound of pleasure when she felt him inside her.

When the peak came, it was as swift and sharp as the ascent had been. Quinn wrapped his arms around her and held her tight against him, both of them shuddering under the force of the waves of ecstasy that tore through them—and left them with barely the strength to remain upright.

Morgan kept her face buried in the curve of his neck, breathing in the heady male scent of him while her pounding heart slowly returned to its normal steady beat. She didn't want to move or open her eyes. All she wanted to do was hold him like this while he held her and luxuriate in the sensations.

It gradually occurred to her, however, that their positions, while amazingly erotic, were hardly comfortable now that passion was temporarily spent. In fact, being Morgan, she was suddenly tempted to giggle. A chair in her living room, for heaven's sake, and in the middle of the day. Even with the carpet, his knees were probably giving him hell, and she'd never felt so astonished at herself in her entire life.

He lifted his head suddenly and looked at her, smiling but with fierce eyes. "If you laugh, I swear I'll strangle you," he told her in a voice that was still husky.

Either she had given herself away somehow, she thought, or else the connection between them was growing stronger.

She cleared her throat and tried to stop smiling. "I'm sorry, but I can't help it. I'm not amused because this is funny, I'm just sort of . . . startled. What happened? I mean, one minute we were having a perfectly rational conversation, and the next minute we were . . ."

"Yes, we were. We certainly were." He kissed

her, then eased away and pulled his jeans up, zipping them but not bothering to fasten the snap. "Let's do it again."

"Wait a minute." Trying to think clearly because something was bothering her, she tapped the middle of his chest with her index finger in a useless bid to get his full attention. "What you told me about your—your sting. You're over here just to catch Nightshade, that's the plan, right?"

"Mmmm," he agreed, nuzzling her neck.

"Then—" She gasped when he gently bit her earlobe, and she felt her eyes starting to cross. "Then why did you take that dagger the night we met?"

"Camouflage," he murmured, but not as if the subject interested him much. "You would have wondered if I hadn't taken anything that night."

"Oh. Umm . . . Alex? I know I asked you before, but . . . did you steal the Carstairs diamonds?"

"No." He stopped exploring her neck long enough to swing her up into his arms. He kissed her and started toward the bedroom, adding cheerfully, "I just borrowed them."

"Why can't she be identified?"

Both Wolfe and Jared looked at Storm, and the latter said, "You mean Jane Doe?" They were still in the computer room and still brainstorming the situation.

"Yeah. Why can't she be identified?"

"No fingerprints, for one thing," Jared began,

then stopped and nodded slowly as he realized Storm's meaning. "Why doesn't the *killer* want her identified."

"It's an important question, isn't it? A piece of the puzzle. He makes damned sure she can't be identified yet leaves signposts all over the place pointing to the museum."

"So," Wolfe said, "either her identity would lead us far from the museum, or else it would get us a hell of a lot closer to seeing a big piece of the puzzle. Another assumption, but a reasonable one."

"The police are working on an I.D.," Jared noted.

"But are they working on the right thing?" Wolfe frowned at the Interpol agent. "The killer went to the extreme of using a blowtorch to obliterate her prints. That says to me that he knew or had good reason to believe the prints were on file somewhere."

"Criminal, police, or military," Storm said. "All are routinely printed. Some states' DMVs are beginning to print drivers, but it's not universal yet. There are other groups with databases, but those are primaries. Covers a lot of territory."

"But it does narrow the field," Jared noted. "Gives the police somewhere to look. If they can ever get a usable print to run against the databases."

"The military tends to be possessive of its information," Wolfe noted. "Max might have to pull a few strings. That's assuming the police forensics people *can* produce a usable print."

Storm said, "It could be just another signpost, you

know. Another way to make us look for something that isn't there. I mean, he's already gone to so much trouble—just planting that knife in the basement the way he did, for instance—that maybe using a blow-torch to destroy his victim's prints is just one more bit of sleight of hand. No pun intended."

"We're spending too much time second-guessing ourselves, that's the trouble," Jared said.

"You've been a cop a long time," Wolfe said, staring at him. "What do your instincts say?"

Promptly, Jared replied, "That knowing who Jane Doe is will give us a very big piece of the puzzle."

"Then I say that's the assumption we follow," Wolfe said rather surprisingly. "What does Alex think?"

"About Jane Doe? He hasn't said much. He's very focused on Nightshade. Maybe too focused."

"Reel him in," Wolfe suggested bluntly.

"It's not that simple."

"Maybe it should be."

Wary that the tentative peace between the two men could end abruptly over this, Storm intervened to say calmly, "Alex is certainly in the best position to track another thief, so until we're absolutely certain Jane Doe or her murder is connected to the museum, it's probably best not to split his focus."

"Morgan already has," Jared muttered.

"Best not to split it a third way, then." Storm smiled. "Can't fight human nature, guys, we all know that. Maybe it is a lousy time for those two to find each other, but we're not really in control of these things." She was smiling at Wolfe. "Are we?"

His face softened. "No. No, we're not."

Whatever Jared might have said to that was lost when a timid knock on the door interrupted them. Chloe Webster stuck her head in without waiting for a response.

"Storm— Oh, I'm sorry. I thought you were alone."

"It's all right, Chloe. What's up?"

"Inspector Tyler just called Mr. Dugan to tell him the forensics team wants to take another look at the basement. Possible points of entry, I think he said. I thought you should know."

Storm nodded. "Okay, Chloe. Thanks."

The new assistant curator sort of ducked her head and hastily withdrew, closing the door softly.

"Am I being paranoid," Jared said, "or was that a pretty flimsy excuse to see what was going on in here?"

"You're being paranoid," Wolfe said, then grimaced and looked inquiringly at Storm.

"She's poking her nose into corners, but that's natural," Storm said. "Trying to learn the place. I haven't seen anything to send up red flags. The background check was clean, you both know that."

Jared sighed. "Yet another tangent, probably. I'm getting suspicious of everyone. Christ, I wish

Nightshade would make his move and get it over with."

"Be careful what you wish for," Storm warned soberly.

It was late afternoon before Morgan could summon the energy to resume their earlier conversation, and when she did her voice was wondering. "Borrowed them. You borrowed the Carstairs diamonds. You're a lunatic, you know that?"

He chuckled softly.

Persisting, she said, "You took an awful chance to steal that necklace. You could have been caught by San Francisco police officers who don't give a damn about your deal with Interpol. Or you could have been killed."

"I needed it, Morgana. Nightshade required a . . . good-faith gesture."

"You stole it for him?"

"I *borrowed* it so he'd think I stole it for him. The Carstairs family will get it back, don't worry."

"If you say so." Pushing herself up onto her elbow beside him, Morgan gazed at his relaxed face and said in bemusement, "It's nearly four in the afternoon, and we're in bed."

He opened one bright eye, then closed it, tightened his arm around her, and sighed pleasurably. "My idea of how to spend an ideal afternoon."

She reached out and began toying with the dark-gold hair on his chest. "Yes, but I haven't even talked to anybody at the museum. And when I *do* talk to them, what do I say? I've taken a whole day off without any explanation at all, very rare for me, and it wasn't because I ran into Nightshade on a fire escape last night."

Quinn opened his eyes. They were still bright and very steady on her face. He was smiling slightly. "Do you care if they know we're lovers?"

She shook her head impatiently. "No, of course not. But will this—our being lovers—cause any problems for you? With Nightshade, I mean."

After a moment, Quinn said, "Not if I can convince him that I seduced you to get information about the exhibit."

Very conscious of the intent, searching look in his eyes, Morgan smiled. "Is that why you haven't asked me any specifics about the exhibit? So I could be sure you *weren't* after information?"

He reached up and brushed a strand of her glossy black hair away from her face, his fingers lingering to stroke her cheek. "Maybe. It isn't something I do, Morgana. I want you to understand that."

Perhaps oddly, she believed him. For all his charm and his undoubted sexual experience, he wasn't the kind of man who would seduce a woman merely for the sake of gaining information from her. Not because it was a dishonorable thing to do, she thought shrewdly, but because it was the more predictable thing—and Quinn would always choose to be contradictory.

"Sweetheart?"

Realizing she'd been silent for too long, she said, "I understand—and I believe you. I just hope Nightshade doesn't realize that trying to get information out of me in any way would have been useless; I don't understand the security system."

"He knows what your area of responsibility is, just as anyone familiar with museums would know, but I think I can convince him that you did provide me with a very important bit of information. That is—if you agree."

"I'm listening."

Quinn frowned a little. "Let me think it through first. Why don't we get dressed and check in at the museum? I know you won't be happy until you make sure the roof didn't cave in today because you weren't there."

"Very funny." But she was smiling. "Sounds like a plan."

CHAPTER
THIRTEEN

They walked about a block away from Morgan's apartment to get Quinn's car, which was where he'd parked it the night before, a distance short enough that it didn't strain Morgan's still-sore ankle. He never parked near the museum when he was being Quinn, he explained to her, so as to avoid having his car noticed.

"That was why you had to carry me all the way last night," she observed.

"Well, it was one of the reasons."

Morgan didn't probe, and she tried to keep their conversation casual. Somewhere in the back of her mind, she had been slowly assembling the bits and pieces of information she had gathered over the last weeks. Discarding some things and reexamining others in the light of more-recent understanding, she was trying to put together a puzzle when she wasn't entirely certain what the finished picture was supposed to look like.

It was a slow and rather frustrating process, but one she had to endure for two reasons: because Quinn was unwilling to tell her all of the truth—at least for now—and because she was too curious to wait to be told. She had an excellent mind, and even if she hadn't been worried about the man she loved, she would doubtless still have been pondering the situation.

But most of the puzzle pieces were still floating about in her mind when they reached the museum, and Morgan put the matter to one side for the moment. With less than an hour before closing, there were far more people coming out of the museum than going in; it looked as if a respectable crowd had visited today.

"I need to check the security and computer rooms," she told Quinn when they were standing in the lobby. "Just in case."

He nodded, then caught her hand and carried it briefly to his lips in a very loverlike caress. "I'll wander around a bit."

Morgan hesitated, but then smiled at him and made her way toward the hallway of offices, wondering what, in particular, he wanted to examine in the museum. She didn't believe for an instant that he'd be as casual as he indicated, of course. It wasn't that she was *suspicious* of him exactly, it was just that she'd developed a healthy respect for his innately devious nature. She had the distinct feeling that he'd never walk a straight line if he could find a curve or an angle.

She checked the security room first, talking briefly with two incurious guards who reported a peaceful day undisturbed by anything except the usual number of children momentarily lost from their parents and a couple of lovers' spats. Morgan had been bemused years ago to discover that a surprising number of lovers chose to work out their differences in museums—possibly believing the huge, echoing rooms and corridors were much more private than they really were.

Given her own knowledge of the security surrounding such valuable things, Morgan was always aware of the watching eyes of video cameras, patrolling guards, and other members of the public, and so museums were not what she considered either romantic or private.

With that thought still in her mind, she went on down the hallway to the computer room, finding Storm frowning at her computer as she typed briskly.

"Hi," Morgan said, deliberately casual as she leaned in the doorway. "What's up?"

The petite blonde finished typing and hit the enter key, then leaned back in her chair and looked at her friend with solemn interest. "We'll get to that in a minute. What's up with you?"

Since she wasn't easily embarrassed, Morgan didn't blush under that shrewd scrutiny. "Well," she offered, still casual, "I'm better than I was yesterday."

"Mmm. Even after being chloroformed?"

"That wasn't the high point of the evening."

"I should hope not. Alex?"

Morgan felt herself smiling. "Does it show?"

"Only all over you." Storm smiled in return. "Sort of disconcerting, isn't it?"

"I'll say. And with all this other stuff . . . Well, let's just say I'm taking things as they come."

"Probably best." Then Storm looked more serious. "Jared said they thought it was Nightshade who grabbed you."

"Yeah. Just my luck, huh? Listen, has Max checked in today? I feel guilty as hell about missing work."

"As a matter of fact he's here. Out in the museum somewhere."

"I'll try to find him. Um . . . where's Bear?" She didn't see the little cat anywhere.

"With Wolfe—who is also somewhere out in the museum." The computer beeped just then, commanding Storm's attention, and she sat up to deal with the electronic summons. "He's getting a bit nervous. Wolfe, I mean."

That surprised Morgan, since she had seldom seen the security expert rattled by anything. "About the trap?" she asked.

Storm keyed in a brief command, then looked back at her friend with a smile. "No. About a church wedding in Louisiana. He was all for us finding a preacher and just doing it, but we can't. After six sons, my mama started saving her pennies for my wedding the day I was born, and I just can't spoil that for her. So, even as we speak, plans are being made back home. And Wolfe's feeling a bit daunted about meeting my family and walking down the aisle."

She didn't sound particularly worried, Morgan thought in amusement. But then—there was no reason she should be. However nervous he might be about the ordeal awaiting him in Louisiana, it was abundantly clear that Wolfe was so deeply in love with Storm it would have taken a great deal more than a gauntlet of relatives to drive him away from her. It would, Morgan thought, take something absolute. Like the end of the world.

Somewhat dryly, Morgan said, "His job and reputation on the line, and he's worried about a little rice and orange blossom."

"Men are odd, aren't they?"

"Ain't that the truth? Listen, is there anything else I should know about, workwise?"

Storm reported the latest findings and their own speculations on Jane Doe, finishing with, "Keane's forensics team was down in the basement for a while, trying to determine points of entry, but they're gone now. Didn't find anything conclusive.

We've beefed up security cameras and alarms on all exterior doors. And windows."

"Sounds good." Morgan frowned. "Does Keane believe they're any closer to identifying Jane Doe?"

"I don't think so, but he did say they were pretty much focusing all their efforts on getting a viable fingerprint from the body."

"Is that even possible with burned fingers?"

"The experts believe they have a shot at it. Let's hope they know what they're talking about." Storm grimaced. "It's actually easier to look for a missing person than it is to I.D. a body when it's dumped somewhere other than a crime scene and the description doesn't match up with any listed missing person. Makes sense when you think about it."

"Yeah. Got to have a place to start."

"That's what Keane says. And he's frustrated as hell about it. Anyway, that's it for now. You're up to speed."

"Thanks." Morgan lifted a hand in farewell and went on down the hall. She stopped at her office, discovering that her clipboard wasn't on her desk where she'd left it, then continued to the curator's office at the end of the hall. She found Chloe Webster there at Ken's desk, frowning down at paperwork. The frown vanished when she looked up to see Morgan in the doorway.

"Hey, are you all right? I heard you got mugged last night."

Which was, Morgan decided, a safer version of what had happened than the truth. "I'm fine. Actually, it all seems like something out of a nightmare now, as if it never happened."

"You could have been killed."

Quinn had said the same thing, Morgan remembered. "I don't know—it happened so fast I didn't have time to be scared. Anyway, it's over now." She glanced around at Ken's cluttered office. "Have you seen my clipboard? It wasn't on my desk, so I figured—"

Chloe moved a stack of papers to one side. "Is this it?"

"Yeah, thanks. Ken must have needed it. I really should have come in today."

"I heard Mr. Bannister say an unscheduled day off never hurt anybody. Besides, as far as I can tell, there haven't been any problems."

"You were frowning when I came in," Morgan observed.

Chloe shook her head dismissively. "Oh, I was just talking to Stuart Atkins—at the Collier Museum?—and he told me that several of the museums in the area have been having problems with their security systems. Alarms going off for no reason, things like that. But everything here seems fine."

"Famous last words," Morgan said.

"I know, that's why I'll tell Mr. Dugan and Mr. Bannister about the call. Just in case."

Morgan nodded, agreeing that would be best. She continued on to her own office to return the clipboard to her desk and check all the status logs. Then she went in search of Quinn.

"I don't like it," Max said.

"I didn't expect you would." Quinn sighed and eyed the other man rather cautiously. "Look, we both know Morgan's impulsive; I'd made her mad and she came to pour wrath all over me. She was smart enough to figure out where I was watching, and furious enough to come storming up the fire escape."

"I know that, Alex." Max shifted his broad shoulders just a bit in a rare movement that gave away his tension. "What I don't know—and what you've been evasive about—is what Nightshade was doing on that fire escape. If it *was* him, of course."

The two men were standing in a gallery near the *Mysteries Past* exhibit, out in the open so that no one could approach unseen, and both kept their voices low.

Quinn hadn't exactly looked forward to this interview, but he'd known it would take place sooner rather than later; Max was far too intelligent to have missed the significance of what had happened last night.

As casually as possible, Quinn said, "Didn't Jared explain?"

"No. He said you were too upset to talk about it last night when he came to relieve you. I got the feeling he had a few questions of his own."

Quinn only just stopped himself from wincing. He thought Jared had more than a few questions by now, having had time to consider what Quinn remembered himself saying: *Maybe he got suspicious of me and showed up tonight looking for me. . . .*

It was the only time in his entire career that Quinn could recall having been so disturbed—by Morgan's close call—that he spoke without thinking. And by now Jared had quite probably reached the conclusion that Nightshade's identity was definitely no longer a mystery to Quinn.

Pushing that aside to be dealt with later, Quinn cleared his throat and spoke in a convincingly frank tone. "Well, it isn't so complicated, Max. Nightshade, if it was him, of course, was probably casing the museum—though I don't know how I could have missed it—and he must have seen me on the roof. I can't know what he meant to do, naturally, but it's obvious Morgan got in his way and so he put her to sleep for a little while. I heard something and came down before he could do anything else—and he left. That's all."

Max never took his eyes off the other man's face. "Uh-huh. Tell me, Alex: Do *you* carry chloroform around at night?"

"I've been known to," Quinn admitted candidly. "It's an efficient and nonlethal way of dealing with unexpected problems."

"Does Nightshade carry it?"

"He did last night."

After a long moment, Max said, "Is Morgan in danger?"

Quinn answered that with genuine sincerity. "I'll do everything in my power to make certain she's not."

Max frowned slightly. "You didn't answer my question."

"I answered it the only way I could. Max, there are a few things I didn't exactly plan on in all this, and Morgan's one of them. It seems to be . . . more than usually difficult to predict what she might do at any given moment, so I can't be sure she won't charge up another damned fire escape. But I won't let anything happen to her."

"Are you so in control of the situation that you can promise that?"

"Max—" Quinn broke off, then sighed. "Look, after tonight, I'll *know* how in control of the situation I am, and until then I can't give you an answer. You'll just have to trust me to know what I'm doing."

"All right," Max responded slowly. "I'll wait—until tomorrow."

"That's all I ask." With any luck, he'd think of something plausible by then. Either that or else figure out a way to avoid Max until this was finished. "Now, if you'll excuse me, I'm going to go find Morgan."

"Tell her I said hello." Max waited until the other man turned away, then added, "Alex? Did you steal the Carstairs necklace?"

Quinn wasn't imprudent enough to conjure a hurt expression or even to sound offended, but he did manage an utterly sincere answer. "No, Max, I didn't steal it."

Max didn't say another word; he merely nodded and watched the younger man walk out of the gallery. A moment later, he didn't react with surprise when Wolfe entered from the opposite end and joined him. Wearing his black leather jacket and a faint scowl, Wolfe didn't look much like a crack security expert—and even less so with a little blond cat riding on his shoulder.

But Max was familiar with the appearance (even to the cat, since Wolfe was often accompanied by Bear these days). Still gazing after Quinn, he said meditatively, "I'm beginning to think Alex is lying to me."

"Now you know how it feels," Wolfe told him, unsurprised and not without a certain amount of satisfaction.

"I never lied to you. I merely withheld portions of the truth."

"Yeah, sure." Somewhat morosely, Wolfe added, "Maybe Alex is doing the same thing. We both know he only lies about something when he's sure he's going to eventually come clean. If he's lying now, I'll bet it's because he's in deeper than he's told us."

"I'd take that bet," Max agreed. Then he sighed. "And we may have another problem. Mother called. She's in Australia—but she's heading this way."

Wolfe's face brightened, but that instant reaction was quickly altered by a scowl. "The timing isn't exactly the best, Max. Couldn't you stop her?"

"Stop Mother?" Max asked in polite disbelief.

"Sorry, I forgot myself." Wolfe shook his head. "Well, maybe it'll be over by the time she gets here."

"Yah," Bear commented in a distinctly sardonic tone.

Max looked at the little cat and sighed. "Bear, I couldn't have said it better myself."

The lobby was nearly deserted when Morgan crossed it to get to the stairs, but she met Leo Cassady about halfway up. The lean and handsome collector smiled as soon as he saw her and stopped when they reached the same tread.

"Hello, Morgan. I hear I unintentionally played matchmaker at my party last Saturday."

She felt a little jolt at the reminder that it had been barely a week since she officially met Alex

Brandon, but she was able to smile at Leo. "Let's just say I have a feeling my life will never be the same again."

"And it's all my fault?"

"Well, it was your party, Leo. But . . . we would have met anyway, I imagine. Collectors have been drawn to the exhibit in droves."

Somewhat wryly, he said, "Yes, I can't seem to stay away from it myself. Is Alex here now?"

"He's around somewhere," Morgan replied casually. "Max too."

"I talked to Max upstairs, but I didn't see Alex. Tell him I said hello, will you?"

"Sure. See you later."

Morgan continued up the stairs as he continued down, and when she was at the top, she paused to look back and watch Leo's elegant figure strolling through the lobby to the front doors. Even his lazy saunter couldn't quite hide the kind of ease and grace that came from muscles under perfect control, like those of a dancer or an athlete.

What had Quinn said? *If you came face-to-face with a man you knew was Nightshade . . .*

Nightshade *was* someone she knew. Probably someone she knew well or at least saw on a regular basis, or else Quinn might have told her who he was. Could it be Leo?

She gripped the massive bannister and looked rather blindly down into the lobby, her thoughts whirling, feeling suddenly very cold. Leo? He was certainly a collector, and though he often made light of it, he had himself termed his hunger for rare and beautiful things an obsession. He had traveled all over the world gathering them, paying incredible amounts to own what no other man could. . . .

Leo . . . Nightshade?

Morgan didn't want to believe it. She didn't even want to consider it possible. Nightshade had killed people—including a young woman of twenty-two whom Alex Brandon had loved like a sister. Nightshade had shot Alex—Quinn.

Nightshade had used chloroform on her.

As hard as she tried to remember, Morgan couldn't recall any identifying characteristic of the man who had held her in an iron grasp and rendered her unconscious. He'd been taller than her, but she wasn't sure how much taller. Strong. Quick. She could remember no scent except the chloroform, and no sound except those made by her own struggles.

Could Leo chloroform a young woman he knew well and the next day meet her with a pleasant smile?

Quinn had said something once about having the ability to lie convincingly under stress. He'd said it took a certain kind of nerve—or a devious nature. Did Leo also possess that brand of cunning?

She couldn't know, not for sure. With a faint shiver, Morgan turned and slowly made her way toward the *Mysteries Past* exhibit, where she expected to find Quinn. She wondered if he would answer with the truth if she asked him whether Leo was Nightshade. She wondered if she could even ask.

When he saw her standing at one of the display cases in the exhibit, Quinn paused for a moment and just looked at Morgan. He was vaguely aware that closing time had been announced and that it would no doubt be wise for him to get out of the museum with all speed and without encountering Max again, but he couldn't make himself hurry.

What was she thinking? Lovely face solemn, great golden eyes intent, she stood with her hands loosely clasped together before her and gazed at the Bolling diamond. She was dressed casually in jeans and a sweater, her glorious hair spilling down her back like black fire, and just looking at her made his heart beat faster.

He wondered if she knew what she did to him. She'd be aware of the physical response, certainly; he could hardly conceal his desire for her, and so he hadn't tried. But did she know the enormity of it? Did she have any idea that he wanted her, needed her, far past the point of reason?

His life, especially in recent years, had made him adept at hiding or disguising his feelings, but he wasn't sure he had been able to hide how he felt about her. Jared certainly knew, after last night.

Max knew, although he hadn't said anything about it since they had talked the night Quinn was shot.

But did Morgan know?

He moved up behind her, instinctively cat-footed because he so often had to be, but she didn't jump when his arms slipped around her. She had known it was him.

"There's a plaque," she said almost idly, relaxing against him. "It tells the story of the Bolling—though not as interestingly as you did."

"Thank you, sweet." He nuzzled her hair aside and kissed the side of her neck. Her skin was particularly soft there, and he loved the way it felt under his lips.

"Mmmm. The point is, I didn't even read it. I mean, I helped put the plaques in place for all the pieces, and I didn't even bother to read them."

"You were busy with other aspects of the exhibit," he reminded her, placing another kiss just beneath her ear. Soft flesh . . . bruised by a cruel grip. That bruise still filled him with a hot, almost murderous fury—he had added it to the tally of Nightshade's many crimes—and he brushed his lips very gently over the small area of discolored flesh.

Morgan made another faint sound, then turned in his arms to gaze up at him, her hands lifting to rest on his chest. She was smiling, but her golden eyes were heavy-lidded in the look of sensual awareness he loved. And her voice was a little husky when she said, "We both know how many security cameras are trained on us right now. I don't know about you, but I'd rather not entertain the guards."

Quinn kissed her very lightly. "No, I suppose not." He stepped back just a little but caught her hand in his and held it firmly. "You do realize the museum's closing?"

She nodded, but sent the brilliant yellow glow of the Bolling a last glance. As they started strolling toward the doorway, she said, "Why would any thief want it? I mean, why would anyone in their right mind want to steal something with the history of the Bolling?"

"Aside from its rather astonishing value, total egotism," Quinn replied succinctly. "Every one of the thieves who tried in the past believed they'd be the one to triumph."

"And now? Does Nightshade believe in curses?"

Quinn answered that more slowly. "Nightshade believes he must own what would destroy other men, and he believes he can. That he's somehow immune to the danger. He believes it's his right, his . . . destiny . . . to possess priceless beauty."

Morgan looked up at him. "What do you believe?"

He shrugged. "I believe he's just trying to fill the emptiness inside him, Morgana. He's a hollow man, emptied out of everything that matters." Aware of her searching gaze, Quinn suddenly felt slightly self-conscious. In a much lighter tone, he added, "Psychology 101."

Morgan didn't respond to that. Instead, amusing him yet again with her singular determination to get all her questions answered (it reared its head at the most unlikely moments, he'd discovered), she said, "I checked the plaque for the Talisman emerald a little while ago. Do you—I mean, does *Quinn*—want it because it's supposed to have belonged to Merlin?"

"Well, a hundred and fifty carats of emerald are worth quite a lot no matter who they once belonged to."

"You know what I mean."

He knew. "Actually, Quinn *has* earned a bit of a reputation for . . . um . . . . taking items with odd or supernatural backgrounds. Not all the time, mind you, just here and there, often enough to make interest in them obvious. And it is something Nightshade was aware of. He found it quite easy to believe that Quinn would have come all this way to try to get his hands on that little bangle."

"And avoid the Bolling?"

"I told him I was superstitious and extremely wary of curses. I'm reasonably sure he believed me."

Leaving the exhibit behind, they walked in silence to the stairs and began descending. Halfway down, Morgan spoke again in a voice that was just a bit unsteady.

"Alex, if I wanted to guess who Nightshade is—"

"Don't, Morgana." He kept his own voice even, but his fingers tightened almost unconsciously around hers. "Your knowing who he is wouldn't help—and could hurt. There's no reason for you to know until you have to. Trust me."

Morgan glanced up at him as they reached the lobby, and a little laugh escaped her. "We've already established that I don't really have a choice about that." Then, before he could respond, she was going on in the same casual tone. "You're free until around midnight, aren't you?"

"More or less," he agreed. "I thought we could get something to eat and then go back to your place."

"Sounds good to me."

After that their conversation steered clear of the exhibit and Nightshade and other troubling matters, and Quinn was glad. He knew he should have kept his attention focused on those matters, troubling or not, but all his concentration seemed taken up by her. She had fascinated him from the first night they'd met, and their subsequent, rather intense encounters had only deepened and increased that fascination.

He thought she was magnificent. Not just in her physical beauty, although that could certainly cause a marble statue with no more than the vague form of a man to leave its base and trail along wistfully behind her. No, what Morgan had was much more than mere beauty. She was unusually vibrant, her inner spirit so bright and strong it shone from her golden eyes and seemed almost to illuminate her flawless skin. Her voice was quick and musical, the tone just throaty enough to make every word a caress. And her mind . . . her mind.

Intelligence was only a part of it, though she certainly had plenty of that. She had a sense of humor that was sometimes ironic or offbeat and always sharp. A keen perception. More sensitivity *and* sentimentality than she wanted to reveal. And she possessed a deep reserve despite her talkative disposition and charm.

Quinn thought she had been profoundly hurt in her life—and not only by the fiancé too unspeakably stupid to look past her surface shine to the pure gold underneath. She had been taken at face value too often in her life, he thought, and that had taught her to guard her vulnerable heart.

Which made it all the more remarkable that she could have fallen in love with him. He still couldn't quite believe it. A part of him even considered that if they spent enough time together, she would eventually decide she'd been mistaken in what she felt. But a deeper part of him saw and recognized a luminous truth in her eyes.

She loved him.

And it was going to cost her.

CHAPTER
FOURTEEN

Late on Saturday evening, Quinn pulled himself reluctantly from the warmth of Morgan's bed to get dressed. It was nearly eleven, and he had to return to his hotel briefly before he could begin his night as Quinn. They had spent most of the evening in bed, and though he hadn't gotten very much sleep during the past few days, he felt peculiarly energized.

Morgan banked pillows behind her and absently drew the sheet up over her naked breasts as she watched him, and in the lamplight her eyes seemed bottomless. For the first time since they had discussed it earlier in the day, she brought up the subject of Nightshade, her voice calm but deliberate.

"Have you thought of a reason why I would have expected Alex Brandon to be on a rooftop at midnight?"

"Only one," he confessed, sitting on the side of the bed to pull his boots on. "If Alex had told you that's where he'd be—not, of course, expecting you to come calling."

Morgan frowned, then realized. "You were dressed as Quinn. All-black cat-burglar attire. Which you wouldn't have wanted me to see if I didn't know you were Quinn."

"That is a bit of a problem in explaining things, yes."

She watched him for a moment, still frowning, then said, "Well, you can always fall back on the unpredictability of women. You tell me you're going to be up there—stargazing, or just checking out the roof of a building you're interested in buying or leasing—"

"In the middle of the night?"

"You had a busy day, and it was the only time available." When he stared at her with lifted brows, she laughed and said, "Most men think that a woman in love will believe anything, so I'm sure you can make it sound convincing. Or tell him I *wasn't* convinced, that I suspected another woman or something, and thank him very much for knocking me out before I could see you in your Quinn costume."

"That's not bad," he noted. "Especially since I plan to get him on the defensive immediately."

Morgan considered that for a moment. "Because *he* shouldn't have been on that fire escape?"

"Right. And with chloroform, no less. There I was, perched on that roof and studying the museum while I planned a way in for *him*, and he came cat-footing along to either check up on me or else do something a bit more permanent. I'd say he demonstrated a distressing lack of trust in his partner, to say the very least. I'm going to be quite indignant about that, I think. So indignant, in fact, that I'm not at all sure I want to share with him the rather vital bit of information I got from you, sweet."

"Ah, I wondered if we were going to get back to that." She eyed him thoughtfully. "If you expect to sidetrack him that way, it'd better be good. Since I don't know much about the security setup for the exhibit *or* the museum, what could I possibly have told you?"

He leaned over to kiss her, lingering not because he was avoiding the answer to her question, but simply because kissing her had become as necessary to him as breathing. When he finally, and very reluctantly, ended the kiss, he had to fight an overwhelming urge to yank his clothes off and crawl back under the covers with her—and that sleepy, sensual expression in her eyes didn't do much to shore up his willpower.

Quinn cleared his throat, but his voice emerged hoarsely even then. "Why, you told me something only a handful of people know, sweet. You told me that Max is planning to break up his collection—and donate it to various museums—even before the exhibit is officially ended."

She was startled for a moment, but then nodded slowly. "I see. Once the collection is scattered all over the country—even the world—he wouldn't have much hope of getting his hands on many of the pieces."

"Exactly. With a little luck, the news will at least give him something to think about. And, if I'm reading him right, it might just cause him to move a bit faster than he planned."

Morgan nodded again, but then bit her bottom lip as she gazed at him. "Alex, be careful. Nightshade moving faster sounds like a deadly proposition."

He kissed her again, managing to keep it light this time. "Don't worry, sweetheart, I can take care of myself. Besides that, I told you I always land on my feet."

Quinn didn't want to leave her, but at the same time he was anxious to confront the man known as Nightshade and divert his attention from Morgan; she wouldn't be safe until those greedy eyes were fixed once more on the Bannister collection.

It was that thought that enabled him to get up off the bed and turn away, but he had to pause in the doorway of the bedroom and look back at her. Unable to help himself, he said, "I'll be looking for a place to rest my weary head around dawn. Do you have any suggestions?"

She smiled slowly, and that luminous truth was in her eyes. "I believe the lock on the front door is easy to pick. And then there's the window; you didn't have any trouble with it either. It's your choice. I'll be here."

Given that enticement, Quinn knew he wouldn't have any trouble getting back here. With Morgan waiting for him, the only question was whether he could endure the long hours until dawn.

"Any problems?" Quinn asked Jared lightly when he joined him just a few minutes after midnight.

"None that I saw."

Since they had to assume that Nightshade had spotted the earlier vantage point, Jared and Quinn had agreed—in a brief phone conversation much earlier in the day—to move to a new position and another building. So they met now in a fourth-floor office overlooking the museum, one of several currently unoccupied spaces they had rented before the exhibit opened.

Keeping his voice casual in what he knew was a vain attempt to avoid a confrontation with Jared, Quinn said, "Okay, then. You'd better go get some sleep while you can."

"Not so fast." Jared perched on a huge old slate-topped desk that had been left in the office by the previous occupants, the position indicating that he wasn't going anywhere for the moment. The room was very dim, but there was enough light to make his expression obvious. Grim.

Quinn leaned against the window frame and peered through venetian blinds at the museum across the street. Well lighted on all sides, the building appeared utterly peaceful. No help there, he thought ruefully, almost wishing for a few armed thugs to storm the place.

"Alex."

"Yeah?" He looked at his brother, still casual.

"I backed you in this from the beginning." Jared's voice was very deliberate. "I bent some laws and broke quite a few rules, because I knew what it meant to you to put Nightshade behind bars. So far, I don't regret that."

"I'm glad," Quinn murmured.

"Wait. I let you lie to Max; I didn't like it, but your reasons made sense. I let you lie to Wolfe, even though I knew damned well it probably meant he'd take both our heads off when he found out the truth. But I will be *damned*, little brother, if I'll let you lie to me."

Quinn didn't move or speak. Familiar with the sound of danger, he heard it in Jared's voice. And though he was an inch taller than his brother, a fraction wider across the shoulders, and arguably more powerful, there was no one in the world that he was less inclined to take on than Jared.

Especially when he knew himself to be in the wrong.

"I want the truth, Alex."

"All right," Quinn said quietly. "I would have told you anyway. Maybe not tonight, but . . . soon."

Jared drew a breath and let it out slowly. "Tell me."

So Quinn told him.

Almost everything.

*   *   *

Still balancing on that high wire, Quinn's second meeting of the night took place in a private home far from the museum, and as he'd discussed with Morgan, he didn't give Nightshade the opportunity to ask awkward questions.

"What the hell do you mean by shadowing me?" he demanded, stripping off his mask.

"Shadowing you? What are you talking about?"

"I'm talking about your little stunt on that fire escape last night. What would have happened if Morgan hadn't got in your way, you want to tell me that? Was the chloroform meant for me, or do you make it a habit to carry the stuff around? Or was it Morgan you were after?"

His host moved slowly to a chair by the fireplace and sat down. "Alex, I didn't go out last night. At all."

Quinn recognized the truth when he heard it. Part of him was relieved—and part of him went even colder. He sat down across from his host and spoke slowly, even though his mind was working at top speed. "And you didn't kill that woman the police are calling Jane Doe. So we have another player."

"It appears so. What was Morgan doing on a fire escape?"

"Looking for me. For Alex."

"And she expected to find you on a rooftop?"

"I didn't say I was on the roof. I'd told her I was meeting a realtor late to look at a building I was considering as an investment. I never meant to be specific about which building, but I must have been.

Apparently, she decided to surprise me with a visit. Either that, or . . ."

"Or she suspected you might be meeting someone else?"

"I wouldn't have pegged her as the jealous type," Quinn mused, then shrugged. "In any case, being Morgan, when she found the front doors locked she tried the fire escape." Quinn felt fairly safe in creating a plausible tale, and it was certainly better than the truth.

"And someone used chloroform on her. An interesting choice, to not simply kill her. Something you'd be more likely to do than I."

Gambling as he often did, Quinn said, "It occurred to me that you might have tried to grab Morgan to have an extra lever against me."

"Alex, I'm surprised at you. Such a lack of trust."

Ignoring that comment, Quinn added, "Still a possibility if we do have another player in the game. But whoever it was couldn't have known Morgan would be there. Unless he followed her."

"Or followed you."

"He didn't follow me."

Nightshade accepted that. "Where is Morgan now?"

"Safe. Being watched. As she'll continue to be watched until this is over."

Smiling faintly, Nightshade said, "Is that a warning, Alex?"

"If you like." Quinn held his host's gaze steadily.

"No one is going to hurt Morgan. No one is going to use her against me."

"Noted." Nightshade shrugged. "At the moment, I'm far more interested in who this new player is and whether he's a threat to our plans. It sounds at the very least as if he has your number, that he knows Morgan is your weakness."

Quinn could have argued with the choice of words, but instead said only, "The murder of Jane Doe points straight at the museum. They even found the murder weapon in the basement, rather . . . creatively placed."

"So whoever it is got inside the museum without tripping any alarms."

"And spent a considerable amount of time in there. Weeks ago. Before the new security went online. Since then, no one has breached the system."

"You're sure of that?"

"Positive."

"And you have no idea who this new player might be."

Quinn shook his head. "Neither do the police, if that's any comfort."

"It isn't."

"You have more resources in this city than I do. Tap them. Find out what's going on."

"We have a timetable. You do remember that, don't you?"

"I do. And everything will be in place by Thursday night. If you choose to go ahead, that is."

"Of course I choose to go ahead. I can't take the

chance that this . . . other player . . . can get in ahead of us."

"It's a risk. To proceed without knowing who's out there. But there's another risk." Quinn saw no reason why he shouldn't go ahead and stoke the fire.

"Which is?"

"Something Morgan told me. Max is planning to break up the collection, donate it to various museums around the world. He says the time for any one man or one family to have such treasures is long past."

"He would," Nightshade commented grimly.

"Yeah, definitely in character. He plans to make the announcement at the close of *Mysteries Past,* but he'll be contacting the other museums well before then to officially donate the pieces."

"I wondered why he was willing to exhibit the collection now, after all these years. One final hurrah. One last opportunity to see all of it together in one place."

Quinn shrugged.

"So you got this from Morgan?"

"Pillow talk. She couldn't know the information was particularly important."

Rather than comment on that, Nightshade said, "So this is the last real chance to target the entire Bannister collection at once."

"Looks like."

Nightshade eyed him. "You don't sound too concerned."

"All I want is the Talisman emerald, remember?

Sending it to another museum could make it easier for me."

"But not for me." His lips tightened. "I don't like being rushed. But I won't take the chance of the collection being put beyond my reach. We move Thursday, on schedule."

"Despite the risk of not knowing who this other player is?"

"Despite that. The Bannister collection is worth the risk. Some things are worth any risk. You believe that, don't you, Alex?"

"Yes," Quinn replied. "Yes, I do."

During the next few days, Morgan was uncharacteristically tranquil—particularly since she woke up each morning with a passionate cat burglar in her bed. Not that she was calm *then,* because her need for Quinn seemed only to grow stronger with every day that passed, but when she reluctantly left him asleep in her bed and went to the museum later each morning, she wrapped serenity around her like a shell.

If any of the others realized that behind her smile and thoughtful eyes a very sharp and observant mind was working, no one said anything about it. Storm teased her about Alex's effect on her, and both Max and Wolfe made rather surprised comments about her newfound composure and the lack of chatter around the museum, but if Alex thought there was anything different about her he hadn't mentioned it.

That was fine with Morgan. She didn't try to hide the fact that she was in love with Alex; she merely remained calm about it. Almost fatalistic, in fact. What would be, would be.

It was, of course, a deceptive appearance.

He came to the museum every day to pick her up—sometimes for lunch, but always by closing time—and they'd spend the remainder of the evening together, until he had to leave to become Quinn. He was always there when she woke in the morning, but he kept his suite at the Imperial and returned there at least once every day. He didn't suggest moving in with her, and Morgan didn't bring up the subject.

She teased him until he began teaching her how to pick a lock, though he claimed he was doing it only to impress her with the level of skill required. (She was impressed.) And, as always, they talked. Morgan didn't ask him too many questions, but she chose those she did ask carefully and timed them with even more caution. And it might have been because he was increasingly tense about the trap—or sting—but Quinn didn't seem to notice that she was gathering bits of information in a discreet but methodical way.

By Thursday, Morgan thought she had figured out at least part of what was happening—and why. If she was right, she also thought she had at last pinpointed the core motivation of Quinn/Alex Brandon, the inner force that propelled him through life and shaped so many of his choices and decisions.

Once she did that, he stopped being *either* Alex

or Quinn to her; she no longer referred to him by name in the third person when they talked about either of his personas. She thought she understood the man he was now, and Alex had finally become as real to her as Quinn had always been.

She had also reached the conclusion that her beloved was in hot water up to his neck—and not only with Nightshade. He was carefully avoiding being alone with either Max or Wolfe, and when Jared appeared at the museum rather suddenly that afternoon just after Alex arrived, it was painfully obvious that there was a very real tension between the brothers.

Morgan stood in the lobby just outside the hallway of offices and watched thoughtfully as Alex spoke to Max near the guards' desk while, a few feet from them, Jared and Wolfe talked. All four men looked unusually serious—not to say grim— and Morgan had the oddest feeling. It was as if her mind was yelling at her that there was danger here, right in front of her, if she'd only *see*. . . .

Then her gaze tracked past them as a movement caught her eye, and she watched as Leo strolled down the stairs. He'd been up at the exhibit, she knew; he visited about every other day, as regular as clockwork. He called out something to Max, casually lifted a hand in farewell, and left the museum without, apparently, noticing her scrutiny.

"Morgan, have you— Sorry. Didn't mean to make you jump."

She turned to find Ken Dugan standing in the hallway, and managed a smile. "It's all right, Ken. I've just got a lot on my mind. What did you want to ask me?"

As usual, the curator was faintly harassed. "Didn't you draw up a list of repair people we could safely call for work while the exhibit's in place? People you've cleared?"

"Yes," she answered slowly. "Why?"

"The air-conditioning system. Morgan, haven't you noticed how damned *hot* it is in here?"

Since she usually felt feverish if Alex was anywhere near her, Morgan honestly hadn't noticed. But now that Ken mentioned it, she thought it was a bit stuffy, even in the vast, open lobby. "I guess it is, at that."

"I think the thermostat must be stuck," Ken told her. "And since the system's practically as old as the building, I think we'd better have it checked out pronto."

Morgan glanced at her watch and frowned. "I'll go make some calls—but I doubt we'll be able to get anyone out here until tomorrow, Ken. We'll probably have to shut the air-conditioning system off until then."

Ken nodded but didn't look happy. "Yes, I suppose that would be best. The weather outside is mild enough, and all the display cases have their own separate temperature-control systems, so we should be all right. Dammit—every museum in the area seems to be having electronic problems of one kind or another."

"Gremlins," Morgan suggested, about half serious.

He agreed with a sigh, then said, "I'll tell Max and Wolfe, just to be on the safe side."

Morgan returned to her office and made the necessary calls, both surprised and pleased when the second repairman she called cheerfully agreed to come within the hour. It would be time-and-a-half, of course, but if the museum didn't mind that . . .

She ruthlessly committed the museum's resources and told the man to come, and after she'd hung up, she sat there looking down at her clipboard with a frown. The Lucite clipboard with its thick sheaf of papers was more or less Morgan's lifeline, containing virtually every bit of information she needed to oversee the exhibit. There was a floor plan of the exhibit wing; design specifications for the display cases holding the Bannister collection; a copy of the insurance inventory of the collection; a long list of people cleared to perform various repairs in the museum should those be needed—and other things.

She was usually careful to leave the clipboard locked in her desk *and* locked in her office whenever she didn't have it, though she hadn't really thought about what information it could provide to someone else.

As she gazed at it now, Morgan's uneasiness began to increase. The clipboard had been in Ken's office on Saturday, she remembered. It had been in Ken's office, where both he and Chloe had worked that day. Why had it been there? She'd forgotten to ask either Ken or Chloe, but now that she thought about it, she couldn't think of a reason why either of them would have needed any of this information. And . . . Ken had always been around whenever Alex was watching someone, she remembered.

It seemed ridiculous to even *consider*—but when Alex had said that Nightshade couldn't go after the Bannister collection alone, he'd also said that *one* reason was because of a lack of electronic skill. What if there was another reason? What if Nightshade dared not use his own inside knowledge, his own security key card and alarm codes, to get at the exhibit *in his own museum*?

God, how ironic that would be! To have such a prize underneath his very nose and know that if he touched it he risked the police being suspicious of it being an inside job. In that situation, Morgan could believe that the arrival of Quinn would be a godsend. To use that other skilled thief's knowledge, to let *him* find a way past the security—and take the blame for the resulting robbery.

And what would be the risk for Nightshade? Quinn might know his identity, but Nightshade also knew who Quinn really was—and that mutual knowledge kept them both relatively safe from each other, at least as far as public disclosure was concerned.

It was possible, Morgan thought. It was definitely possible. She couldn't imagine Ken gloating in secret over his cache of priceless objects, or holding a chloroform-soaked cloth over her face, or shooting Quinn as they both crept through the night—but then, she couldn't imagine it of Leo either. In fact, she couldn't imagine it of anyone she knew.

After a while, she locked the clipboard up in her desk and left her office, locking the door behind her. She glanced across the hall into Ken's open office, and for a moment she didn't move a muscle. Then, slowly, she headed toward the lobby, pulling on her mask of tranquillity as she prepared to tell Ken that the repairman was on his way.

She thought she'd be able to keep all her thoughts and speculations to herself. She hoped. But she couldn't help wondering if anyone else had noticed the drooping rose in a crystal bud vase on Ken's desk.

It was only a little after eleven that night when Alex began dressing to leave her, after explaining that he had to return to his hotel briefly. Morgan lay and watched him dress, admiring and unselfconscious. She thought he was beautiful. She also thought he was wired, even after he'd expended a considerable amount of energy in their bed.

"Is it tonight?" she asked quietly.

He sat on the side of the bed and looked at her steadily. "I don't know, Morgana. Perhaps."

"If you knew, would you tell me?"

He leaned over to kiss her. "Probably not," he admitted with a slight smile. "There's no reason for you to worry, sweet. No reason at all."

Morgan eyed him. "I guess you heard me tell Ken

that a repairman was coming for the air-conditioning system?"

"I heard."

She was getting better at reading him, she decided; there had been a flicker of reaction in his green eyes. She was suddenly positive that *something* was going to happen tonight.

"Alex—"

He kissed her again, then rose quickly to his feet. "I'll be back by morning. Sleep well."

Morgan didn't reach to turn off the lamp on the nightstand, even though she was physically weary. Instead, she gazed at the doorway, acutely conscious of his absence, and tried to get her thoughts organized.

Tonight. It was tonight. And, somehow, the air-conditioning system at the museum was important. Because it had malfunctioned? Because it had been repaired? She assumed it had, anyway; Ken and Wolfe had decided to remain at the museum until the repair work was finished. But if Ken was Nightshade . . .

Morgan had the awful, clenched-stomach feeling that she was missing something, something vitally important. It had nagged at her since this afternoon, and now it was getting stronger, getting unbearable. What *was* it? It had started, she remembered, when she'd stood at the head of the hallway gazing across the lobby, suddenly and inexplicably conscious of danger, as if her instincts or her subconscious had been trying to warn her.

What was it?

She closed her eyes, concentrating, trying to re-create what she had seen in her mind. The men standing in the lobby. The guards at their desk. Leo coming down the stairs. Ken approaching behind her—had she sensed him nearing?

She'd just been watching everybody, idly, not thinking about anything except how grim they looked. . . .

It was then that the final piece of the puzzle dropped quietly into place, and Morgan sat up with a gasp. Well, for Christ's sake. *Now* it made sense, all the vague little things that had bothered her all along. Now she understood.

But even as surprise and relief and annoyance chased one another through her mind, another and far more disquieting realization reared its head.

If *she* had seen the truth, then it was always possible someone else had as well. The wrong someone. Because either of them had her knowledge, she thought. At least her knowledge and maybe more. All either of her suspects had to do was put a couple of things together, as she had, and look at the sum.

One wrong trick of the light, and Nightshade would know without doubt that he was being lured into a trap.

Morgan glanced at the clock on her nightstand even as she was bolting out of bed and hurrying to dress. Not yet midnight. Could she make it?

She didn't have a cell-phone number for Alex, a belated realization that made her kick herself mentally. She tried calling Alex's hotel as she dressed, but there was no answer in his room, and when she got the desk clerk she was informed that Mr. Brandon had left for the evening.

Which told Morgan absolutely nothing. It was doubtful that Alex openly returned to his hotel after an evening out only to depart again dressed as a cat burglar. He probably had a quiet way in and out of the hotel and used that to come and go as Quinn.

Morgan grabbed her cell phone, but it wasn't until she was in her car that she realized the battery was dead. Great, that was just great. The universe really did hate her.

Where was Alex heading tonight? Which man was Nightshade?

Morgan sat in her car and closed her eyes, trying to relax and let that extra sense open up, to feel Alex as she had so often been able to feel him, to sense where he was. If he was entirely focused on what he had to do tonight, not consciously blocking her, then—

The certainty was abrupt, and so clear that it was almost an image in her mind.

Morgan didn't waste any time marveling at how much stronger this odd sense of hers had grown since she and Alex had become lovers. There would be time later, she hoped, for that. She started her car and headed north.

She had to make it. She had to.

CHAPTER
FIFTEEN

The only reason she took the chance, Morgan explained later, was because she was reasonably familiar with the place. She even knew the security code for the garden gate, because she had fairly recently helped organize an outdoor benefit and he had the best garden in town.

Of course, being Morgan, she didn't stop to think either that he might have changed the code (he hadn't) or that security for the house itself would doubtless be much tougher.

In any case, her newly established lock-picking skills were not put to the test. She managed to make her way through the fog-enshrouded garden all the way to the terrace, but two steps from the French door that she knew led into the study, a pair of strong arms grabbed her and pulled her somewhat roughly away from the door and up against a very hard body.

This is getting to be a habit, she decided as relief made her legs suddenly weak. She turned in his arms and threw her own up around his neck.

Quinn held her for an instant, then yanked her arms down and softly, fiercely demanded, "What the hell are you doing here?"

"That's a fine greeting," she whispered in return.

Unmasked but wearing the remainder of his cat-burglar costume, he scowled at her. "Morgana, dammit, you're supposed to be safely in bed."

"I had to come," she insisted, still whispering. "Alex, I just figured out—"

"Shhh!"

He was so still and silent that Morgan could hear the dripping of the fog-wet ivy climbing the wall beside them. She couldn't hear anything from the house, but he must have, because the tension she could feel in him increased. Then his gloved hands lifted quickly to frame her face, and he gazed at her with such intensity that his green eyes were like a cat's in the dark, alight and vibrant.

"Sweetheart, listen to me. There's no time—he'll be in the study in just a minute. I want you to stay here, right here, and don't move. Do you understand?"

"But—"

"Morgan, *promise* me. No matter what you see or hear, no matter what you think is happening in that room, you stay here and don't make a sound until you're absolutely sure he's gone. Promise."

"All right, I promise. But, Alex—"

He kissed her, briefly but with such overwhelming hunger that she felt her knees buckle. "I love you," he whispered against her lips.

Morgan found herself leaning back among wet ivy, shaken and momentarily confused, wondering if she had really heard him say that. She fought to clear her mind, suddenly more afraid than she'd ever been before, because she had the cold idea that he wouldn't have said it unless he thought he might not get another chance.

Her promise kept her silent, and by the time she could gather her thoughts, he had swiftly and skillfully opened the French doors and gone into the house. He'd left the door just barely ajar; she'd be able to hear what went on in the study. From her position she could see him as he moved draperies aside to the right of the door and reached up a gloved finger to punch numbers on a keypad.

The security system, she realized vaguely. He knew the codes? Well, of course he did. He was Quinn.

Then he moved away from the doors, and Morgan shifted around carefully until she could—just barely—see into the room. With the lamplight in there, and the darkness of the foggy terrace, she knew she was invisible to anyone in the room, but she was wary enough to keep her body back and just peer around the edge.

Quinn, his expression perfectly calm and that inner tension she had felt completely hidden, was standing by a fireplace where a dying fire crackled softly. He was still wearing his gloves, and the black ski mask was tucked into his belt. He looked across the room when the hall door opened and another man walked in, and he said with faint impatience, "You're late. If your man did his job, all the guards in the museum should be passing out in another hour."

Morgan was a bit startled by his voice; it wasn't the one she was accustomed to hearing from him. Quicker, sharper, faintly accented, and subtly vicious, it was the voice of a man who could easily be a world-famous criminal.

Leo Cassady, also dressed all in black, walked to his desk and bent forward to study a set of plans laid out there. His handsome face was hard and expressionless. "We have plenty of time," he said flatly. "The gas cartridges are set to fire at one-thirty, and we can be at the museum long before then."

"I don't want to take any chances," Quinn insisted. "We have to cut the power in case one of the guards realizes he's being gassed and gets to the alarm. Even though we've been tripping alarms and shorting out electrical systems all over the city for a week, that's no guarantee Ace will automatically assume there's another glitch in one of their systems."

So that's why so many museums have been having problems, Morgan realized.

"We have plenty of time," Leo repeated. Then,

head still bent over the plans, he said, "Tell me something, Alex."

"If I can."

"Why don't you carry a gun?"

Quinn laughed shortly. "For two very good reasons. Because *armed* robbery carries a stiffer penalty—and because I'm a lousy shot. Good enough?"

"It's a dangerous weakness."

"Is it? Why?"

"Because you can't defend yourself. Suppose, for instance, that I decided your usefulness to me had ended. After all, I'd much rather keep the Talisman emerald myself—no need to break up the collection. And I hardly need your help now that I have the proper identity codes to placate Ace for an hour or so."

Rather grimly, Quinn said, "I didn't give you those codes."

"No, you very wisely kept them to yourself." Leo looked at him with a faint, empty smile. "But you forget, my friend—I've been doing this a long time. Longer than you, if the truth be told. I took the precaution of cultivating my own source inside the museum—though I didn't sleep with him."

"Who?"

"Ken Dugan. He's such an ambitious man. So eager to please. And I'm so eminently trustworthy, of course, so respectable. I'm sure he never thought twice about leaving me alone in his office once or twice for just a few minutes while he took care of a little problem out in the museum."

"Let me guess. He has a lousy memory and had to write down the codes and passwords?"

"So many people do, you know. And *hide* those little slips of paper in such obvious places. The codes weren't hard to find. Not hard at all."

Quinn took a step toward the desk but halted abruptly when Leo reached into his open desk drawer and produced a businesslike automatic.

Morgan felt her heart stop. The gun, a shiny black thing with a long snout—a silencer, she realized dimly—seemed to her enormous. She wanted to cry out, to do something. But the harshly whispered warning echoed hollowly in her mind. *No matter what you see or hear, no matter what you think is happening in that room . . .* She had promised him.

"This is not a good idea," Quinn was saying evenly, his face expressionless.

Leo walked around his desk, the gun fixed unwaveringly on the other man. "I beg to differ," he said in a polite tone. "I'm not wildly enthusiastic about killing you in my own house, you understand, but it seems the best way. I don't have the time tonight to take you somewhere else, and I won't make the stupid mistake of trying to keep you alive somewhere until I can make other arrangements."

"I hate to sound trite, but you'll never get away with it."

He knows what he's doing . . . please, God, he knows what he's doing. . . .

"Alex, you disappoint me. Of course I'll get away with it. I have so often before. And this time, since I plan to make certain the authorities believe the mysterious Quinn pulled off the robbery of the century—and then fled the country—I'll make very sure your body is never found."

"Oh, I couldn't possibly take the credit for something I didn't do."

"The one flaw in my grand design; I'd much rather take the credit myself. But you see how it is. Living right here in San Francisco, well, I just can't take the chance that any of the bright boys and girls at Interpol will link me with this particular robbery. So you'll get the kudos, I'm afraid."

"Leo, we can talk about this."

"That's the mistake the villains always make in movies and on television," Leo mused thoughtfully. "They let their victims talk too much. Good-bye, Alex."

He shot Quinn three times full in the chest.

It wasn't her promise that froze Morgan on the terrace; it was soul-deep shock and a pain so great she was literally paralyzed by it. The three shots— so soft, almost apologetic as they issued in whistling pops from the silenced gun—slammed Quinn's powerful body backward with stunning force, out of her sight when he crashed heavily to the floor, and she could only stare numbly at the place where he'd stood.

Leo, sure of his marksmanship, didn't bother to check the fallen Quinn. Instead, he glanced at his watch, then got an extra clip for the automatic out of his desk drawer and left the room with a brisk step.

Again, it wasn't her promise that kept Morgan still until she heard the sound of his car leaving the house; it was simply that, until the sound jarred her loose, she'd been trapped in a dark and horrible place. With a moan like that of an animal in agony, she stumbled forward, wrenched the door open, and rushed into the study.

"*Damn, that hurt.*"

Dropping to her knees beside him, Morgan stared incredulously as he sat up, pulling his gloves off and probing his chest with a tender and cautious touch. He wasn't even pale.

"You're alive," she said.

"Of course I'm alive, Morgana. I never make the same mistake twice." He pulled the neckline of his black sweater down several inches, revealing the fine but exceptionally strong mesh of a bullet-proof vest. "I've been wearing this thing every night since the bastard shot me the first time. Had the devil of a time hiding it from you that first night at your apartment. Thank God you decided to take a shower before things got intense."

"You're alive," she said again.

"Like being kicked by a mule," he grumbled,

getting somewhat stiffly to his feet. Then he reached down, took her icy hands in his, and pulled her up into his arms.

She was crying, Morgan realized, clinging to him.

"I'm sorry, sweet," he said huskily, holding her very tightly. "I thought he'd probably do that, but there wasn't time to warn you. I'm sorry. . . ."

She could feel where the bullets had struck him, the brutal indentations on the armor plating in the vest, and it was several minutes before she could even begin to stop shaking. He stroked her back gently, murmuring to her, and when she finally lifted a tearstained face from his chest, he rubbed at the wetness with his fingers and kissed her. As usual, when he did that, all she could feel or think about was how much she loved him and how much she wanted him.

Then, with a sigh, he said, "I hate to repeat myself, but what the *hell* were you doing here tonight?"

Morgan sniffed as she looked up at him. "I thought if I could figure it out, then Leo probably could—and then he'd *know* it was a trap."

"Figure what out?"

"Who you really are."

Quinn looked at her with a smile playing around his mouth, then shook his head a little as if in wonder. "You're a remarkable woman, Morgana."

She sniffed again and rubbed her nose with the back of one hand. "Yeah, right."

He gave her his handkerchief. "Use this."

"Thank you."

While she blew her nose and wiped away the last traces of tears, Quinn stepped to the desk and used Leo's phone to place a call. "He's on his way, Jared," he reported. "No, he thinks he killed me. I'll be black and blue tomorrow, but that's all. Yeah. Okay, we'll be there shortly."

Jared must have asked who "we" was, Morgan decided, because Quinn winced and murmured, "Well, Morgan's here." Then he jerked the receiver away from his ear—and she could hear unidentifiable sputtering sounds.

Without putting the phone back to his ear, Quinn merely dropped it onto its cradle. "He's going to kill me," he said with a sigh.

"If he hasn't by now," Morgan told her beloved, "then he never will. But you'd try the patience of a saint, Alex."

"*I* would? Shall we count up how many times *you've* gone charging into danger, sweet?"

Morgan dismissed that with a wave of his handkerchief. "What I want to know is—what happens next? Leo's on his way to the museum and . . ."

Quinn rested a hip on the corner of Leo's desk and answered obediently. "And—he'll find what he expects to find. That the gas canisters his so-called repairman slipped into the air-conditioning system have laid out all the guards."

"Not really?"

"No, Wolfe got the canisters out after the guy left earlier tonight."

"So the guards are just playing unconscious?"

"The regular guards are. The extra ones and all the cops are placed at strategic points throughout the museum. Seems they got a tip that someone was going to try to break in, and after finding gas canisters in the air system, they decided not to take any foolish chances."

Morgan eyed him. "I see."

"Yes. So Leo—Nightshade—will cut the museum's electricity, which seems easy enough. He will then call Ace Security and, using all the proper codes and identity numbers, tell them that the system's going to be off-line for about an hour. Which will give him plenty of time to steal everything except the fillings in the guards' teeth."

"He thinks."

"Right. In reality, he'll never get near anything of value, because of a number of very conscious guards and a rather clever little welcome mat Storm designed into an internal security system that Leo knows nothing about."

"But, if he cuts the power—"

"The secondary system has its own power supply; it's ingeniously hidden in the subbasement, and he couldn't find it even with a map."

Morgan drew a breath. "Then you've got him. But . . ."

"But?"

"If he never gets near anything of value, then

you won't be able to get him for anything except breaking and entering, will you?"

Quinn smiled. "Morgana, all we want is enough probable cause to search this place—something we couldn't get before, because he hadn't put a foot wrong. Breaking into the museum tonight will make the police rather anxious to find out if he might have a few secrets hidden here—which he certainly has. In addition to the safe behind that painting over there, he's got a concealed vault below our feet, and it's stuffed with priceless things, virtually all of which were stolen."

"You know this because you've seen it?"

"Yes. He doesn't know I have, mind you. I checked out the house thoroughly one night while he was . . . otherwise occupied."

"Something else the police will never know?"

"I certainly hope so. Leo's also still using the same gun that killed at least two of his previous victims, something a ballistics test should easily prove. Plus he has a few other guns on the premises that will have to be tested. And, if that isn't enough, the police will also find the Carstairs diamonds here."

Morgan found herself smiling back at him. "You were going to get him one way or another, weren't you?"

"One way or another," he agreed. Then his smile faded. "He killed a lot of people, Morgana. And what he meant to do tonight is going to deeply hurt someone who called him friend."

"Max."

Quinn nodded and got off the desk. "Max. Now—why don't we get going? We don't want to miss the final curtain."

They didn't, but as the virtual end of a rather famous career, Nightshade's final curtain was rather tame—and peculiarly apt. The "welcome mat" Storm had cleverly designed had turned a short and unassuming corridor on the first floor of the museum into a literal cage. Perfectly ordinary and innocent whenever the primary security system was in operation, the activation of the secondary system meant that the slightest weight on pressure plates triggered steel grates to drop from the ceiling at either end of the corridor.

Morgan was astonished; she had no idea that Storm had taken old equipment meant to close off various corridors and had wired in sophisticated electronics to create a cage.

And in that cage, Leo Cassady had no choice but to drop his gun and surrender to the police and guards waiting for him. He was very calm about it, obviously thinking they couldn't hang much of a charge on him. Until he caught a glimpse of Quinn, that is, when he was being led through the lobby. Then it must have occurred to him that there was much more to this than he had thought, because he went white.

Quinn, the black costume and bullet-proof vest

having been swiftly exchanged for dark slacks and a casual denim shirt he'd had in his car, gazed at Leo with the cool satisfaction of a man who has seen a difficult job completed smoothly.

Leo didn't comment to or about Quinn, perhaps already considering how best to structure his defense in the coming courtroom battle and saving his knowledge of the other man's activities for that. But when the police led him past Max, he paused to look up at the other man.

Leo's hard mouth twisted just a bit, but his voice was steady and without much expression when he said, "If you'd only left the collection in the vaults, everything would have been fine. But you had to display it." Then, calmly, he added, "It wasn't personal, Max."

"You're wrong, Leo." Max's deep, soft voice held both pain and loathing. "It was—and is—very personal."

Leo glanced at the other faces around Max. Quinn was calm; Wolfe grimly pleased; Jared expressionless. Storm was obviously satisfied that her trap had worked. Even Ken Dugan and his assistant, Chloe, were there, both clearly shocked and Chloe more than a little bewildered.

And Morgan, who had thought she had known Leo, stood in front of Quinn. Both his arms were around her, and she leaned back against him as she met Leo's gaze with all the steadiness she could muster. She thought she probably looked as unhappy as Max obviously was; her intellect told her this man was evil, but she couldn't help remembering all the times he had made her laugh. She didn't understand how it was possible for him to be the man she had known—and a ruthless thief and murderer.

Then, in a moment that clearly revealed the streak of cruelty in his nature, Leo glanced at Quinn, then said softly to Morgan, "You don't know what he is."

She felt Quinn stiffen behind her, but Morgan never took her eyes off the handcuffed man. Just as softly, she said, "No, Leo. *You* don't know what he is."

Keane Tyler gestured slightly to the police officers on either side of Leo, and said, "Get him out of here." When the handcuffed thief was led away, Keane said, "I'm sorry, Max."

"So am I," Max responded.

"I won't need any of you at the station tonight. Paperwork should keep us up until dawn, but there's no reason the rest of you need to lose any more sleep."

"Paperwork," his partner, Gillian, said with a sigh. "Great. Not that it won't be a pleasure to book that slimy bastard."

They followed their fellow officers from the museum.

And Chloe, sounding as bewildered as she looked, said, "I hope nobody expects me to go back to bed!"

*   *   *

Since Max had managed to get a reliable electrician to come to the museum in the middle of the night and reestablish power to the security system, they didn't have to remain there for long, but it was still after three A.M. when the museum was finally locked up again, regular guards in place. Ken and Chloe left for home, with the young woman still murmuring something about how it would be impossible for her to sleep.

None of the others was particularly sleepy either, and most had questions, so Max suggested they return to his and Dinah's apartment for coffee and explanations.

However, the first explanation, the one Morgan had figured out on her own, was waiting for them at the apartment, clearly and justly incensed at having been persuaded by her eldest son to wait tamely for their return.

"As if I couldn't be trusted," she said in annoyance.

"Mother, we've been over this," Max said patiently. "And I explained all the reasons."

"The principal reason being that you didn't want me seen," Elizabeth Sabin sniffed, unconvinced. She was a delicate woman, still incredibly beautiful in her sixties, with a figure many a much younger woman would have envied and gleaming fair hair a lovely shade between gold and silver. She also bore a striking resemblance to Quinn—which

was explained when he caught her up in an enthusiastic bear hug.

"Mother, how long have you been here?"

"Since yesterday," she replied, returning the hug
and kissing him. "I saw Max, of course, and Wolfe
last night, but they thought I shouldn't call you or
Jared until this thing you're all involved in was
over. I gather it is? Alex, have you lost weight?"

"Pounds," he confirmed cheerfully, and caught
Morgan's hand to draw her forward. "Meet the
reason."

He followed that blithe comment with a more
reasonable introduction, and Morgan found herself
gazing into the warmly sparkling green eyes of the
mother of four of the most remarkable men she'd
ever known. Since that was what Morgan had finally realized earlier in the night, she wasn't surprised—but she was still a bit dazed.

"Half brothers, all of you," she murmured to
Quinn a couple of minutes later when they gave
way for Jared to greet his mother. "Different fa-
thers, different last names, different lives. But the
same mother. The same blood."

Leading her to a comfortable chair in the huge
sunken living room, Quinn said, "How did you figure that out, by the way? You hadn't met Mother,
according to Max."

"No, but I'd seen her picture; he has it here in his
study." She shook her head and settled onto the
arm of the chair when he would have put her some-

where else, adding in a murmur, "I won't be able to think if I sit on your lap."

His eyes gleamed at her. "That's one of the nicest things you've ever said to me, sweet."

"Mmm. Anyway, in the museum today—I mean yesterday—I was looking at the four of you, and I realized it was the first time I'd seen you all together in the same room. I think I knew then, subconsciously, but it didn't really hit me until later."

"That I looked more like Max's mother than he did?"

"Something like that. You were talking to Max, and Jared was talking to Wolfe . . . and there was something about the way you all stood, or the way the light was hitting you. . . . A bell went off in my mind. Later, when I realized, I remembered seeing Elizabeth's picture here, and I thought either Leo or Ken might have too; they've both been here. I knew Max and Wolfe were half brothers, and I knew their mother had been married several times, so it was at least possible. Nightshade, he might think of it, might have even seen her photograph here. It scared the hell out of me."

"When did you know Leo was Nightshade?"

"When I went out looking for you. I did—used—tapped into—that thing between us. That connection. And it was really strong this time. I could almost *see* Leo, and I knew without a doubt that's where you were."

Quinn didn't comment on her use of the connection

between them, though he did smile a bit wryly. But all he said was, "Which is why you came creeping through Leo's garden?"

Sighing, she said, "Well, it occurred to me that if Max didn't know it was *Leo* you were after, and he didn't know that Quinn and Nightshade were supposedly in cahoots, then he probably also didn't know that it would be important to make sure Leo didn't find out you guys were brothers. Because if he knew that, he'd be certain that Max's brother would never steal from him. I mean, you just wouldn't. And he'd know that. So he'd know it was a trap."

Before Quinn could respond to that tangled explanation, Max said rather bitterly, "Obviously, there was too damned much that Max didn't know."

Morgan glanced around the room, finding the others beginning to settle into chairs and couches. Dinah and Storm, both having spent the previous evening here getting to know Elizabeth, were handing out coffee to the others. There were a number of expectant faces in the room, and more than one frown directed at Quinn.

Somewhat hastily, Quinn said, "Jared, why don't you start the ball rolling?"

With a faint shrug, Jared did, setting up the situation very briefly by explaining how he and Alex had believed they could construct a trap to catch Nightshade.

"We know that," Max told him, very patient.

"What we don't know is at what point Alex identified Leo as Nightshade."

"Ask him," Jared advised dryly.

Quinn sent him a glance, and murmured, "Traitor."

Max, unamused by the byplay, said, "Alex?"

"It was . . . fairly recently." Quinn hurried on, hoping Max wouldn't demand too many specifics. "I thought I might have some luck if I approached him directly and proposed a partnership. After all, I was a virtual stranger here with no professional contacts, and it was well known—within the trade—that Nightshade tended to avoid sophisticated electronic security systems, while I specialized in them. It seemed obvious a partnership would be mutually beneficial."

Quinn shrugged. "Of course, from his viewpoint it was even simpler and far more attractive a proposition, since he always intended for me to take the blame. He was too close to Max, too close to the art world here in San Francisco, to take the chance of pulling off the robbery unless he could pin it on someone else. Someone the police could be counted on to believe was capable of pulling it off."

"Someone who would seemingly vanish in a puff of smoke afterward," Wolfe said. "Quinn."

"Exactly," Quinn confirmed.

CHAPTER
SIXTEEN

Of course, the reason he gave me was simply that he was too close to Max and the museum to take any chances, plus that he wasn't particularly adept with cutting-edge electronic security systems. Since I had never hesitated to take the credit—or blame, rather—for past robberies, it was understood I wouldn't mind taking it for stealing the Bannister collection, even if all I actually walked off with was one piece of it."

"I guess he never mentioned that he intended to kill you to make certain you could never be a threat against him in the future," Wolfe commented.

"Well, no," Quinn said. "I naturally assumed it was a risk and took sensible precautions."

"And you never let the rest of us in on this because . . ." Wolfe's voice was dangerously quiet.

Quinn cleared his throat. "I thought the fewer of

us who knew, the less likely there could be a slip. A problem."

"Jesus Christ, Alex. Teaming up with a vicious killer? One *slip* and you end up with your throat cut."

"Look, I thought it was worth the risk. Just setting a trap in the museum and waiting to see if he decided to rob the place seemed to me awfully chancy, especially given his avoidance of sophisticated electronic security. Besides which, he could have waited weeks to make his move, and I didn't think any of us wanted to wait and pace the floor that long."

"So you decided to push him," Max said.

"Well, more or less. After I made contact with him, I assured him I could find a way into the museum, and he wanted the collection badly enough to let me try. And it worked," he added lightly. "He was caught breaking into the museum, and the police will certainly find plenty of evidence they can use against him when they search his house."

Morgan frowned. "But Leo also knows a few things that could hurt you. He knows that Alex Brandon is Quinn." She sent a quick glance toward Elizabeth, marveling that the older woman hadn't seemed upset by any of this, but Elizabeth smiled at her with utter calm.

"Does he?" Quinn smiled up at her. "He *says* Alex Brandon is Quinn. But all he really knows is that I told him I was Quinn, and he can't prove that; there hasn't been a single robbery attributed to Quinn here in San Francisco. So it's my word against his. If he tries to implicate me in any way, my sterling reputation should protect me. Besides, Interpol will report that the man they strongly suspect of being Quinn never left Europe. And since, also thanks to Interpol, there have been a couple of robberies on that side of the Atlantic publicly attributed to Quinn during the past week or so—while Alex Brandon was blamelessly over here—well, who would you believe?"

Mildly, Max said, "Lucky for you the Carstairs family decided not to go public about losing their necklace."

In a tone of great innocence, Quinn said, "No, it's just lucky that the police will find that necklace in Leo's safe. Obviously, Nightshade stole the thing."

"Obviously," Wolfe grunted.

Storm giggled suddenly and, to Quinn, said, "I'll say this for you, Alex—you keep your balance on a high wire."

"Practice," he told her.

"So what now?" It was Max who asked, his steady gaze on his younger brother.

Quinn shrugged. "Well, there are lots more thieves in the world, some of them pretty good at eluding the police. I imagine Interpol can use someone of my . . . talents."

Max looked at Jared, who nodded. "Probably. This little adventure, with its highly successful outcome, will look good to my superiors—since they don't know what went on behind the scenes. He's more valuable to us outside a prison cell than in."

"On the road to redemption," Quinn murmured.

"Don't push it, Alex," Jared warned.

"I was being serious." Quinn realized he was being stared at and cleared his throat. "Well, reasonably serious."

Eyeing him, Wolfe said, "Sounds to me like you'll be in indentured servitude to Interpol. And that was never your style, Alex."

"People change."

"Uh-huh."

"Look, I'm not saying I'm going to always enjoy playing on Interpol's team, but I can do it."

"Can. But how long will you?"

"As long as . . . necessary."

"How long will that be?" It was Max who asked now.

Quinn sighed. "If you want to know whether I intend to return to thieving, the answer is no. Been there, done that."

"And earned the infamous reputation as a master thief," Storm murmured.

"Exactly," Quinn said. "I have nothing to prove. And, truth to tell, I enjoyed these last months."

"Even getting shot?" Wolfe demanded.

"Alex!" Elizabeth scolded, for all the world as if a small son had come home with a black eye.

Her youngest, though far from small, looked a bit

sheepish, contritely accepting the blame for having gotten himself shot. "Sorry, Mother," he murmured.

"It could continue to be an occupational hazard," Max pointed out. "Getting shot at. A dangerous life, Alex."

"Maybe. But a life I enjoy, Max. A life I'm good at."

Morgan very deliberately didn't enter the discussion, her gaze moving among the brothers as they talked about the future of Alex—and Quinn.

"You broke the law," Wolfe said.

"And now I'm being punished."

"Punished, hell. You're enjoying yourself too much to call it punishment."

"All right, then say I'm working to redeem myself."

"And all the loot you stole over the years?"

"What about it?"

"Goddammit, Alex, you know what about it."

"You surely don't expect me to give it back?" Quinn shook his head, smiling faintly. "Even Interpol didn't expect that."

"Well, we tried," Jared said.

Max lifted a brow at him. "And?"

"And . . . it was decided that his willing cooperation was worth more than reclaiming whatever valuables it was even possible to track down after all these years."

"I never hoarded," Quinn explained. "Unlike Leo Cassady, it was never about having a vault somewhere stuffed with pretties only I could look upon. It was never about the money."

"What was it about?" Max asked.

Quinn flicked a glance at Morgan but answered readily. "The thrill, I suppose. Pitting my skills and smarts against the best security systems in existence."

"Which he can still do," Jared murmured. "In a manner of speaking."

"It's certainly a far better life than one inside a prison cell," Quinn said. "And I'm willing."

Max looked at Jared. "Can you control him?"

"God knows. But I'm willing too. To try."

Wolfe sighed explosively. "Am I the only one who's still hung up over the idea that Alex broke the law? Repeatedly?"

"Yes," Quinn said. "Get over it."

Max said, "Nobody's happy about that, Wolfe. But it was Interpol's decision, and they made it. I'm sure even you would rather see Alex working to help them rather than the alternative."

"If you think I'm buying this whole redemption thing, think again." Staring at Quinn, Wolfe said, "The next time *I* catch you with your hand in a safe, I won't stop to ask if you're still playing on Interpol's team. Got it?"

"Got it." Quinn paused, then grinned. "Assuming you ever do catch me again."

* * *

Since they were all still up at dawn, it was tacitly decided that they might as well remain up. They did go home for showers and fresh clothing, to say nothing of breakfast, but by eight-thirty they were back at the museum.

Morgan had continued to deliberately avoid any discussion of the future—Quinn's or theirs—and he hadn't said anything about that beyond what was said in the discussion with his brothers. She didn't know if he would stay or go. She thought he wanted to stay, at least for a while, which was probably as much of a commitment as Quinn could make.

She didn't know if that would be enough for her, honestly didn't know. She knew she wasn't looking for an ivy-covered cottage with a white picket fence and happily-ever-after, at least not right now.

But she hadn't been looking for a fling either.

Clearly, her relationship with Quinn fell somewhere in between.

In the meantime, she tried not to think too much about it. She'd burned her bridges, and whatever was meant to happen would. She'd deal with it.

"So even with Nightshade safely out of action," she said as she stood near the guards' station with Storm, Quinn, and Wolfe, watching the first of the day's visitors beginning to trickle in, "the exhibit will continue to run."

"Yeah, Max considers that a given," Wolfe said, more resigned than anything else. "Which means we can't let down our guard."

"Still a lot of thieves out there," Quinn said. "Trust me on that."

"And unanswered questions," Morgan reminded them. "The Jane Doe, the knife in the basement—we still don't know what that was all about."

"Maybe we do," Keane Tyler said as he reached them. "Where's Max? And Jared?"

Morgan didn't like the look on his face. "What do you— Never mind. Steve?" she called out to one of the guards. "Page Mr. Bannister, will you, please? Private page. Tell him we need him and Mr. Chavalier in the lobby."

"Yes, ma'am." He immediately picked up the phone to call Max's pager.

Morgan looked back at the other men in time to intercept a glance between the police inspector and Quinn, and she abruptly realized something. "You weren't surprised to find Alex here last night," she said slowly. "You know, don't you, Keane?"

The men exchanged glances again, and Keane said in a lowered voice, "Max wanted at least one cop to know exactly what was going on. Two, actually. The commissioner and me. So, yes, I know who Alex is. And who Quinn is."

"Jesus, I'm surrounded by actors," she muttered. "I never guessed you had a clue about Quinn. You hunted down all the information for me, and—"

"Information?" Quinn said curiously.

"Never mind." Somewhat dryly, she added, "An

awful lot of people seem to know your secret identity. I'd watch that if I were you."

"You might have a point."

"We could all wear decoder rings," Wolfe suggested, deadpan. "Or have a secret handshake just so he can keep up with who knows."

To Morgan, Quinn said, "Thanks so much for helping him to take me even less seriously."

"Happy to oblige."

"I couldn't possibly take you less seriously," Wolfe told his brother.

Keane said, "I thought it was Jared who was mad as hell at you. Do you piss everybody off?"

"He tries," Morgan said.

"I have a host of friends," Quinn murmured.

Jared and Max arrived then, and Max lifted inquiring brows at Keane. "You have the look of a man who's having a very bad day," he noted.

"The worst." Keane had at least smiled faintly at the byplay between Morgan, Wolfe, and Quinn, but now he was serious again. His face was strained. "The forensics people finally pulled a usable print from Jane Doe. We ran it against the criminal and police databases and got a match. She is—was—Gillian Newman."

It was Morgan who spoke up first, saying, "Wait a minute. *Inspector* Gillian Newman?"

"Yes."

"Then who was that with you all this time?"

He shook his head. "Whoever she was, she left

her desk to get coffee about four this morning and vanished. After the I.D. came in, we checked her apartment. Empty. Boxes everywhere, which means the real Gillian at least had time to move her stuff in. But not to unpack. And there was no sign anybody ever lived there."

Quinn took a step toward him. "A cop. She impersonated a cop."

"Looks like," Keane agreed grimly. "Did a pretty goddamned good job too. Presumably to get inside the department. And inside this museum, on the pretext of investigating the very murder she committed. She killed the real Gillian and then left us all those nice, clear signposts pointing here. Ever since we found that body, she's been cleared to come and go here as she pleased. We rolled out the fucking welcome mat for her."

"Jesus Christ," Quinn said. "The collection."

Ten minutes later, with the *Mysteries Past* exhibit closed to the public and guards stationed at the doors, Keane and the others watched Max and Quinn, the two most familiar with the Bannister collection, move from display to display, studying the individual pieces.

Not surprisingly, it was Quinn who found it.

"Here," he said. "Shit."

The others joined him immediately.

"The Talisman emerald?" Morgan said. "But it's here. It looks—"

"It looks real. It isn't. Storm, the display alarms?"

"Off. Just a second." She opened a concealed access panel in the display's base and punched in a code. There was a soft click, and the case opened. "Okay, that kills all internal alarms as well. You can pick it up."

Quinn reached inside, using his handkerchief in lieu of gloves. "I guarantee there are no prints," he said. "Still . . ." Carefully, he lifted the wide gold bangle with its oval emerald and held it up so they could all examine it.

"Are you sure?" Morgan asked. "It looks real."

"It's a good copy. A damned good copy." He turned the bangle slightly to see the underside of the setting. "The workmanship is too new; the genuine piece showed faint hammer marks in the gold." He turned it back so that the "emerald" flashed green fire. "And the stone is just one shade too pale."

"How did she get into the case?" Storm demanded. "None of the alarms has been tripped."

"I don't know. Christ, Max, I'm sorry."

"It isn't your fault, Alex."

"No? I asked you to risk the collection. I told you I'd keep it safe."

"You did keep it safe—from the threat we knew about. None of us saw this coming."

"I should have," Quinn said. "I should have."

*　　*　　*

It was after midnight when Morgan woke to see Quinn standing at the window gazing out on a chilly, foggy San Francisco night.

"Alex?"

He stirred slightly and then returned to the bed, sliding in beside her and drawing her into his arms. "Go back to sleep, sweet."

"Alex, stop blaming yourself. You did everything you could to safeguard the collection."

"Everything except keep it safe."

"The only piece missing is the Talisman emerald. It's valuable, sure, but look at what the thief *didn't* get."

"I knew there was someone working behind the scenes after the police found that body. I *knew*, Morgana. But all I could think about was trapping Nightshade."

"Which you did."

"And cost Max the emerald."

"And saved lives, Alex. We'll never know how many lives you saved. If the price was the emerald, then so be it. You heard Max. He doesn't care."

"Maybe not, but—"

"He doesn't care."

After a long moment, the tension seemed to leave Quinn and he pulled her even closer. "Yes. I know."

Feeling the effects of the previous night without sleep, Morgan yawned and snuggled closer. "Besides, you'll be able to find that other thief and the emerald. Set a thief to catch a thief, remember?"

"I remember. Go to sleep, love."

Halfway there, Morgan chuckled drowsily. "That's the first time you've ever called me that. I like it."

"So do I." He kissed her forehead. "Good night, love."

When Morgan woke late the next morning, Quinn was gone. She knew it the instant she opened her eyes. She knew he wasn't in the apartment. She doubted he was even in the city.

"Set a thief to catch a thief," she murmured. "Me and my big mouth."

He'd gone after the emerald.